'This wonderful, wonder-*full* book is a fable and phantasmagoria of the sources of our century. Mr. Millhauser possesses a bountiful imagination, and an ability to catch his perceptions in a bright butterfly net of prose' *New York Times Book Review*

'His true strength is in magic realism ... Brilliant parodies, pastiches, and comments on Alice in Wonderland, Sinbad and T S Eliot show how this gifted craftsman can stretch the boundaries of the form'
Time

'This magical adult fairy tale is both an exploration of the dark side of the American dream and an evocative recreation of late nineteenth-century New York when horses were still seen in the city streets and elevators always had smartly-jacketed operators ... The story of Dressler's life is the story of pre-war America, told here with a poet's eye by a writer who, although new to these shores, has published six books in the States and who won the Pulitzer Prize for Fiction in 1997'
Publishing News

'[A] beautifully written morality tale of a man who wants too much' *Evening Standard*

'His prose is exuberant ... Millhauser enthusiastically recreates something of the spirit of turn-of-the-century aspirations found in, say, H G Wells's novel *Mr. Kipps*, and successfully conjures up the perceived glamour of hotels of the period ... evoked in a rich, energetic prose ... immensely readable' *Spectator*

'A truly remarkable achievement, *Martin Dressler*, which earned its author the 1997 Pulitzer Prize for Fiction, imprints itself delicately, indelibly on to the reader's mind, leaving a dark residual phantom set of memories, echo recollections of places never seen'
Mail on Sunday

'This is the Great American Novel in understated, quietly skilful mode – a straightforward, good old read with brilliant historical detail' *Esquire*

Steven Millhauser is the author of *Edwin Mullhouse*, *Little Kingdoms* and *The Knife Thrower*, among other books. He won the Pulitzer Prize in 1997 for *Martin Dressler*. He teaches at Skidmore College and lives with his wife and two children in Saratoga Springs, New York.

Martin Dressler
The Tale of an American Dreamer

STEVEN MILLHAUSER

PHŒNIX

A PHOENIX PAPERBACK

First published in Great Britain in 1998
by Weidenfeld & Nicolson
This paperback edition published in 1999
by Phoenix
an imprint of Orion Books Ltd,
Orion House, 5 Upper St Martin's Lane,
London WC2H 9EA

Reissued 2001

A CIP catalogue record for this book
is available from the British Library.

ISBN 0 75380 542 1

Printed and bound in Great Britain by
The Guernsey Press Co. Ltd, Guernsey, C.I.

To my sister, Carla

CONTENTS

Martin Dressler

The Tale of an American Dreamer

DRESSLER'S CIGARS AND TOBACCO

There once lived a man named Martin Dressler, a shopkeeper's son, who rose from modest beginnings to a height of dreamlike good fortune. This was toward the end of the nineteenth century, when on any streetcorner in America you might see some ordinary-looking citizen who was destined to invent a new kind of bottlecap or tin can, start a chain of five-cent stores, sell a faster and better elevator, or open a fabulous new department store with big display windows made possible by an improved process for manufacturing sheets of glass. Although Martin Dressler was a shopkeeper's son, he too dreamed his dream, and at last he was lucky enough to do what few people even dare to imagine: he satisfied his heart's desire. But this is a perilous privilege, which the gods watch jealously, waiting for the flaw, the little flaw, that brings everything to ruin, in the end.

One hot morning in the summer of 1881, when

Martin was nine years old, he was standing in the window of his father's cigar store, looking out at the street. He liked the striped, shady awnings across the way, the sunshiny cobbles, the heavy bent-head drayhorse pulling a delivery wagon. He watched the sunshot ripple of muscles in the shoulders of the horse and a lady with green feathers in her hat who had stopped to look at the window of the silk and ribbon shop. A gleaming wet clump of horsedung lay steaming in the sun. Along came a jogtrotting cabhorse, the upright bouncing cabby somehow reminded Martin of a dice box – and as he watched the bright enchanting world of the street, separated from his nose by a single sheet of carefully washed glass, he almost forgot why he was standing in the window. An excitement came over him, as he remembered. Already that morning he had helped his father crank down the dark green awning and wheel out old Tecumseh into the warm shade. Under the far edge of the awning he saw Tecumseh standing on the sidewalk, shading his eyes with one hand, holding in the other a bundle of wooden cigars topped by a plug of wooden tobacco. In the brown, dim store his father had walked behind the dark counter with its glass-knobbed jars of tobacco. Picking up the big key to unlock the iron cashbox, he had again given Martin permission to place the cigar tree in the window, while warning him not to disturb the row of cigar boxes on display.

In the narrow window-space Martin began walking carefully up and down among the open boxes, with the colored pictures on the inner lids, searching for a good place for his tree.

The cigar tree was a wooden rod set in a round base, with sixteen branches of twisting copper wire. From the end of each wire hung a cigar. The tree was Martin's own invention, but he had borrowed the idea of a gorgeous display from the windows of the big department stores that he passed with his mother on their Sunday afternoon walk, when she put on her best dress and feathered hat to stroll along Broadway and look at the store windows. Martin's mother almost never allowed him to cross Broadway, where great red or yellow omnibuses pulled by teams of two horses came clattering by; once she had seen a man hit by the wheel of an omnibus, and another time she had seen a horse lying in the middle of the street. She herself shopped at the less expensive stores on Sixth Avenue, where high in the air the Elevated tracks stretched away like a long roof with holes in it for the sun to come through. But the line of stores and hotels on their side of Broadway between the two big shady squares, Union and Madison, was almost as familiar to Martin as his own street. At Madison Square Park his mother liked to sit on a wooden bench under the trees and look up at the big seven-story hotels, before heading back to their rooms over the cigar store, where she changed into her second-best dress and went down to straighten the boxes and dust the tobacco jars while his father sat bent over the account book. It was after one of these Sunday walks that Martin had begun to think of improving the window display of his father's store. Otto Dressler had at first refused, for he disliked anything that smacked of the frivolous or extravagant, but he had come round, as

Martin knew he would, under the pressure of reasons presented in an orderly way and without excitement. Martin was especially proud of one argument: he had reasoned that the sale of even a single additional nickel cigar each week would result in increased sales revenues of two dollars and sixty cents in the course of one year, which even after subtracting the cost to the wholesaler would leave enough for three thirty-five-cent fares on the steam train from Prospect Park to Coney Island.

Although Martin liked the sunny world beyond the window, he also liked the brown dusk of the cigar store, which even in summer was lit by gaslights on the walls. He liked the neat rows of cedarwood boxes with their lines of orderly cigars packed twenty-five and fifty and one hundred to the box. His father had once taken out the cigars from a box of fifty to show him how they were stacked: there were three top rows of thirteen cigars and a bottom row of eleven, with wooden inserts to make up for the missing two cigars. Still better were the colored labels on the inside lids, showing pictures of all sorts of things: an Indian on a horse, with teepees in the background; a boy and his dog by a swimming hole; an Egyptian woman with bare breasts and a gold bracelet on her upper arm, sitting in a little white boat and trailing her fingers in flowering lily pads; a gleaming black train puffing black smoke. He liked the names of the smoking and chewing tobaccos: Bull Durham, Lone Jack, Winesap, Diadem of Old Virginia, Daniel Webster. He liked the dark-shiny briarwood pipes in their velvet cases, the cherrywood pipes with the bark left on them, the tall Alsatian pipes with shiny porcelain bowls and silver lids, the big-bowled meerschaums carved with faces. Then there were the boxes of chewing tobacco, plug and twist, the jars of sweet-smelling pipe tobacco with knobs on top, the cigar lighter on the counter with its tulip-shaped globe and its two alcohol burners where a customer could bend to light a cigar. His father had started out as a cigarmaker in two rooms over a mirror-frame-maker's shop in an alleyway off Forsyth Street in Kleindeutschland. Otto Dressler had worked at a bench at home, using his own cutting board and knife on tobacco leaves that were prepared by strippers and delivered from the shop in pads of fifty. He showed Martin the art of rolling a cigar: you handled the leaf carefully to prevent tearing, rolled the wrapper so as to cover holes in the leaf, and used both hands to shape the cigar over the filler and binder.

Martin himself could roll a pretty fair cigar, an art he had demonstrated more than once to admiring customers. His father had both admired and disapproved of these displays, which were well done in themselves but smacked of showmanship. But Martin knew that he'd won his father's solid respect as a helper in the store. Customers who were at first amused by the well-mannered boy behind the counter were quickly impressed by the thoroughness of his knowledge of cigars, pipes, and tobacco. And he had a gift that surprised people: he could swiftly sense the temperament of a customer and make sensible, precise suggestions. He himself, he well understood, was a kind of attraction in the store; men liked him and trusted his judgment, even as they were amused and faintly disturbed by the idea of relying on Otto Dressler's youngster.

And yet, standing in the window as he adjusted one of the copper wires in his tree, Martin had to admit that in the brown peacefulness of the store he sometimes had ideas that he had to keep carefully out of sight – ideas that his father, with his heavy shoulders and thick brown mustache, would have judged to be extravagant. The cigar tree itself was a much quieter version of Martin's original idea, which he had known he'd better keep to himself: he had imagined a window filled with elegant French dolls, all smoking cigars. When his father grew angry he never shouted but seemed to harden himself, as if he were holding in an explosion, and his voice became thin and hard; and sometimes when he was angry with Martin's mother he would tell her to lower her voice, to control herself, to stop being excited. His mother, like Martin, helped out in the store, which stayed open six days a week from seven in the morning to nine at night. But in the parlor over the back of the store was an old upright piano, with a dark bench covered in wine-red brocade, where now and then his mother would sit and play 'Für Elise,' and a dreamy look would come over her: at the end of a phrase she would lift her hand in an odd, graceful way, and leave it suspended in the air for a moment before it seemed to wake up and then plunged down to the yellowish keys. His mother told him that she had played the piano as a girl in Darmstadt and that when she married Otto Dressler he had vowed she would have a piano: he had

6

insisted on renting one by the week in the old neighborhood, at a time when they sometimes had only black
bread for supper. Martin liked to hear his mother tell
that story, for he saw that his serious father, in his own
way, had a touch of the extravagant.

He gave a final bend to one wire branch, moved the
tree slightly back so that it stood behind and between
two open cigar boxes, and stepped down from the
window. Then he opened the door and walked out under
the awning. On the sidewalk old Tecumseh stood
shading his eyes, staring out at the street. Martin saw
instantly that the cigar tree in the window was wrong: it
looked funny and spindly, hardly like a tree at all – it
gave off an air of poverty, of failure. It was stupid and
ugly. It hadn't even been what he'd wanted anyway. His
eyes began to prickle, anger and disappointment flamed
in him, and in the dark window he caught sight of his
face. It looked thoughtful, even calm, utterly unlike the
feeling in his chest. The sight of his calm face calmed
him. He felt a moment of anger at his father and then
complete calm. He felt calm and clear and wise and old.
He was old, old and calm, calm as old Tecumseh by the
door.

2

CHARLEY STRATEMEYER

Martin's first successful business venture took place not long after. Charley Stratemeyer, one of the day clerks at the Vanderlyn Hotel, had a fondness for a particular kind of fancy panatella that he couldn't get at the lobby cigar stand, and for the past few months he had taken to strolling over to Dressler's Cigars and Tobacco during his lunch hour and chatting with Martin before walking over to a little chophouse he knew on Seventh Avenue. Martin, who liked the humorous young man with the melancholy eyes, and who had been struck by something Charley had said, turned things over in his mind and at last decided to make a proposal. He pointed out that Charley had to walk from the Vanderlyn to the cigar store and then turn around and pass the Vanderlyn on his way to Seventh Avenue, so that he was losing valuable time on his lunch hour. But if Martin delivered the cigar to Charley at the Vanderlyn each day, then

Charley would save time on his walk to the restaurant. In return he asked only one thing. Since the cigar stand in the hotel lobby had disappointed Charley, it must also disappoint many people who stayed at the hotel, and he asked Charley to put in a word for Dressler's Cigars and Tobacco. At this Charley laughed aloud and clapped Martin on the back, saying he was a sharp little devil.

Now every day at noon Martin walked from the cigar store to the Vanderlyn Hotel, where he delivered Charley's cigar and took in the great lobby with its chairs of maroon plush, its pillars carved at the top with leaves and fruit, its ceiling decorated with gilt hexagons, the plants in stone pots, the shiny brass spittoons on the marble floor, the cigar stand in the corner. One day he walked over to the stand, behind which sat an old man reading a newspaper, and saw that it was a careless mix of expensive and cheap cigars, displayed without plan, the whole affair badly thought out from start to finish. Soon the first new customer from the Vanderlyn entered Dressler's Cigars and Tobacco; and business began picking up in a small but noticeable way.

Martin liked the hot noon walk down his street to the Vanderlyn at the corner of Broadway. He knew each window and awning well: the paper and twine window under its green-and-white-striped awning, the window of derbies and fedoras under its red-and-white-striped awning, the window of umbrellas and walking sticks under its brown-and-white-striped awning, the window of ladies' dress trimmings, the stone steps going down to the linen draper's shop, the window of bolts of cloth past which he could see old Grauman the tailor, the window of ladies' hats, the barbershop window with the reflection of the turning pole – and then the fringed awning, the rounded stone entranceway, the high glass doors of the six-story Vanderlyn Hotel. Martin was soon friends with the doorman in his maroon-and-gold jacket, who for some reason reminded him of old Tecumseh, and the lobby no longer seemed like one of the colored pictures in the *Arabian Nights*, but a familiar place filled with interesting details: the heavy room keys hanging on a board behind the desk clerks, the chairs grouped in twos and threes around small tables, the gentleman with gloves and a fancy walking stick who sat smoking a second-rate cigar. Sometimes when Martin handed Charley his cigar he would stand talking for a few minutes before returning to the store, but one day Charley said he'd like to show Martin something. He led Martin through the lobby past a group of pillars into what seemed another lobby, with half-open doors giving glimpses of smaller rooms, and turning a corner he came to a row of three elevators.

An elevator boy in a dark green uniform was pulling open the shiny door. Inside Martin saw polished dark wood. Two benches covered in dark red velvet stretched along the walls. 'Fifth floor, Andy,' said Charley. The door slid shut, followed by a rattling brass gate that unfolded like a bellows. There was a deep rumble, and Martin had the odd sensation that he was falling upwards. Once, coming downstairs to the cigar store, he had reached the bottom and started forward, only to discover that it wasn't the bottom, there was nothing at all, and he had been about to fall when he suddenly understood that he had miscalculated the number of steps – and this sense of being about to fall, while understanding that you weren't going to, was what the elevator was like. He was beginning to enjoy it when they came to a clunking stop. The elevator boy pulled open the brass gate. The floor of the elevator was too low. They lurched up; the boy pulled open the heavy door; Martin stepped out after Charley Stratemeyer onto a landing with stairs in front and doors on both sides. He followed Charley through a door and down a red-carpeted dusky hall lit by gas brackets with blue glass globes, past high doors with brass numbers on them. He heard voices. Charley held up a hand in warning, and when Charley turned the corner they both stopped abruptly.

Martin saw men and women sitting on the floor against both walls and standing in open doors. In the middle of the corridor a woman in a black dress with yellow flowers in her hair was pacing up and down, wringing her hands. A man with a brown beard stood with his arms folded on his chest, glaring at a younger man in a silk hat who carried a walking stick. The woman covered her face with her hands and began to weep. Suddenly she fell to the floor, the young man in the silk hat dropped to his knees beside her. Martin, watching in terror, saw that no one was doing anything: a woman sitting on the floor was peeling an orange, a man in a doorway bent over to brush something from his shirt front, someone was smoking a perfumed cigarette. A few faces turned toward Martin and then looked away. He had the strange, melancholy sense that something terribly wrong was happening, it was as if he had stepped into someone's dream, but already Charley was tugging at his arm and whisking him back along the way they had come. In the elevator, which suddenly began to fall, so that Martin stumbled back against a bench, Charley explained that a troupe of actors and actresses had rented a row of rooms on the fifth floor. They liked to rehearse at strange hours, sometimes they didn't come in till four in the morning, you saw all kinds of queer things in this line of work, and as Martin stepped out into the hot sunlight of the street he recalled with sudden vividness a curious detail: through one of the half-open doors he had seen the corner of a bed with a pair of crossed feet on it, one of which was naked and white and one of which wore a shiny black button-up shoe.

3

WEST BRIGHTON

Although Martin's father kept the store open fourteen hours a day, six days a week, once a year during the hottest part of the summer he put up a sign in the window and took his family to West Brighton for three days. Almost to the moment of departure his father gave no hint that anything extraordinary was about to happen, but at closing time on the evening before the holiday he put up his sign in the window, and that night there was a great scraping of drawers and clicking of luggage locks. The next morning Martin would wake eager to crank down the dark green awning and roll out old Tecumseh into the shade, and as the knowledge of the holiday entered him he felt for a moment a little burst of disappointment, before excitement seized him.

Martin liked the sound of the reins slapping the cabhorse, the thump of baggage on the roof over his head, the shaking bouncing seat and the shaking bouncing window from which he looked out at buildings that bounced and shook in the rattle of high wheels and the bang of horsefeet. At the ferryhouse there was a smell of tar and fish. Masts stuck up over the roof. The fat tower of the almost completed bridge rose into the sky like a gigantic hotel. On the other side of the ferryhouse he looked down through spaces in the planking at the green-black water under his feet. Gulls lazed in the sky on motionless outspread wings. Gulls floated on the gleaming dark water like wooden shooting-gallery ducks. Suddenly the ferry lurched backward. Martin stood at the side rail feeling the spray on his face and taking in the bright red ferries, the sun sparkling on the black coalheaps of the barges, the thick cottony smoke-puffs from the tugs, the trawlers at the fishmarket, the sand scows, the high three-masters thick with rigging like floating telegraph poles. A man held a red lunchpail that grew smaller and smaller. When Martin turned his head he saw the ferryhouse on the other side getting bigger and bigger. A bell banged. There was a jolt as the engine reversed, chains rattled – and no sooner had Martin stepped onto the planks of the wharf than the loading gates of the ferryhouse swung open and men and women rushed from the waiting room toward the ferry. In the street on the other side of the ferryhouse there were snorting cabhorses and horsecars on tracks and two-wheel pushcarts heaped with bananas and hats and apples under big umbrellas. The tower of the great bridge rose over the top of the ferryhouse. In a horsecar with screeching wheels and a clanging bell they rushed along the streets of the other city, the one that was always unaccountably there, on the wrong side of the river. It was too much, too much – the whole world was trembling – at any moment it would crack apart – but already they were climbing into a steam train, already they were hurtling along in the Prospect Park & Coney Island Railroad, soon the land would flatten out and he would smell a change in the air. For they were going down to the ocean.

As Martin came down the big iron steps of the train he heard band music, as if he were stepping into a parade. The depot opened onto a plaza where the band was playing, and straight ahead rose a high iron tower, where you could ride to the top in a steam elevator – he saw one elevator rising and one falling, high up in the blue sky. As they walked along a big street with their bags, Martin took it all in: the lobster and hot corn vendors, the crayon artists, the peanut stands and chowder pots, a man selling little bottles of beach sand, the towered bathing pavilions, the flag-topped cupolas of the big hotels on the beach. Their parlor and bedroom was in a small hotel on a side street that had a shooting gallery and a fortune teller's tent with a sign showing a hand divided into zones. As Martin walked with his mother and father from the hotel across a wide avenue to the beach, he seemed to feel the shaking flow of the train and see the trees rushing by the window and taste the coalsmoke on his tongue and hear the roar of the engine, or the rushing world – or was it the sound of the surf? In the two-story bathing pavilion on the beach he changed into a heavy dark-blue flannel suit with itchy straps over his shoulders. The ocean was warm on his feet. Farther out he could see people standing up to their knees, while lines of surf broke in different places, and far out in the water he saw people up to their chests. An iron pier came out over the water. There were shops and booths on the pier and the roof had towers with flags. He stood a little apart from his father and mother, and tried again to take it all in as the water rose and fell against his stomach: the great pier rising high above their heads, the fancy beach hotels like palaces in the distance, the white-headed gray-winged gulls skimming the waves, his mother suddenly laughing in the water, the salt-and-mud smell of ocean mixed with wafts of chowder cooking on the pier, the iron tower at the railroad depot looking down at the little people in the ocean. Here at the end of the line, here at the world's end, the world didn't end: iron piers stretched out over the ocean, iron towers pierced the sky, somewhere under the water a great telegraph cable longer than the longest train stretched past sunken ships and octopuses all the way to England – and Martin had the odd sensation, as he stood quietly in the lifting and falling waves, that the world, immense and extravagant, was rushing away in every direction: behind him the fields were rolling into Brooklyn and Brooklyn was rushing into the river, before him the waves repeated them-selves all the way to the hazy shimmer of the horizon, in the river between the two cities the bridge piers went down through the water to the river bottom and down through the river bottom halfway to China, while up in the sky the steam-driven elevators rose higher and higher until they became invisible in the hot blue summer haze.

4

THE VANDERLYN
HOTEL

In the summer of Martin's fourteenth birthday it happened that the Vanderlyn Hotel was in need of a bellboy. Charley Stratemeyer walked into Dressler's Cigars and Tobacco with the news. The assistant manager, Mr. George Henning himself, had asked Charley to see whether Martin was interested. They all knew Otto Dressler's boy, a hard worker who stayed out of trouble, and after bad luck with two bellboys who had loafed on the job and had been careless about their uniforms, the management was inclined to hire someone whose character they could count on. They were looking for a boy to work the six-to-six shift, though in view of Martin's age Mr. Henning would be willing to consider a half-time six-to-noon arrangement, at least for the time being. The salary itself wasn't much to write home about, said Charley, though the tips made up for it. But the whole point was that it was a foot in the door – if it was a door you wanted to get your foot in. If they liked you, and Henning already liked Martin, and if you showed you had the stuff, you could work your way up: already the Vanderlyn employed two day clerks and a night clerk, and there was talk of hiring a mail clerk to take some of the pressure off. And there were openings all the time in other hotels, especially the new uptown joints that were springing up as fast as you could blink an eye. Martin ought to think it over.

Martin didn't have to think it over, since the idea was as fantastic and crackbrained as the idea of joining a circus, and as he dismissed the offer with a shrug he suddenly imagined himself walking along the red-carpeted corridors of the Vanderlyn, past the high doors, looking up at the brass numbers; and for a moment he saw so vividly the half-open door, and the two feet crossed on the bed, that a confusion came over him, as if he were waking from a dream to find himself in a brown, dusky shop. Charley stood with his hands in his pockets and his head tipped at a jaunty angle. His father's face was thoughtful. And seeing his father's thoughtful face, Martin had the sense that he was slipping back into his dream of the dim red corridor, the high doors, the actors and actresses sitting along the walls.

That night Otto Dressler proposed to Martin that he accept the bellboy job at the Vanderlyn Hotel. Although Martin had all the makings of a first-rate cigar man, and would one day inherit the store, Otto wanted him to have the chance to better himself. Wasn't America the land of opportunity? And wasn't the Vanderlyn Hotel a golden opportunity? Sure, the cigar store was doing well enough, but the hours were long and hard and life was an endless battle to pay the lease. And it wasn't as if Martin would be leaving home, or quitting the store; he'd simply devote his mornings to the Vanderlyn and the rest of his time to the store. He would then be in a position to choose. To his mother's objection that the job would mean an end to Martin's education, which would never go beyond the eighth grade, his father replied that there were other ways to get an education, that he himself had gone to work at the age of twelve, and that in any case Martin could quit his job after a few months or a year and return to school if the job proved disappointing. As for the odd hours: he himself would walk Martin down the block to the hotel at twenty of six each morning. Martin would be home for lunch.

Two days later Martin began work at the Vanderlyn Hotel.

In his dark green uniform with maroon trim, he sat on a bench near the check-in desk with three other bellboys and watched the main door. When he was at the end of the row it was his turn to spring up whenever the desk clerk rang a bell, unless the buzzer rang and the bellboy captain ordered him up to a room. Martin, who enjoyed the drama of sliding along the row and wondering what fate had in store for him, was astonished by the immense variety of things people carried: leather Gladstone bags with nickel corner protectors, slim leather dress-suit cases, soft alligator-skin satchels, pebble-leather club bags, English cabinet bags, canvas telescope bags with leather straps, hatboxes, black umbrellas with hook handles, colored silk umbrellas with pearl handles, white silk parasols with ruffles, packages tied with string; and one morning a woman wearing a hat with fruit on it came in with a brass cage containing a monkey. The idea was to offer people immediate relief from their oppressive burdens, while never seeming to insist. But there was more to it than that: Martin saw that after the signing in it was his job not merely to carry the bags, but to lead the way to the elevators – and this meant being careful not to walk too quickly, especially in the case of those who were clearly new to the hotel and seemed a little uncertain, although the opposite error of being overly familiar must also be avoided, while at the same time the bags, however heavy or clumsy, had to be carried without an appearance of struggle. Once in the elevator, it was important to stand in silence beside the bags, to erase oneself behind the dignity of the uniform, while at the same time not seeming cold or indifferent and indeed remaining alert to any sign of helplessness in the traveler. At the door of a room, Martin set down the bags, opened the door with the key, and led the way in, setting the bags down wherever he was requested to do so. After that he checked to see that the shades were raised and the curtains open, tested the faucets in the washstand, and made sure the maid had left clean towels. Then he placed the key in the inside keyhole and hesitated ever so slightly as a reminder that he should be tipped.

It was also his task to answer the buzzer that sounded when a guest pushed a button in the wall beside the bed: one ring for the bellboy, two for ice water, three for the chambermaid. Guests usually wanted a pitcher of ice water, which Martin fetched from a table outside the kitchen, but they might want anything: a newspaper from the newsstand in the lobby, another hand towel, writing paper and envelopes from one of the writing rooms, help with a stuck shade. Sometimes Martin was sent out of the hotel on short errands: to buy a bottle of cough syrup at a drugstore or a shirt collar at a haberdasher's, to deliver a shoe with a loose heel to a cobbler, to find a safety pin or a spool of white sewing silk. For all these services he received tips of a dime or a quarter, or even thirty-five cents, so that in the course of a week he found that he made over ten dollars in tips alone.

As in the cigar store, where Martin sensed that people liked him, so too in the lobbies, the elevators, and the rooms of the Vanderlyn Hotel he moved in an atmosphere that, despite its briskness and even harshness, was one of welcome, of swift smiles and appreciative glances. Among those smiles and glances Martin was aware of the smiles and glances of women: elderly, imperious women in expensive hats who were grateful for polite, flawless attention, young wives beside portly husbands, little girls in straw hats with black ribbons, exasperated matrons with creaking corsets and furious eyes, bored-looking girls of sixteen attended by maiden aunts. At fourteen Martin was tall and broadshouldered, with smooth dark hair and a shadow on his upper lip; in his uniform he carried himself with a certain authority. But if people liked him, if he attracted appreciative glances from women, it wasn't at all, he decided, because he was striking to look at: his face, for example, was even-featured in an unremarkable way that some would consider handsome but that he, for his part, found irritating. No, if people smiled at him, it was because of something else, some quality of sympathy or curiosity that made him concentrate his deepest attention on them, made him sense their secret moods. People were grateful for such attention, and rewarded Martin with looks and smiles. Sometimes he received a different kind of look, a more penetrating, more ambiguous gaze, flashed out from a pair of coffee-black or smoke-blue eyes that an instant before had glanced at him coolly. Such looks Martin received respectfully, even gratefully, though in themselves they seemed to belong to a different version of himself, a version that hadn't yet come into being. It was a version of himself that he was willing to wait for, without impatience.

In the early mornings that grew darker and darker, Martin walked with his father down the half-sleeping block to the well-lit lobby of the Vanderlyn Hotel. Even at quarter to six the world was up and about. Milk wagons clattered over the cobbles, hacks pulled by clopping horses rattled along. In the near distance he could hear the rumble of the Sixth Avenue El. His father left him at the rounded stone entranceway that made him think of a castle. In a basement room he changed into his bellboy uniform, dark green with brass buttons, a maroon stripe running down each trouser leg. He liked to keep his buttons brightly polished and to fit the flat round hat carefully to his head. From his bench in the lobby he would watch the morning grow brighter, hear the world fill with the sounds of day: the jingling bells and grinding wheels of the new Broadway horsecars, the rattle of dishes in the dining room, the clank of a maid's bucket on the marble stairs. As the day grew brighter and louder Martin felt himself filling with light and sound, so that by noon he was ready to burst with energy. Sometimes, after changing back into his clothes, he sat for a few minutes in a soft chair in the main lobby and took it all in: the people walking about or taking their ease, the shiny mahogany desks in the writing rooms, laughter in the ladies' parlor, the gilt hexagons on the ceiling, the great marble stairway. The spectacle interested him, interested him deeply, though it came over him that he wasn't particularly eager for a way of life represented by marble and gilt and feathered hats. No, what seized his innermost attention, what held him there day after day in noon revery, was the sense of a great, elaborate structure, a system of order, a well-planned machine that drew all these people to itself and carried them up and down in iron cages and arranged them in private rooms. He admired the hotel as an invention, an ingenious design, a kind of idea, like a steam boiler or a suspension bridge. But could you say that a bridge or a steam boiler was an idea? In the warm, bright lobby Martin's thoughts would grow confused, as if he had been falling into a fantastic dream, and with an inner shake of the head he would force himself to stare at a solid table leg, a brass spittoon on the marble floor, an ash-burn on the arm of a chair, an empty glass, clear and hard, sitting beside a folded newspaper.

In this way Martin passed his fifteenth year.

5

ROOM 411

The Hamiltons, husband and wife, had returned to the Vanderlyn for one of their sudden and prolonged stays, and among the bellboys, the room clerks, the chambermaids, the elevator boys, the waiters, and the cooks, the grumbling grew louder and more insistent. Even the assistant manager, a master of the unruffled countenance, had moments of abruptness, even of snappish ill temper. The trouble wasn't the husband, an impeccably tailored graying man with plump well-manicured hands and a boyish face, who was always removing his gold watch from his waistcoat pocket, snapping up the lid, staring at it with a slight frown, and holding it to his ear, and who never stayed for more than two days before dashing off on mysterious business trips to Philadelphia or Baltimore. No, the trouble was the wife, Mrs. Louise Hamilton, a buxom bustling handsome dark-haired lady whose large black eyes were skilled in the expression of disdain, outrage, dissatisfaction, and astonished disbelief that the simplest request had been handled with such ineptitude. She sent back food, discovered dust on the mantel shelf over the parlor hearth, complained to the management about noise in the halls, and rang incessantly for the bellboy – a towel was missing, a drawer refused to open, she needed still another pitcher of ice water in order to endure the terrible stuffy warmth of her wretched rooms. If she was bad when her silent husband was with her, she was worse when he was away, for then she had nothing to distract her from the unsatisfactory state of her surroundings, from the mouse-sized clumps of dust under the bed to the inedible white paste that was set on her plate at dinner under the laughable pretense that it was fresh scrod. The elevator boys made unpleasant jokes about her bursting bodice and plump rump, the bellboys complained about her iron stares and stingy tips; and it was said that her quiet husband with his boyish smile fled her side not for business in Baltimore, but for the brothels off Sixth Avenue near the roar of the El.

To all such talk Martin listened with a certain detachment, for in his year at the Vanderlyn he had learned to distrust the gossip that swirled around hotel guests, while something reserved and respectful in his nature prevented him from enjoying mocking allusions to the bodies of women. Besides, he felt a kind of sympathy for Mrs. Hamilton, the subject of so much malicious talk. Yes, she was fussy and difficult and cranky, and yes, she liked to queen it over the hotel staff, but it was also true that the scrod had been served lukewarm, as the chef had admitted, that the maids, as he himself well knew, were often careless about dusting, that service in the Vanderlyn might be improved in all sorts of ways. It was also true that Mrs. Hamilton never spoke rudely to Martin himself, exempted him from her general disdain, treated him with a kind of haughty politeness that, without being in the least friendly, carried with it a hint of approval. Once or twice he defended her to Charley Stratemeyer, who said she was a high-class bitch who walked as if she had a poker stuck up her corset – what she needed was a well-aimed fist to knock her high-class teeth down her well-fed throat. Martin, who had noticed in his mild-mannered friend a tendency to speak violently and contemptuously of women, let it go, while in his mind he leaped in front of Mrs. Hamilton, as if to protect her from a blow to the face.

And then one day Mrs. Hamilton came down with a cold. If she was bad before, she was impossible now, pushing the buzzer every five minutes to demand pitchers of ice water, softer towels, throat lozenges, cough medicines. The bell-boys were up in arms; Martin offered to go up each time, even when it wasn't his turn. In the dim parlor darkened by lowered shades and drawn curtains, Mrs. Hamilton in a long dress half-sat and half-lay upon the sofa, her legs stretched across the cushions and covered with a small blanket, one arm lying limply across the back of the sofa, her head flung back, her eyes half closed, her other hand dabbing at her nostrils with a scented handkerchief. 'Please set the pitcher down over there, Martin, no, a little closer. And if you'd be kind enough to fill my glass, but not to the very top: of course I know I can trust you to do it just right. I must say it's a comfort, Martin, when one is simply slaughtered with aches and fevers, to know that someone in this disastrous place understands how to pour a proper glass of water. I really do sometimes think there must be a conspiracy in this impossible hotel to kill me through sheer blundering stupidity. My hanky is sopping, simply sopping. Do you think you could fetch me another from my bureau, in the upper left-hand corner of the second drawer from the top? But of course you remember: you never forget. It isn't every woman who would trust a stranger in her bedroom, Martin. Thank you, young man. Did you close the drawer all the way, but not too tight? These drawers have an unfortunate tendency to stick: have you noticed? My pulse is racing. I'm sure I'm coming down with a flu. Are the windows closed tight? A draft would kill me, I'm sure. It would finish me off. I really do think my pulse is dangerously fast. Come here, Martin. Feel my wrist. Oh, for heaven's sake, I'm not going to eat you up. I'm not going to devour you. And yet one might say that your hesitation is a sign of good breeding, Martin: you respect people, I've noticed that. Tell the truth, now. Is my pulse dangerously fast? Conceal nothing from me. Would you mind fetching me my shawl? I feel such a draft.'

As her cold worsened, her demands increased; no sooner had Martin returned to the lobby and sat down on the bellboys' bench beside the check-in desk than the buzzer would ring: Room 411. Martin was irked, and even took to rolling his eyes in mock exasperation, but in his mind he defended Mrs. Hamilton: her husband was away, she was alone and sick in a big city, for all her air of crossness and imperiousness she really seemed quite helpless. But this was not all of it. Martin had never met anyone so demanding, so difficult, as Mrs. Hamilton, and in part his patience, which at times surprised him, came from a desire to meet a challenge, to rise to an occasion. And there was something else, which he sensed without quite putting it clearly to himself: Mrs. Hamilton, this powerful and far from unattractive woman, was drawing him close to her in some puzzling, secret way. She gave him an occasional look that made him lower his eyes, sent him into her dusky bedroom for scented handkerchiefs, seemed, without moving from her sofa, somehow to be circling round him – and this sense of a secret adventure, of something intimate and slightly dubious that must never be spoken of, something dusky and hidden that at times made a tremor ripple across his stomach, drew him willingly to her side.

And she was burning up: there was no doubt about it. Over and over again she took her temperature and rang for Martin to read the thermometer, since she could never find the miserable column of mercury in the insufferable glass rod. She waited anxiously while he stood by the edge of a curtained window and turned the glass rod slowly in his fingers. 'You see,' she said, 'I really am burning up,' as the number rose to 101, to 102,

to 102.5. Martin handed her the two blue pills prescribed by her doctor, dampened towels that she pressed
to her forehead.

On the third morning of her fever, when Martin
entered the dusky parlor with a pitcher of ice water at
seven o'clock, he saw Mrs. Hamilton lying on the sofa
with a blanket pulled up to her chin and her head
resting on two bed-pillows in ruffled shams. Martin
poured a glass of water, full but not to the very top, and
set the pitcher down carefully on the table behind her
head. She lay with heavy-lidded eyes, her hands pale and
almost luminous on the dark blanket; below her eyes
the skin was waxy and blue-dark. 'I've had a simply
abominable night, Martin. I feel heavy as a lump of lead.
Be a dear boy and check the curtains, I feel a wretched
draft. I really don't think I can bear much more of this
wretched abominable fever. I really do believe I won't
ever get well. I'll just lie here and burn to ash and be
swept out with the fireplace cinders. They can boast till
they're blue in the face about the incandescent lamp,
but they can't even invent a cure for a simple fever.
That doctor is the most stupendous fraud – even his
whiskers look false. My pulse is racing; I have a
throbbing in my head. Everything's burning, burning –
and cold, I feel cold. Are you cold? I feel it's all up with
me, Martin; it's far more serious than these fools can
possibly know. Everything seems like a dream. That's
what they say, you know: life is a dream. As in that
child's song – how does it go? Merrily merrily. Life is
but a dream. My pulse is absolutely racing. If you could
bring me a glass of ice water: yes. Just hold it: right

there: yes: and lift my head. That's it. Now set the glass down and take my pulse. Is this a dream? My heart's racing, racing: can't you feel it? Can't you? Silly boy, what's wrong with you? Here, place your hand here, on my poor racing-away heart. Yes. Yes. Don't you know anything? Come here now. Here now. Yes.'

And Martin entered her fever-dream, at first awkwardly, then easily: it was all very easy, easy and mysterious, for he barely knew what was happening, there in the dusk of the parlor, in a world at the edge of the world – Mrs. Hamilton's dream. The silk-smoothness of her skin surprised him, and under the skin was bone, lots of bone, skin stretched over bone, and then a sudden warm wet sinking and sinking, and somehow he was standing in his uniform with an empty pitcher in his hand and Mrs. Hamilton was looking at him with wide-open eyes over which the lids came slowly down halfway. And she said, 'Mind you don't catch a fever, Martin,' and raised a forefinger that she waggled lightly. Then her eyelids closed decisively.

Later that morning, when Martin returned to the bell-boys' bench from delivering a pitcher of ice water to another floor, he learned that Mr. Hamilton had just returned from Baltimore or Philadelphia and was riding up in the elevator at that very moment. The buzzer from Room 411 remained silent, a cause for ribald comment by the bellboys and Charley Stratemeyer, and later that day as Martin was delivering a tray of drinks to the fifth floor he suddenly sneezed and nearly upset a glass. By four in the afternoon he felt heavy-headed; that night his temperature rose to 103. He struggled to lift his head from the pillow, and finally sank back into confused dreams. When he woke it was growing dark. He returned to work the next morning, despite burning eyelids and a heaviness in the temples; the Hamiltons had checked out the day before. Mr. Henning took him aside and said that Mrs. Hamilton had commended Martin to him – he wished to pass on the compliment. 'A good job, my boy: you've done well. A difficult proposition, if I may say so. Well now: don't let it go to your head.' 'I won't, sir.' Martin felt drowsy; he could feel his heavy eyelids closing, but forced them open.

6

A Business
Venture

A few weeks after Martin's sixteenth birthday, Mr. Henning summoned him into the small office located behind an oak door between two pilasters near the ladies' parlor. Seated at a high-backed desk with envelopes sticking out of every pigeonhole, Mr. Henning motioned for Martin to sit down in a mahogany armchair upholstered in green morocco, opened a cedarwood box, and began to remove a fancy Havana. He paused to offer the box hesitantly to Martin, and seemed startled when Martin bent forward and removed one. 'Strictly between us, of course,' he said. 'Your father –' Martin, who had never smoked a cigar in his life, despite sampling hundreds of them in his father's presence since the age of thirteen, but who didn't like to refuse a challenge, sat rolling the cigar under his nose and admiring the smoothness of the wrapper before he thrust it decisively into the pocket of his bellboy jacket.

Mr. Henning quickly closed the box, clipped his cigar, rolled it on his tongue, removed it, and seemed to forget about it as he swiveled in his chair, thrust a thumb into the pocket of his vest, and began to speak.

'I'm not going to beat about the bush, Martin: 'tain't my style. Fact is, you've done a pretty good job here at the Vanderlyn. I suppose you know it. We've been keeping an eye on you, lad, watching you, you might say – well, we'll speak no more about that. Pretty soon a fellow gets all full of himself and then his hat won't fit on his head. Has to get himself a new hat, or maybe a new head, old one isn't good enough for him any more. You catch my drift. Cochran – clerk – little guy, up to here on me, you may have run into him – Cochran's been given notice, not up to the mark and so forth, no concern of yours. We'll move Charley into the night slot where he won't have to get up at five in the morning and you can take Charley's spot 'longside of John. He'll show you the ropes. You'll catch on quick. Well, then. What do you say?'

Martin, who had been distracted by the aroma of the cigar in his pocket, an aroma that reminded him of a familiar one he couldn't quite place, realized suddenly that he had just been offered a promotion. He sat up straight, was about to accept, felt a sharp hesitation, and said he'd think it over. To his surprise, Mr. Henning grew angry.

'Think it over, by God. Sure sir very good sir I'll just think it over a bit sir thank you sir will that be all sir. By God, boy, you don't think over a thing like this. You seize it by the scruff of the neck and hold onto it and pray it don't get away.'

Martin realized that he had been careless, that by appearing cool he had hurt Mr. Henning in his pride. He was irked at himself, and at the stupid cigar, but the hesitation had been powerful and couldn't be ignored. He knew perfectly well that the promotion was a great chance; what caused him to hold back was something else, something that had to do with his relation to this hotel and to any hotel. He needed time to think it over. He said, 'What I meant was, I always talk these things over with my father.'

Mr. Henning raised his eyebrows and threw up his hands, one of which still held the unlighted cigar. 'And do you think for a minute I haven't spoken of it to your father?'

It struck Martin that Mr. Henning was shrewder than he'd given him credit for: the assistant manager had sensed a crucial thing. Martin agreed to finish out the week as bellboy before taking up his new position, and that night, seated in the parlor over the cigar store, listening to his mother and father talking down below, it suddenly came to him: he had hesitated because his life in the hotel was a dream-life, an interlude, a life from which he would one day wake to his real life – whatever that might be.

Meanwhile Mr. Henning had plans for him, and that was fine with Martin, who threw himself into his new duties with a zest that surprised him. It was as if, having acknowledged the dream-nature of his life in the Vanderlyn Hotel, he was able to sink wholly into the dream without any fretful hankering to wake up. He liked his new hatless uniform, with its chocolate-brown jacket and brass buttons, and the shiny mahogany counter, and the rows of heavy keys hanging from numbered hooks. Mr. Henning hovered erratically behind the desk before vanishing on mysterious errands. It was John Babcock, the other day clerk, a polite and reserved young man of eighteen whose thick pale eyelashes gave him a slightly blurred look, who helped Martin with the details of his new job, such as presenting the leather-bound hotel register for guests to sign, distributing mail to the rows of wooden boxes, and operating the handsome new cash register, with its jumping-up numerals that appeared behind the glass at the top and the satisfying bing of its bell. It all seemed very clear to Martin, as if he'd been working behind the desk for a long time. He enjoyed attending to newly arrived guests, answering questions, soothing ruffled tempers – talking to people. Was it so different from the cigar store, really? People talked to you, and you talked back. You tried to imagine the confusion of strangers, satisfy their desires, make things simple and orderly and clear. And people liked him back: he could feel it in his bones. Guests began relying on him, coming to him for advice. John Babcock was an efficient room clerk, but Martin saw that he didn't really like anyone; he spoke to everyone in the same polite toneless voice, which seemed the echo of his eyelashes.

Mornings, Martin arrived at a quarter to six, changed into his uniform, and took over from Charley Stratemeyer, whose skin beneath his melancholy eyes was the color of plums and who had taken to greeting Martin with ironical flourishes. 'Ah, young Lochinvar is come out of the West,' he would say, or 'Up bright and early to greet the dawn, eh, Martin?' There was a new coolness about Charley, which shaded at times into an air of mockery, mixed with something murkier that felt like a sort of spiteful respect. It occurred to Martin that at twenty-two his old pal must sometimes wonder whether he was going to spend the rest of his life as a room clerk. Charley had already received two warnings from Mr. Henning for arriving late; the plum-dark patches under his eyes, the waxy skin, the talk of hookers under the El and the joys of bought love in borrowed rooms, a touch of harshness about the mouth, all this gave Martin the sense that Charley was turning into someone else before his eyes.

From his position behind the front desk he had a clear view of the glass doors before him, through which he could see a strip of awning and the clattering traffic on Broadway. He also commanded a view of the great lobby stretching away to the left and, in an alcove of the lobby, the news-stand and an edge of the cigar stand. Everything about the cigar stand irritated Martin: the choice of cigars, the display, the dullness or indifference of old man Hendricks, who never offered customers advice and sat on a stool reading a newspaper through small square spectacles worn low on his nose. Once or twice Martin had tried to strike up a conversation with him, in an effort to win his confidence and offer a suggestion or two, but the old man had looked up from his paper with red-rimmed hostile eyes. After that,

Martin had no qualms about sending cigar-smoking guests to Dressler's Cigars and Tobacco, conveniently located just down the block. He wondered how the concession could possibly pay, though of course it was more convenient for a guest to step out of an elevator and walk three steps to purchase a morning paper and a so-so cigar than to leave the hotel for even a short walk down the street. The hotel rented lobby space to three other concessions – the news-stand, a florist's shop, and a railway ticket agency – all of which seemed to Martin to be operated far more skillfully than the cigar stand. When he asked the assistant manager whether the hotel couldn't enforce higher standards, since it owned the space, Mr. Henning looked at him with amusement. He said that there had been no complaints, that the hotel wasn't in the cigar business, and that so far as the lobby concessions were concerned, the hotel was simply a landlord, who demanded from the concessionaires only the rent check and behavior appropriate to the reputation of the Vanderlyn Hotel. Martin argued that the Vanderlyn was in the business of attracting guests, and that the lobby concessions were part of that business, and that therefore – but here Mr. Henning laughed and said that all this talk about cigars was making him hungry for a smoke, and if it made Martin feel better, there was talk that old man Hendricks would be giving up the concession when the lease ran out at the end of the year. 'Then I'll take it over myself,' Martin said irritably. Mr. Henning burst out laughing, then looked at him sharply. 'Go easy, lad. One thing at a time.'

The old man gave notice before the end of the year:

John Babcock said he was moving out to Brooklyn to live with his widowed sister, a milliner who owned the house over her shop and took in boarders. And Martin, after thinking things out for two months, explained his plan to his father, presented it in detail to Mr. Westerhoven, the hotel manager, and took over the cigar concession. For the past two years Martin had been giving half his salary to his father and putting the other half in the bank; although he had saved enough money for a month's rent, he needed his father's signature as guarantor of the lease, which ran for one year. His father agreed to advance Martin a sum of money good for six months' rent, after which Martin had to pay the rent himself or give up the lease. And Martin, who had no intention of giving up either the lease or his post as day clerk, had in addition to pay the salary of the cigar vendor. He wanted someone young and vigorous, someone who knew cigars, and Otto Dressler had just the man for him: Wilhelm Baer, the twenty-year-old son of Gustav Baer, a cigarmaker on Forsyth Street in the old neighborhood. Wilhelm, who had no trace of a German accent and called himself Bill, had worked as a cigarmaker and a packer before clerking in a cigar store on Third Avenue under the El; he was out of work and would jump at the chance. Martin took an immediate liking to Bill Baer, a friendly man with alert blue eyes and copper-colored hair brushed hard to the side. He seemed grateful for the job, agreed with Martin in principle about the display of cigars but had strong opinions of his own, and seemed untroubled by the idea of working for someone three years younger than himself – although Martin at seventeen, with his serious dark eyes and soft brown mustache, looked like a man of twenty-one.

Bill Baer fell in happily with a secret plan of Martin's, and one Sunday a few weeks before the cigar stand was to change hands, the two men took the Second Avenue El down to the old neighborhood, getting off at Canal and walking east toward the river. The old neighborhood was changing. Poles and Bohemians stood in doorways and leaned out of windows, ragged children sat on the curbs, and everywhere you looked you saw the black-eyed Ostjuden, dark and curly-bearded, gabbling their harsh tongue, crowding the streets, filling the tenements – forcing the Germans north, Bill Baer told Martin, into the quiet German streets around Tompkins Square, which the old people still called Der Weisse Garten. On a cobbled lane lined with furniture shops and clothing stores they came to a narrow alley. Baer led Martin along the alley to a small courtyard of workshops, where over an open doorway hung a wooden griffin with faded red wings and a blue tongue. Inside the dusky shop there was a sharp smell of fresh wood and varnish. Pallid sunlight swirling with sawdust penetrated partway into the gloom. They walked along a twisting path that led among shadowy life-sized figures, leaning wooden signs, upside-down barrels heaped with pawnbrokers' balls, a wooden lion with open jaws – and always the stern Indians, standing erect, eyes glaring out their defiance. Martin heard scraping sounds. They came to an open door that led into a small workroom. A short, thick-chested old man in a leather apron stood planing a rough figure beside a workbench. Another man stood in a corner, applying paint to the face of an Indian. On the bench lay an ax, a spokeshave, scattered chisels, a mallet, piles of sandpaper of different roughnesses. The woodcarver, Asmus Friedländer, spoke only German. Bill Baer questioned him and led Martin back into the shop.

'He says we can pick any one we like, except the fellows over there by the windows, with the tickets around their necks. They're sold. Or he can knock one out for us. Any style.'

'If we can't find the right one. But I have a feeling –'

Together they walked among the wooden Indians, who in the half dark stared at them with a kind of melancholy fierceness. Some stood stiffly with their arms close to their sides, some leaned forward on one foot and shaded their eyes like old Tecumseh, some held an arm straight out, but however they posed, they clutched in one fist a bundle of wooden cigars. Bill explained that all the Indians were made of white pine; the logs came from the waterfront spar yards. Martin imagined a barge loaded with white pine logs floating down the East River to a loading dock, where they were piled onto a delivery wagon and drawn clattering over cobbles by a team of big-hoofed truck horses to the workshop of Asmus Friedländer. There were stern chiefs and brave young scouts and bosomy squaws, and here and there a different sort of figure who also held out a bundle of cigars: a Blackamoor with a brilliant red turban, a Highlander in a kilt, a fashionable lady wearing boots. Martin was surprised to see a Chinaman

41

in a pigtail holding a large box in both hands; Bill explained that it was destined for a tea store. After a while Martin stopped before a figure and stood looking at it with his chin in his hand and his head tilted slightly. The Indian was a chief, a little smaller than life-sized. Both elbows were pressed close to the sides and both forearms extended: one hand held a tomahawk, the other a bundle of cigars.

'What do you think of this noble warrior?' he asked Bill.

'Oh, he'll bring 'em in. He'll do just fine. With a little more color in his feathers –'

'Exactly what I was thinking,' Martin said, and placed his hand on the Indian's shoulder. 'Old fellow, you're about to move uptown.'

One week later the new Indian, with his brightly painted headdress and his emerald-green tunic, stood before the cigar stand in the lobby of the Vanderlyn Hotel, holding out in one hand a bundle of pinewood cigars. To the handle of the upright tomahawk was attached a white sign that announced in large red letters: GRAND OPENING. The washed and sparkling display case was filled with an entirely new selection of expensive and medium-priced cigars. Before each open box rested a small card advertising the virtues of the tobacco ('smooth, rich flavor for the discriminating smoker'). In an attempt to attract the patronage of female guests, the display included half a dozen packages of the newly fashionable little cigars called cigarettes, which Otto Dressler refused to carry. Beside the new cash register stood several arrangements of cigars bound in ribbons and suggested as gifts for a beloved husband or friend. On the wall behind the display case hung a framed painting of a band of Plains Indians riding across a desert.

The day before, Martin had placed in every hotel mail-box a printed circular announcing the grand opening, advertising an improved and expanded line of outstanding but moderately priced cigars, and introducing the new sales clerk, William Baer, expert tobacconist.

Opening day was a modest success; Martin, who had hoped for a spectacular showing, was disappointed. But the new cigar stand with its handsome Indian and its alert, cheerful young salesman continued to attract customers, and by the end of the second week it was clear that the stand was making an impression. Bill was doing a brisk business in cigarettes, for which orders had tripled, and at the request of hotel guests he began to stock a variety of smoking tobaccos and a selection of sundries: embossed leather cigar cases, ebony tobacco boxes, briar and meerschaum cigar holders with amber mouthpieces, nickel-plated match safes with spring covers. Martin watched the busy stand from his post at the front desk and spent part of his lunch hour going over accounts with Bill, who liked to bring in lunch from a delicatessen and eat on the stool behind the cigar stand; and once a week they had dinner at a restaurant on Sixth Avenue. The stand had caught on, there was no doubt about it. Martin raised Bill's salary, and they made plans to add a small wing to the display case and put in wall shelves.

7

LITTLE ALICE
BELL

Not long after the cigar stand had begun to flourish in its lobby alcove, Martin became aware that a Mrs. Margaret Bell, from Boston, who had arrived at the hotel with a great deal of luggage and a ten-year-old daughter in a black straw hat, had taken to lingering at the front desk several times a day. There she would inquire after mail, ask directions to various points of interest, question Martin about the weather, and engage him, with many flutterings of her long and beautifully curved eyelashes, in bouts of light conversation. Mrs. Margaret Bell was a handsome woman in her early thirties. She liked lavish hats trimmed with bunches of cherries, strode decisively through the lobby with her daughter in tow, and seemed always to have an appointment in a different part of town. Martin had the sense that she wanted to ask him something, and one morning she did: she said that she had to be out for two hours, that she would return absolutely no later than eleven o'clock, and that she wondered whether Martin might do her the favor, the really tremendous and prodigious favor, for which she would be eternally grateful, of keeping an eye on her daughter, who would do nothing but sit in the lobby in his direct line of sight and keep out of his way until Mrs. Bell returned. Martin, who liked the little girl with the blond ringlets and the blue serious eyes, agreed to watch her from his post at the front desk, while secretly disapproving of the request. Carefully he explained that he was required to remain behind the desk and couldn't leave to follow Alice if she wandered from view, nor could he promise that he would be able to watch her at every moment. 'Oh, Alice is very good at sitting in chairs,' replied Mrs. Bell. 'She knows how to take care of herself. You won't have anything to do but glance over at her from time to time. I do appreciate it. It's so hard, sometimes, with a child.'

That was the beginning; and now every day, and sometimes twice a day, Mrs. Bell asked Martin to keep an eye on little Alice, who sat with her legs dangling from a big red-plush chair or took little walks about the lobby, glancing obediently over her shoulder to make certain she didn't wander out of Martin's sight. Sometimes she came over near the front desk and stood watching Martin as he turned the leather-bound register toward a new guest, or lifted a big key from its hook, or called orders to the bellboys. Martin, turning back from the mailboxes, would catch sight of the serious blue eyes of Alice Bell staring up at him from beside a potted plant, and sometimes he would invite her to sit on a high stool behind the desk off to one side and watch him while he worked. The slightest sign of attention seemed to touch her deeply; and one day she handed Martin a small package, wrapped in pink tissue paper, which contained a slightly melted piece of chocolate wrapped in gold foil.

As Martin waited for Mrs. Bell and her daughter to return to Boston – a return that was bound to take place any day, he assured himself, as the mother thanked him profusely, fluttered her handsome eyelashes, and hurried out onto Broadway – he began to notice in Alice a number of puzzling looks. She had grown fond of him in the course of their two-week friendship, but in her large, serious, beautiful eyes he sometimes saw, or seemed to see, a look that made him avert his own eyes. It was a look that could only be described as tender or adoring, as if – but it was precisely the 'as if' that stopped him short, for he didn't know how to think about it, though he understood clearly enough that he was the accidental repository of the girl's baffled affection. She took to wearing handsome ribbons in her hair, and blushing furiously when her mother suggested that it was for Mr. Dressler's sake; and sometimes he would exchange with Alice Bell, past her mother's shoulder, a look of mournful understanding.

One morning she gave him a little flat package wrapped in blue tissue paper. When Martin opened it, he discovered a lock of blond hair. He was on the point of saying something witty when he raised his eyes and saw little Alice Bell staring at him tensely. Without a word he nodded gravely at her, gently wrapped up the curl of hair, and placed it in his pocket.

A day came when Mrs. Bell failed to return to the hotel at noon. Martin paced in the lobby, trying to suppress his anger, while Alice walked a little bit out of his way, casting at him looks of shame and mortification. He strode over to the cigar stand and talked for a few minutes with Bill Baer, who gave him an apple and half a hard roll, then resigning himself to a ruined hour he sat down in a red-plush lobby chair and watched the guests walking purposefully, striding in and out of parlors, sinking flamboyantly into armchairs and couches. Beside him Alice kneeled by the arm of the chair and seemed to try to see what he was seeing. Martin knew that she felt his irritation and, glancing down at her as she kneeled there, he had a moment of pity for the lobby orphan and of anger at himself. He let his left hand drop over the side of the chair and touched her on the shoulder. Alice grew suddenly tense – turned to him with a startled, almost violent look – her shoulder trembled – and all at once Martin felt something pass over him, his heart beat fast, there was an inner bursting, and the entire lobby was transformed: he became aware of the soft underswish of petticoats, the faint creak of stays, the rub of silk stockings, a dark alluring undersound of silk and lace, a sudden dark flash of glances – and as they strode past or sank sighing into soft couches, the ladies of the lobby began shedding their long dresses, unlacing their tight corsets, flinging up their petticoats like bursts of snow, throwing back their heads and breathing sharply as veins beat in their

47

necks, while Martin, rippling with terror, started to rise and knocked something over that began rolling away and away and away along the wavy pattern of the marble floor.

8

ADVANCEMENT

Three days later the Bells, mother and daughter, returned to Boston. From Mrs. Bell, Martin received a box of cream-filled chocolates, and from Alice he received – suddenly and secretly, as Mrs. Bell's back was turned – a small heart-shaped gold locket, still warm from being clutched in a fist. He watched them follow the doorman along the shade of the awning. The locket contained a hand-painted photograph of Alice Bell, with eyes too blue and hair too yellow, staring thoughtfully and a little sadly at the viewer. Martin kept it at the back of his shirt drawer in the bedroom over the cigar store.

With relief he watched them disappear beyond the glass doors, and also with the conviction that something needed to be done about a part of his life he rarely gave much thought to, and then only in a vague, shadowy way. At dinner he spoke briefly and directly to Bill Baer, and a few nights later he accompanied his friend to a house Bill Baer knew on West Twenty-fifth Street off Sixth Avenue. You had to be careful to choose a good house, Bill said, because some of the houses hired creepers who stole your money through secret panels in the walls. In the gaslit parlor with plush chairs and couches and a yellow-keyed piano, Martin chose a dark-haired girl with heavy shoulders, who reminded him of a younger, coarser, sadder Mrs. Hamilton. He followed her up the nearly dark stairs and had a moment of hesitation as he entered the dim-lit bare-looking room with pink-flowered wallpaper and a drawn yellow shade. Against one wall was a wooden washstand with a zinc basin, beside which stood an enameled white pitcher with a red handle. When she sat down on the bed he walked over quickly. Three things stayed with him: the violent rattle of the window behind the drawn shade as the El train roared past, the girl's look of fear as he made a sudden gesture with his hand, and the odd feeling of gratitude to Mrs. Hamilton, for teaching him what to do in a brothel.

He began visiting the house with rattling windows regularly, once or twice a week, at first choosing only Dora, the dark-haired girl, out of a sense of loyalty. One night when she remained upstairs he chose a big blond girl in a blood-red robe called Gerda the Swede, and in time he made his way through the remaining four girls, though he always chose Dora when he could. Martin looked forward to the night strolls up the sidewalks of Sixth Avenue, past the high columns of the El. Bursts of piano music came from the concert saloons. Rushing trains shook the overhead tracks, spewed out coalsmoke shot through with red flames. It was a world of top-hatted swells and toughs in reefer jackets, of brazen-eyed women standing in doorways, of sawdust smells through swinging saloon doors mingling with the tang of horsedung thrown up by clattering wheels and ironshod hooves – and then the sudden plunge into darkness under the high tracks. One night a man with a black scarf around his neck lurched out at him from behind an El stanchion, holding a knife. Martin, fright-ened and outraged, swung from the shoulder. He left the man kneeling on all fours, coughing blood onto the dropped knife. In the sudden glare of an arc light Martin saw his split-open knuckle crusting with blood. But for the most part his walks were undisturbed; he welcomed the red streetcorner lamps casting their glow over the fire-alarm boxes, harsh laughter from the saloons, the familiar doorway with its red lantern, the gaslit parlor with its yellow-keyed piano on which stood a pair of double-branched tarnished brass candlesticks contain-ing four white candles, the girls in low-cut robes and half-bare breasts walking in and out or sitting on the chair-arms. It struck him that the parlor and the girls were night versions of the hotel lobby, as if these were the same women who by day walked about in long dresses and wide-brimmed hats heaped with fruit. Sometimes he found himself imagining how, at night, all the hotel ladies loosened their hair and put on blood-red robes and walked back and forth, showing their breasts, leaning close, giving off warmth and a sweetish, sharp smell of liquor and perfume.

Meanwhile he was working harder than ever at what he called his triple life: day clerk at the Vanderlyn Hotel, lessor of the cigar concession in the hotel lobby, and part-time assistant in his father's cigar store. From Monday through Friday he clerked full time at the Vanderlyn, from six to six, and on Saturday and Sunday half-time, from noon to six, for a total of seventy-two hours. He worked at the cigar store four nights a week, from seven to nine, and two or three hours on Saturday mornings, for a total of ten or eleven more hours. Three nights a week – Wednesday, Friday, and Sunday – were his own, as well as Sunday mornings and two hours on Saturday mornings when he didn't work in the store; much of this time he spent with Bill Baer, walking about town, riding the horsecars and the El roads, exploring the city. Martin was fond of taking the Sixth Avenue El all the way up to the 155th Street terminus and emerging in a world of picnic grounds and beer gardens and dance halls, with a flight of steps up to Washington Heights. But what struck him most on such trips was the vast stretch of land between the Hudson River and the Central Park – a strange mix of four-story row houses and weedgrown vacant lots with rocky outcroppings, of isolated châteaux and clusters of squatter's shacks, of unpaved avenues and tracts of sunken farms like canyons. He had heard a good deal of talk about this wilder and newer part of town; it was said that speculators were holding on to lots in expectation of a boom.

One day shortly before his eighteenth birthday, two

years after he had gone to work as day clerk at the Vanderlyn Hotel, Martin was called into the manager's office, located off the lobby not far from Mr. Henning's office. Alexander Westerhoven was a big man with a plump jowly face and a surprisingly ·sharp profile, as if he had grown thick layers of distorting softness over a sharp hard frame. With a flourish of his right hand he invited Martin to sit in a plumply upholstered oak armchair trimmed with tassels. He began by praising Martin's service behind the desk, referred obscurely to several testimonials to his loyalty and hard work, and broke off with a wave of the hand to thrust at Martin a sheet of blank white paper.

'Your name,' he said, pushing toward Martin a bottle of black ink.

'My name?'

'Your name, your name. You do know how to write your name, Mr. Dressler?'

Martin, irked, dipped the pen in the ink and wrote his name boldly across the middle of the paper. Mr. Westerhoven snatched up the paper and held it up to his face. He studied it for a few moments before thrusting it down.

'Never,' he said, 'underestimate the power of good penmanship.'

Martin looked hard at him, and Mr. Westerhoven, placing the tips of his fingers together, looked hard at the ceiling. Still looking up, he offered Martin the position of personal secretary to the manager at double his present salary. Martin's secretarial duties would be confined largely to Mr. Westerhoven's far-reaching correspondence, although they would include miscellaneous duties as well, such as the reading of the assistant manager's daily reports concerning problems that required prompt attention, the preparation of memoranda for staff use, and the reading and summarizing of each day's correspondence. His new hours would be seven to six Monday through Friday, with a half day from seven to noon on Saturday, and Sunday off.

At first Martin missed the noise and bustle of the desk, the double view of the street through the doors and of the lobby stretching away, the weight of room keys in the palm, the smart uniform buttoned to his chin, the ring of the electric buzzer and the leaping up of bellboys, the snatches of talk, the sheer splendid sound of things – shuffle of suitcases, clank of keys, swish of dress trains, rattle of cab wheels through the suddenly opened doors – from his post behind the polished mahogany counter, but Martin, wearing a new cutaway coat over a shiny vest with a watch chain looped across the front, threw himself into his new duties with helpless zest. If, out at the desk, he had seemed to be in the lively center of things, it was true only in a special and limited sense, for in fact he had been a minor employee in one department of a vast and complex organization that he had scarcely bothered to imagine. Sitting in Mr. Westerhoven's quiet office, reading through piles of correspondence, or taking dictation from Mr. Westerhoven, who liked to walk up and down in the small space between his broad desk and Martin's narrow one with a thumb hooked in his vest pocket and the other hand tugging at his chin, Martin, bewildered but deeply curious, exasperated by his ignorance, vowing to sort things out, to bring disparate details into relation, gradually began to see his way. One thing he saw was that the work of running the hotel was divided far more carefully and precisely than he had imagined, all the way down to the seamstresses and linen-room attendants of the housekeeping department. The bell-boys, the day and night clerks, the doorman, and the elevator operators constituted the front office, and were directly under the supervision of the assistant manager, but the maintenance and smooth operation of the elevators was the direct responsibility of the assistant to the chief engineer. The engineering department also looked after the plumbing, the electric push-button buzzers, the gas lighting fixtures, and the new incandescent lights in the public rooms. Martin, wanting to see for himself, needing to arrange it all in a pattern, went with the chief engineer, Walter Dundee, to look at the new electrical plant in the basement that powered the incandescent lamps in the lobby and main dining room. Standing before the big 120-horsepower dynamo that Dundee said could light up a whole city block, Martin listened carefully to the engineer's prediction that the old push-button buzzers would be driven out by telephones within ten years. Dundee, a lean vigorous man with a gray mustache, and a carpenter's folding rule weighing down the side of his coat pocket, liked to explain things in detail, in a slow serious voice, and Martin liked to listen. The voice reminded Martin of his father explaining to him as a child how to roll a cigar without tearing the wrapper or how the back-and-forth motion of the piston in a steam engine became the circular motion of the flywheel. Martin warmed to the intelligent engineer, who in turn seemed to take an interest in Martin, and asked precise questions of his own about the management of the cigar stand.

But Dundee was only the most likable member of a large hotel staff. Martin visited the poorly ventilated staff dining room, spoke with the headwaiters, the steward, and the managing chef, listened to the complaints of the Irish chambermaids, visited the chief accountant and arranged to take lessons in the elements of bookkeeping. The details interested him, from the operation of the old steam elevators with their winding drums to the washing of the knives and forks, but they had no meaning until they were connected to the larger design. Then he grasped them, then he held them in place and felt a deep and almost physical satisfaction – and in his mind, in his chest, in the veins of his arms, he felt a secret exhilaration, as when in his childhood he had gone shopping with his mother and had realized not only that all the toy fire engines and diamond necklaces and leather gloves were different parts of one big department store, but that the store itself was part of a block of buildings, and all the blocks went repeating themselves, rectangle by rectangle, in every direction, until they formed a city.

As he threw himself into his new duties, which took him away from the life of the lobby but placed him close to the inner workings of the hotel, he sometimes had the sense that he was being led by friendly powers toward a destination they had marked out for him. The management, in the person first of Mr. Henning and then of Mr. Westerhoven, had shown him unusual favor, had singled him out and raised him up from the lowly rank of bellboy to his present position as personal secretary to the manager, all in the space of a few years. There had been rumors from time to time of Mr. Westerhoven's retirement, of Mr. Henning's promotion to manager, of the creation of a new position above assistant manager and below general manager, and Martin, who disliked rumors, which struck him as the exasperating equivalent of speculations about what would have happened if Lee had won the war, or if Booth had been a bad shot – Martin sometimes found himself wondering whether there might be something in the rumors after all, whether the friendly powers might be moving him in a direction. Then the dream-feeling would come over him, as if his real life were not here, where it seemed to be, but over there, a little off to one side, just over there.

Meanwhile the cigar stand was turning a nice little profit. Martin increased the amount of display space for cigarettes and added gift items that proved popular: alligator cigarette cases lined with satin, porcelain figurines of humorous pipe-smoking farmers, cast-iron clown faces that blew streams of little smoke rings. He and Bill Baer discussed ways of drawing women into this mostly male domain: on the cigarette counter they placed a chromo of a well-dressed woman smoking a cigarette, and alongside brightly lacquered boxes of specially selected cigars they set advertising cards directed at a woman in search of the perfect gift for the man in her life. Purchases by women had tripled over the last three months; and Martin added a new line of silver ashtrays, with the hotel insignia, a tiny Vanderlyn, engraved in black and red.

Martin had money now, more than ever before, even after his monthly rent for the cigar stand, his monthly contribution to his father's store, his dinners with Bill Baer, and his visits to the house of rattling windows. In his free hours on the weekends he walked the streets of the city or rode the four Elevated lines, emerging at random from El stations to descend the graceful iron stairways with their peaked roofs, their slender columns ornamented at the top with lacy ironwork. He walked everywhere, alone or with Bill Baer – on sun-striped shadowy avenues under the El tracks, out on East River wharves, past fire escapes hung with blankets and joined by washlines, along new uptown row houses facing weedgrown bushy lots. As he walked, looking about, taking it all in, feeling a pleasant tension in his calves and thighs, he felt a surge of energy, a kind of serene restlessness, a desire to do something, to test himself, to become, in some way, larger than he was. He wasn't sure what it was, this thing he wanted to be, but one day not long after his twentieth birthday he had a little idea that began to occupy his deepest attention.

9

THE PARADISE
MUSÉE

He had learned from his father that the old Paradise
Musée was going to shut down. It stood at the other
end of the block, on the other side of the street, where
he never walked as a child except when his mother
took him to see the exhibits. Moved by memory and
curiosity, Martin paid a visit during his lunch hour to
the gloomy old building with its dark rooms full of
melancholy wax figures and its third-floor hall of
dungeons and prisons. The museum was deserted except
for a single heavyset man in a silk hat who walked
slowly about with his hands behind his back. On the
shadowy second-floor landing, beneath an arched window thick with dust, Martin passed a guard in a dark
green uniform who stood leaning an elbow on the
window embrasure. The guard stared at him with an
expression of hostility and rudely ignored Martin's
question. Martin, feeling a burst of anger in his neck,

began to ask the question again sharply, before he saw that the guard was made of wax. A small spiderweb hung over his mustache. The real guard sat dozing in a chair on the second floor not far from a hooded executioner holding an ax. Downstairs the elderly ticket seller knew only that the lease was up in a few months and that the museum's proprietor, Mr. Toft, was not planning to renew. He had already sold the whole lot of wax figures to an establishment in Coney Island off Surf Avenue. No one knew the landlord's plans, but Martin could ask for himself: Mr. Toft was somewhere in the museum at that very moment, a big man in a silk hat.

Mr. Toft seemed sunk in some private grief and turned to Martin a pair of gloomy dark eyes over folds of tired flesh like melted candlewax. He changed immediately when he learned who Martin was – he remembered buying cigars from him when Martin was a mere slip of a boy. And how was Otto? And his fine mother? In a small restaurant off Third Avenue he listened to Martin's proposal, burst into a sudden sharp laugh, then narrowed his eyes and agreed to lease the building to Martin if Martin could come up with a rent check before the end of the month. He named a large sum that Martin at first thought was a joke. Mr. Toft wiped his mustache with a napkin, removed his watch from his vest pocket and slipped it back in, and asked to be remembered to Martin's father and mother.

Martin watched Mr. Toft's broad back retreating down the street and tried to recall him from the old days, but saw only the present Mr. Toft with his melancholy eyes, bushy mustache, and candlewax eye-pouches. He gave up the idea of the lease as a stupid mistake, then changed his mind and paid a visit to his bank, where he was well known. In a small neat room with a big dark desk that reminded Martin of a great slab of chocolate, the banker explained that under the circumstances a loan would have to be guaranteed by a co-signer.

'But I can guarantee it myself,' said Martin. 'Down to the last nickel.'

'Not in the way we mean,' replied the banker patiently, with a slight smile.

Martin, who was determined to act without his father's help, angrily abandoned his crackpot scheme. So that was how it was! Despite his success at the Vanderlyn, in the eyes of the world he was nothing at all. It occurred to him that the world was of course right. All very well and good to be the private secretary to the manager of the Vanderlyn Hotel, and to put a little vim into a dead cigar stand, but measured against his own confused desires, these were the accomplishments of a boy. Mr. Toft's sharp laugh came back to him, and the patient dry tone of the banker, and he wondered what kind of young dummkopf they supposed he was. In his boyhood bed over the cigar store he slept badly for two nights, and at noon the next day he had lunch with Walter Dundee.

He laid out his plan carefully before the chief engineer, whose good will he had felt from the beginning and whose clear hard sense of how things worked was never dry or dreary. Martin described his interview with the banker and presented the plan in its entirety: a lunchroom on the first floor and a billiard parlor on the second and third floors. Dundee listened thoughtfully, then put down his fork and asked detailed questions that soon revealed flaws in Martin's thinking. It would take much more money than he had imagined to build the ground-floor lunchroom, which couldn't simply be inserted into the existing structure but would require the knocking down of interior walls. And the building was an old one, fitted for gas. It would have to be wired for electricity – had he thought of that? Martin, who had wanted advice about securing a loan and had secretly hoped that Dundee himself, after hearing the scheme, might be willing to serve as guarantor, now felt irritable and idiotic. He scraped back his chair and was about to rise when Dundee began scribbling figures on a piece of paper, tapping the pencil eraser against his upper lip, and scribbling again. He slid the paper across to Martin. 'This is a rough estimate – very rough, since I haven't been inside the place in ten years. You never know about those old buildings. What I propose is this. I'll put up the money myself in return for a partnership: fifty-fifty. Even Steven. Goes without saying I'll have to check the place first.'

Martin, who was still irritable and whose first impulse was to refuse the offer, accepted in confusion, and that night in bed he tried to understand his odd impulse of refusal and the slight disappointment he continued to feel in the center of his exhilaration. What irked him was the idea of the partnership itself, for he had wanted to do something on his own steam. He felt a kind of inner straining at the leash, an almost physical desire to pour out his energy without constraint. This secret ingratitude, which in one sense disturbed him, in another pleased him immensely, for wasn't it the sign of his high desire? And from somewhere in the region of his stomach came a burst of gratitude to Walter Dundee, for permitting him to know his desire.

Martin now flung himself with full energy into his new scheme, eating quick dinners at the hotel dining room and hurrying over to the Paradise Musée with Walter Dundee. Within a week he confessed to himself that his partner was invaluable. Martin had known exactly what was necessary in a well-run cigar stand, but his sense of a desirable lunchroom, though clear and precise in certain respects, was weakened by small failures of imagination. Dundee, striding up and down the ground floor of the Paradise Musée, pausing to take measurements and make sketches, tackled one technical matter after another: the gas fixtures needed to be replaced by modern incandescent lighting, the walls needed to be knocked down, the window openings enlarged and fitted with sheets of plate glass. One of the marble fireplaces might be retained as a decorative touch, but steam radiators fed by a boiler would provide the heat. Dundee examined the floors and walls, which were solid, prowled in the cellar, noted a loose baluster on the stairway leading to the third floor. The yellowing cold-water washstand in its dank closet was thirty years out of date. Dundee proposed brand-new plumbing, a big new lavatory with marble washstands having two ivory-handled faucets and hot-and-cold running water, and private pull-chain toilets for the use of customers.

Martin followed each idea closely, placed it in the general plan, evaluated it in relation to the larger scheme; and though he deferred to the older man's superior knowledge, Dundee in turn listened to Martin's sharp, vigorous sense of what customers would find attractive in a lunchroom. Dundee, whose impulse was always in the direction of the practical and efficient, wanted to seat as many customers as the available space permitted; Martin persuaded him to sacrifice a number of seats for the sake of an elusive but crucial principle: the slippery element, created from a combination of many small precise decisions, known as atmosphere. A hungry man would stop anywhere for a bite to eat. What Martin wanted was the kind of lunchroom that would attract a man who wasn't hungry.

'You want to lure 'em in, do you?' Dundee said, looking at Martin with amusement.

'I want more than that,' Martin said. 'I want to keep 'em in. I want people to return. I want them to be unhappy when they're not here.'

'That's a tall order,' said Dundee.

'It's a tall city,' Martin said quickly.

One Saturday about a week after workmen began to arrive at the Paradise Musée, Martin took Bill Baer to look at the work. He had spoken to Walter Dundee about his friend, with a view to including him somehow in the project, and as he stepped among workmen's tools and piles of lumber and old sawhorses he tried to make Baer see the new lunchroom – the gleaming windows, the curve of the polished oak counter, the pedestal tables, the steady glow of electric lights. Later, at

64

dinner, he made his proposal: Bill would give up the cigar stand and come to work on the first of the year for Martin and Dundee. They needed a man to oversee the daily operation of the lunchroom and billiard parlor, to keep close track of expenses and profits, to be on the premises, to settle problems and keep his eyes open – to serve in short as a kind of managing assistant, at a salary nearly double his present one. Martin, who had expected to see a look of bewildered gratitude on Bill Baer's face, was puzzled to see him stare down at his plate with a small tense frown. He looked up and said, 'It's not for me.'

Martin gave an impatient little lift to his shoulders and turned both hands palm up.

Bill said, 'Oh, I could probably learn the ropes well enough, and not shame myself or let anyone down. And God knows I can use the money. But I'd never feel – it would never suit me, Martin. I'd always feel I was in over my head. Cigars are what I know – it's in my blood. I'm a cigar man, every inch of the way.'

'You're any kind of man you damn well want to make yourself,' Martin said, surprised by the sharpness in his voice.

'Then I damn well want to be a cigar man.'

'Then what you damn well want –,' Martin began, but gave it up. Bill was explaining how he wanted to have a cigar store of his own one day, maybe down in the old neighborhood; he was saving like crazy. He too broke off and looked sharply at Martin.

'Look here, Martin. Say someone offered to let you

run a carriage factory, or a big city bank. The whole shebang. Would you do it?'

'Like that,' Martin said, snapping his fingers.

Bill burst out laughing. 'I think you really would.' He shook his head. Martin expected him to say something more but Bill took a long drink of beer, and the next day, as Martin reported the conversation to Walter Dundee, he didn't know what irked him more: the sharp tone he had taken with his friend, or Bill's bewildered, slightly sorrowful shake of the head. Dundee, who had had misgivings about hiring an amateur, was visibly relieved, and Martin turned his attention to a part of the business that Dundee had failed to consider at all.

Martin had been studying the rows of advertising cards that adorned the inside of every car on the horse railway lines, for he had immediately sensed their tremendous power: people trapped in the slow-moving cars, with nothing to look at except the face of some stranger across the way, let their gaze drift to the advertisements, which attempted to seize their attention with bold lettering and clever pictures calculated to make a sharp, decisive impression. The Jap-a-lac lady in her white apron, painting a window frame and smiling at the viewer over her shoulder, or the man in the ad for Sapolio soap, staring at his face reflected in the shiny back of a pan, were the daily companions of thousands of horsecar riders, who saw the same ads in daily papers and weekly magazines, on cards in shop windows, on posters stuck on hoardings and the walls of El stations, until they were as familiar as the nose on George Washington's face. One afternoon Martin paid a visit to one of the new downtown ad agencies, which placed ads in newspapers and did business with a dozen different streetcar lines, including the new Broadway cable cars. The art director agreed to prepare some sketches for him.

Martin envisioned a single, striking image that would draw people to the lunchroom: a bowl of soup with wriggly lines indicating warmth and, just above the bowl, a man's face with half-closed eyes and a smile of rapture.

Meanwhile his work at the hotel was going well. Mr. Westerhoven knew the hotel business thoroughly, took pride in the Vanderlyn, and behaved with scrupulous fairness toward every member of the staff, though he proved to have one flaw: he liked his hotel just as it was, and was indecisive over the question of costly innovations. He understood that times were changing, that steam radiators were replacing hot-air vents, that room telephones were bound to replace electric buzzers, but he questioned the necessity of such changes even as he bowed, rather stiffly, to the inevitable. He seemed to enjoy hearing Martin's view of such things, as if this permitted him to maintain his opposition while passing on to his youthful secretary the responsibility for each disastrous turn to the modern. Martin, who believed that the Vanderlyn was in danger of becoming antiquated, argued that up-to-date improvements weren't luxuries but necessities of the modern hotel, though he acknowledged that the spirit of a hotel was larger and more complex than technology alone could account for: people liked telephones and the new electric elevators and private toilets and incandescent lights, but at the same time they liked old-world architecture, period furniture, dim suggestions of the very world that was being annihilated by American efficiency and know-how. People needed to be assured that they weren't missing the latest improvements, while at the same time they wanted to be told that nothing ever changed. Hence the cleverness, the sheer genius, of a little invention like the electric chandelier, with its combination of Mr. Edison and the courts of Europe. To Mr. Westerhoven's objection that this was a hopeless paradox, Martin answered that that was the point: people wanted the paradoxical, the impossible, and it was the Vanderlyn's job to provide it. The solution, Martin argued, was to move in both directions at once – to introduce every mechanical improvement without fail, and at the same time to emphasize the past, especially in decor. He had seen the same idea at work in the El trains: miles of iron girders and columns, the whole thing a masterpiece of modern engineering, the cars equipped with up-to-date running gear – but step inside those cars and you saw old-world mahogany paneling on the walls, tapestry curtains on the windows, and Axminster carpets on the floors. He had been told that the old-fashioned curtains were hung on concealed spring rollers.

At night in his boyhood bed over the cigar store, beside his old chest of drawers on which stood a hand-painted photograph of himself at the age of six, a dark-haired boy with clear serious eyes, Martin thought of iron El trestles winding and stretching across the city, of department store windows and hotel lobbies, of electric elevators and streetcar ads, of the city pressing its way north on both sides of the great park, of dynamos and electric lights, of ten-story hotels, of the old iron tower near the depot at West Brighton with its two steam-driven elevators rising and falling in the sky – and in his blood he felt a surge of restlessness, as if he were a steam train spewing fiery coalsmoke into the black night sky as he roared along a trembling El track, high above the dark storefronts, the gaslit saloons, the red-lit doorways, the cheap beer dives, the dance halls, the gambling joints, the face in the doorway, the sudden cry in the night.

10

CAROLINE
AND EMMELINE
VERNON

The Metropolitan Lunchroom and Billiard Parlor opened on a Saturday in mid-October of 1894, six weeks after Martin's twenty-second birthday. The facade had been painted a cheerful shade of blue, with yellow trim, and on the sidewalk near the door stood a wooden Pilgrim in breeches and buckle shoes, holding a horn of plenty. The success of the first weekend wasn't surprising to Martin, who said to Dundee that people were curious and would try anything once; the trick was to get 'em to stick. When they stuck he refused to celebrate, arguing that it was too soon to be sure, though customers were praising the lunch special: corned beef hash served with German browned potatoes fried in butter, with a slice of hot apple pie for dessert. The pies, ordered fresh each morning from a nearby bakery, were three inches thick and flavored with cinnamon. A dip in the fourth week's revenue convinced Dundee that

Martin had been right all along, but Martin gave a shrug and said it was nothing. The same thing had happened with the cigar stand and would happen again. By the end of the sixth week Martin was willing to sit down to a celebratory steak dinner with Dundee, but even as he raised his stein of beer he argued that it would be a serious mistake to stop advertising simply because they were having an early success: now that ads were everywhere you looked, people were starting to feel that the very fact of repeated ads was a sign of success. When Dundee appeared doubtful, Martin proposed that they prepare a questionnaire for customers, asking how they had first heard of the Metropolitan Lunchroom and how many times they had patronized it.

Martin himself had begun to study the classified pages of three daily papers and to make occasional trips north on the Sixth Avenue El, and one day he made up his mind. Without telling anyone he rented a parlor-and-bedroom suite in a new apartment hotel in the West End that seemed to have sprung up overnight on a vacant side street with a view of the Hudson. He had searched the streets and lanes all through the 60s but kept moving north through the 70s until he had found what he wanted: an impossible building set down in the middle of nowhere by an enterprising developer inspired by the example of the Dakota but with his eye on a middle-class clientele. The nine-story hotel, with its medieval turrets and oriel windows and its modern hydraulic elevators, faced a stretch of weedgrown lots where goats roamed behind ramshackle fences. Martin felt he had moved to another city, one younger and more rural, a world he had glimpsed from the El road as he rushed north on his voyages of exploration.

Everything seemed new: the smell of the river through his half-open bedroom window, the runny bright-yellow yolks of poached eggs in the hotel dining room, the wintry early-morning walk over to the El station on Columbus Avenue. He still thought of it as Ninth. Up here, in the wilderness, even the names changed: the northern extension of Broadway was the Boulevard, a wide avenue of hard-packed dirt. From the high platform of the Eighty-first Street station he could see to the west the half-iced Hudson and the red-brown Palisades, to the east the thin dark river and the bluish-brown hills of Brooklyn. Below the Park the train swung east, the track split into the Ninth Avenue and Sixth Avenue lines, already he could hear the bang of his heels down the iron steps of the station and feel steam heat on his cold cheeks as he entered the Vanderlyn. They all thought he was mad, banishing himself like that to the remote north. You'd have thought he had moved to the land of igloos and polar bears. But even as he bent over his desk in a corner of the manager's office, even as he entered the old Paradise Musée and saw with approval the men standing shoulder to shoulder at the polished oak counter of the Metropolitan Lunchroom, Martin looked forward to the night ride into his untamed neighborhood. Row houses were rising on graded side streets, but here and there a decaying farmhouse sat in a field of pricker bushes and Queen Anne's lace.

Sometimes, when he walked over to the cigar store on his lunch hour, he felt, as he stepped inside, a sudden impatience, as if the brown dusk, the tulip-shaped globes of the cigar lighter, the jars of sweet-smelling tobacco were part of a world he had left long ago, a world of red horsecars carpeted with straw, of short pants and bedtime stories, of his mother's hand as they walked up Broadway past big windows and clattering omnibuses. And he longed for Saturday afternoon, for Sunday, when he could walk for hours along the six avenues of his new West End world, under the brown bare elms of the Boulevard or up along the wilder reaches of the Central Park, where tarpaper shanties sprouted in the scrub; when he could walk wherever he liked, turning at a whim to explore the cross streets, many of them muddy lanes, or weedgrown paths between cliffs of rock.

On Sunday evenings he took to having dinner in the dark-paneled dining room of the Bellingham, at a small table near a window looking out on a vacant lot. Beyond the lot came snow-streaked vegetable gardens and the backs of four-story row houses. At his window Martin would read over reports or settle down with a newspaper before rising from his chair and nodding at clusters of fellow diners. Among them were three women who sat always at the same table, two tables distant from his own. They appeared to be a mother and two grown daughters, whom he never saw at breakfast, although one Saturday, when Mr. Westerhoven dismissed him early and he took lunch at the Bellingham, he saw them entering the dining room as he was rising to leave. What struck him about the picturesque group was that the mother and the older, dark-haired daughter talked easily together, while the pale-haired daughter with the pretty face sat eating in silence, with lowered eyes, which she raised only sometimes to look out the window. And whereas Mrs. Vernon – he had caught the name as a waiter delivered a dish – and the dark-haired daughter had begun to look his way, and to smile when Martin entered or rose to leave, the quiet daughter never looked toward him and, if she did not entirely ignore his greetings, restricted her acknowledgments to brief unsmiling nods, during which her gaze would fall to the left or right of his face.

One night when Martin returned to his hotel at about ten o'clock, after going over accounts with Walter Dundee and discussing the possibility of opening a second lunchroom farther uptown, he saw in one of the parlors off the main lobby the three Vernon women sitting in armchairs around a small dark table, on which sat three slender glasses filled with amber-colored liquid. As he passed the open doorway on his way to the elevators, he nodded at Mrs. Vernon, who smiled at him in so inviting a way that he hesitated in the doorway as he said 'Good evening' – and moments later he found himself seated in an armchair between the mother and the fair-haired daughter, facing the dark-haired daughter. Mrs. Vernon laughingly introduced herself and her daughters: Caroline (fair) and Emmeline (dark). Martin formally introduced himself, felt irked at something stiff in his tone, immediately shook it off, and entered the spirit of Mrs. Vernon and Emmeline, both of whom were quick and intelligent and asked precise questions about his work at the Vanderlyn and his role in the transformation of the old Paradise Musée. Caroline Vernon, on his right, remained silent and apart, in a way that the others seemed not to mind. The dimmed light glowing through dome-shaped porcelain lampshades painted with landscapes, the quietness of the nearby lobby, the dark-red armchairs patterned with wavy gold leaves, the shine of dark wood and of the amber liqueurs in the longstemmed glasses, the quiet laughter of the women, the sense of intimacy about the small table, all this soothed something deep in Martin, who found himself speaking about his life and his plans until he suddenly stopped short with an apology and began asking questions of his own. Mrs. Vernon said that she was from Boston, where both girls had grown up. Mr. Vernon had been an attorney, who two years ago had been transferred to a big New York law firm and whose sudden death had been a devastating blow, though fortunately he had left his little family well enough provided for, though heaven knew you couldn't be too careful, and on the advice of a family friend she had moved uptown into the wilderness, where the rents were half what they were downtown. Of course things were a bit slow out here, especially when you knew no one and had to watch every penny; and sometimes it seemed as if they were becalmed, simply becalmed, waiting for the wind to pick up and fill their sails. 'So you're a traveler, are you?' Martin asked Mrs. Vernon with a smile. 'Oh,' Emmeline answered, 'we've traveled extensively in the lobby of the Bellingham Hotel' – and she looked at him so playfully, so expectantly, that Martin felt he ought to make a witty reply, but he could think of nothing, and burst out laughing. Suddenly Caroline rose, said she was tired, and walked out of the room.

There was a moment of awkwardness, which Mrs. Vernon quickly covered with talk; and now that Caroline had left, Martin yielded entirely to the warm friendliness of the little circle in the lamplit parlor. When the evening ended nearly an hour later, with Martin's discovery that it was practically midnight, he felt that an understanding had been reached: they liked each other, they had begun a friendship. And he had learned one fact that struck him: it was Caroline who was the older daughter, by two years, though she looked five years younger. Perhaps it was her small and almost childish features, especially her little girl's nose, that made her seem younger than Emmeline, whose strong straight nose and black thick eyebrows gave her a look of masculine energy; her shoulders were broader, her voice deeper and more resonant, than Caroline's. It struck him too that Emmeline in some sense watched over her sister, filled in gaps left by Caroline's silence, took upon herself the task of speaking for both of them – while Caroline, with her pale hair pulled tightly back, so that it seemed to pull painfully against the skin of her temples, Caroline, with her delicate pale face and small mouth and large brown eyes looking away, Caroline Vernon, sunk in her dream, seemed the younger sister, protected by mother and older sister from unwelcome disturbances and intrusions.

Now every evening when Martin returned to the

Bellingham after late hours at his office in the Vanderlyn, or supper with his parents in the small kitchen over the cigar store, on the familiar old plates with the blue Dutch children on them, or his weekly visit to the brothel on West Twenty-fifth Street, he would glance in at the lamplit parlor off the main lounge. There the Vernon women sat night after night, sipping bright-colored liquids from thin glasses. At a smile from Mrs. Vernon or a wave from Emmeline he would enter the parlor and sink into a waiting armchair, before the dark-gleaming table with its glowing dome-shaded lamp, an ivory-colored lamp with little Nile-green sailboats and a Nile-green island on the translucent porcelain shade and, on the porcelain body, little Nile-green houses on a Nile-green hillside – an admirable lamp, a really first-rate lamp that, he assured the Vernon women, with its removable oil fount and its excellent center-draft burner, was as hopelessly antiquated in the new world of incandescent lighting as the stage coach in a world of steam trains. Had they noticed, incidentally, that the overhead lights in the lobby and dining room were all electric, even the chandeliers? For it was interesting, it was a subject that never ceased to fascinate him, how the two worlds existed together, the world of oil lamps and incandescent lights, of horsecars and steam trains, one world gradually crowding out the other. Mrs. Vernon and Emmeline encouraged him to continue such discussions, Emmeline putting in a sharp, thoughtful question whenever something wasn't absolutely clear to her, and both continued to question him closely about his work. Martin felt pleased and soothed to recount the minor adventures of his day: the resistance of Mr. Westerhoven to everything new, along with a secret willingness to give way in the face of superior argument; the slackness of the new bellboy, who had been caught smoking a cigarette in a fourth-floor corridor; Dundee's brilliantly meticulous mind, which foresaw every expense and left nothing to chance, but which resisted anything daring or unusual, such as Martin's suggestion that one of the two floors of billiard tables be reserved for women. His own father, a tobacco man of the old stamp, they didn't make them like that any more, his own father still wouldn't hear of stocking cigarettes – could anyone believe it? And he turned to Caroline, as if he were asking whether she was able to believe it; and Caroline lowered her eyes.

Caroline Vernon's quietness had quickly come to seem part of the nature of things, a form of reserve rather than of sullenness. Besides, she was by no means silent, but now and then spoke a few quiet words, to which Martin listened with deep attention, as if a remark such as 'I prefer warm weather, but not too warm,' or 'It was the Sunday we were walking in the park and there was a sudden shower' were a revelation of her innermost nature. She no longer ignored Martin, but nodded at him when he joined the group or rose to go – a small, not unfriendly nod and a brief brushing of his face with her large, half-closed eyes, which shone vividly in the lamplight and might have seemed startlingly vivid had it not been for the heavy eyelids, which gave her a languorous and almost sleepy air.

One evening when Martin returned from the Vanderlyn a little later than usual – it was getting on toward
eleven, he had been studying the report of expenses
provided by the head of housekeeping – he glanced in at
the parlor and was surprised to see four empty armchairs about the familiar table. He hesitated, then
stepped inside. At the far end of the parlor an elderly
woman looked up from a book. Martin, who recognized
her from the dining room, nodded and sat down. He
unbuttoned his coat and removed from his vest pocket a
silver-cased watch. At the touch of a pin the lid opened.
It was 10:52; they had often sat until midnight. He
closed the watch cover, replaced the watch in his vest
pocket, and settled back. A moment later he sprang up
and looked into the lobby, where a few guests sat
reading newspapers. Martin glanced in at the other
parlor and the small library, returned to the first parlor,
and at last checked with the night clerk, who said that
the Vernons had taken a late supper, gone for a walk,
and returned to their rooms a little past nine. They had
not come down.

Martin sat in the lamplit parlor for twenty minutes,
looking at the three empty armchairs, in which he could
almost see the three Vernon women: Mrs. Vernon, with
her dark combs glinting in the lamplight as she laughed;
Emmeline, with her sharp intelligent eyes and slightly
too large mouth; Caroline, with her hair pulled back
tight and her eyelids lowered. As he stared at Caroline's
chair, which showed in the dark-red gold-flowered seat a
faint depression that seemed to hold her ghostly form,
he saw on the red-and-gold arm of the chair a single long

yellow hair. Martin rose, looked quickly about, and bent down to examine it. He saw that it was a trick of the light on the raised gold flowers of the dark-red arm. He felt such an unexpected shock of desolation that a few minutes later when he stepped from the elevator and began walking down the corridor he couldn't remember whether he had said good night to old Jackson, the elevator man, and later that night he woke from a dream in which he bent to kiss the hand of Mrs. Vernon and saw, on the back of her long black glove, a bright yellow hair that suddenly began to wriggle away.

11

A SUNDAY
AFTERNOON
STROLL

They were there the next evening, seated around the little table with its dome-shaded lamp, and as Martin stepped through the open doorway Mrs. Vernon looked at him anxiously, as if to implore his forgiveness. Caroline had been unwell – a headache and low fever – and she and Emmeline had stayed with her in her room, even though Caroline had told them she only needed rest, had in fact urged them to go down and wait for Mr. Dressler in the parlor. But Emmeline had insisted on staying by Caro's side, and she herself – well, the truth of the matter was that they were all rather fatigued after a long day of walking. But it was so good to see Mr. Dressler again. They had missed him, indeed they had. For surely she did not exaggerate if she said that he had become a regular member of their little family.

Martin, who had been irritable all day, felt so soothed by her words that he experienced a sharp desire to leave immediately for his room, so that he could lie down with his arm over his eyes and repeat the words carefully to himself, listening to them with close attention, examining them for meanings that might have escaped him in the pressure of the moment.

Instead he turned abruptly to Caroline and said, a little too loudly, 'I hope you're feeling better tonight.'

'Yes,' said Caroline, 'a little better, thank you,' looking at him a moment with her heavy-lidded, slightly moist eyes, with their dark lashes that did not match her straw-colored hair and, in the lamplight, shone with a faint blue sheen; and as she returned her gaze to the small table, Martin seemed to feel, in the skin of his cheeks, in the tips of his fingers, a faint prickle, as if she had brushed the edges of those sharp lashes across his face and fingertips.

One Sunday afternoon when he returned to the Bellingham from the Vanderlyn, he saw the three Vernon women in the parlor, drinking tea. Martin had been planning to have lunch at a riverside roadhouse near the railroad yards and then walk up Riverside Drive to watch men blasting a twenty-foot-high ledge of rock to make way for a new shipping magnate's mansion. Instead he asked the Vernons whether they would like to walk over to the Boulevard and watch the Sunday bicyclists. 'Oh, I'd love to!' cried Emmeline, clapping her hands; Caroline lowered her eyes; and Mrs. Vernon said she thought it would make a lovely excursion.

It was a bright blue day in late March. On the bare-looking branches of the thin new trees in front of the Bellingham, a yellow-green shimmer showed against the sky, like an exhalation. A few brown leaves hung down like scraps of old wrapping paper. They walked two by two along the new cut-stone sidewalk that ended at a vacant lot, Martin and Mrs. Vernon in front of Emmeline and Caroline. Martin, feeling splendid in his new chocolate-brown derby and his new chocolate-brown spring overcoat, looked admiringly at Mrs. Vernon, all decked out in her flower-heaped hat tied with a green ribbon under the chin, her long green coat with its black cape. The weather, Mrs. Vernon said, was simply treacherous, hot one minute and cold the next – a person had no idea how to dress. She had insisted that Emmy and Caro dress for winter, and now it would be her fault if both of them had to take to their beds with a cold. As she spoke she glanced back at her daughters, and Martin followed her glance, struck with admiration at the sight of the two sun-brightened Vernon daughters with their faces in shadow under flower-heaped hats tied under their chins: Emmeline in a long dark-blue coat trimmed with black wool, Caroline in a long brown coat with a black shoulder cape and a small black muff pushed up onto one wrist.

They crossed West End Avenue and came to a built-up block. Sunlight shone on red brick and tawny brick and cream-colored brick, flashed on copper and tile trim, sparkled on the tall second-floor bay windows. In the windows Martin could see reflections of black branches and red brick and blue sky, and through the branches and the brick a dim vase, the glowing top of a chair, a shadowy oval photograph on a dark piano. Streaks of old snow lay in the shadows of stoops and on the dark squares of dirt under the yellow-green leaf buds. At the end of the street, on the Boulevard, Martin saw high-seated cyclists passing on their tall wheels. People stood watching on the corner, watching and cheering on the wide strip of grass and elms that divided the Boulevard into two cycling roads. On the other side of the grass, cyclists passed the other way. Behind Martin, steamboat whistles sounded on the river, beyond the Boulevard he heard the rumble of the El on Columbus Avenue, somewhere an organ grinder played his bright, melancholy tune, and in the mild air chilled by river breezes he caught a faint peppery smell of horsedung from the daily wagonloads stored down by the wharves. Suddenly a burst of brassy music filled the air. As Martin turned the corner onto the broad side-walk running along the elm-lined Boulevard he saw a German band under the trees on the central strip, and above the watching faces the high-seated cyclists moved on sun-sparkling spinning-spoked wheels, and past the tall bare elms and the riders in their cycling costumes he could see down the far street to the dark band of the El track and, farther away, the bare trees of the Park hung with a pale green haze; and turning excitedly to look for Emmeline and Caroline, who might, he thought, wish to walk along the sidewalk in search of a better place from which to view the pageant of cyclists, he felt his turning shoulder strike the brim of a hat and saw Caroline's suddenly exposed sun-dazzled pale hair and startled eyes before she raised both hands and pulled the hat in place, shading her face as he shouted an apology in a blare of trumpets and trombones.

12

THE RADIATOR

The warm weather turned cold, a light snow fell, and when Martin stepped into the lobby of the Vanderlyn in the early mornings or the lobby of the Bellingham in the late evenings his cheeks tightened and tingled in the dry warmth. Mrs. Vernon said it would be the death of her, simply the death; and Martin agreed that it had been an unusually treacherous winter.

One cold evening when Martin entered the lobby of the Bellingham he was surprised to see Mrs. Vernon step from the parlor and hurry toward him. Her expression was anxious; she began with an apology. Martin, suddenly alarmed, glanced into the parlor and saw four empty armchairs about the little table. His alarm seemed to alarm Mrs. Vernon, who urged him not to worry. 'But what is it?' he said. 'What's happened?' The story emerged slowly: Caroline's radiator had banged away all night, Caroline hadn't slept a wink and was on the verge of nervous prostration, the young man who had come to fix it in the morning hadn't done a bit of good. They were at their wits' end. 'But it's a simple matter,' Martin said. 'There's water in the radiator and it has to be let out. Did he check the valve?' She couldn't remember whether the young man had checked the valve or not, and begged Martin to rescue them.

In the Vernons' lamplit parlor on the fifth floor, Caroline lay back with half-closed eyes on a blue-green sofa, patterned with long, curving ivory leaves and twisting silver vines. Her face against the blue-green damask looked very pale, as if she were a little girl lost in a blue-green forest. Two little lines of strain showed between her dark eyebrows. Emmeline, tired and humorous, led Martin into Caroline's room, where the offending radiator stood under a windowsill, between the mahogany bed and a mirrored wardrobe. Martin squatted beside the radiator and Emmeline bent over, hands on knees, to watch. He checked the valve, which was open.

'The banging comes from steam hitting water in here,' Martin said, tapping the radiator with a knuckle. 'There shouldn't be any water in the radiator. It's supposed to flow out through this pipe down here.' He pointed to the pipe under the inlet valve. 'All we have to do is tilt the radiator toward the inlet valve. You don't happen to have a block of wood or a brick?'

'I might have one in my purse,' Emmeline said, and Martin looked at her with surprise before it struck him that she had said something amusing.

Five minutes later Martin returned to the Vernons' apartment holding in his hand a dark book. In Caroline's bedroom he knelt down, lifted the unattached end of the radiator, and slipped the book under. 'That should do the trick,' he said, slapping dust from his hands. Still squatting, he looked up at Emmeline. 'Does anyone ever fiddle with this valve?'

'Caroline turns the heat off when it gets too hot.'

'Well,' Martin said, 'there you have it. You should never turn this knob unless the radiator is cool. If you turn it off when the radiator's hot, the steam gets trapped in the pipes and can't drain out when it condenses into water. Better just to leave it alone.' On a mahogany dresser with an oval bevel-edged mirror lay Caroline's flowered hat.

'I think I see. And your book?'

Martin burst out laughing. '*An Introduction to the Art of Typewriting*. I taught myself last year. This is as good a place for it as any.'

'Well,' said Emmeline, leading him back into the parlor, 'the mystery has been solved. You're quite the hero, sir.'

'I should say so,' said Mrs. Vernon. 'How can we ever thank you?'

'Please,' Martin said, holding up a hand and shaking his head. 'It's nothing at all.' He glanced at Caroline, who murmured 'Thank you' and, turning her cheek toward the blue-green sofa-back, sank into the curving leaves and twisting vines.

13

INTIMACIES

Now on late Sunday mornings in the warming air, Martin led the Vernons on excursions about the neighborhood, stopping with them for a late lunch in a shady beer garden or outdoor cafe and then pushing on into the lengthening afternoons. He took them up along the park by the river into a world of turreted granite mansions and ivy-covered red-brick villas rising among tall oaks and lush lawns. They walked in the winding park with its steep bluffs and sudden open riverviews, passed through an orchard of apple and peach trees, ate a picnic lunch while sun and shade moved on their hands. Through the trembling leaves Martin pointed to boys fishing on a sun-flooded wharf. Three-stacked steamers moved on the river. Suddenly a train came clattering past on the open tracks between the park and the river, a smell of animals was in the air; Mrs. Vernon wrinkled her nose. But Martin had come to like the harsh smell of cattle riding in cars toward the slaughterhouses down in the west thirties. Through the upper trees he pointed to a flash of yellow: the cab of a steam shovel sitting in a cleared side-street lot. The West End was growing, it was growing even as they sat like people in a picture eating their picnic lunch on a lazy Sunday afternoon – lots were being cleared, streets graded, rocks blasted, excavations dug. Row houses were springing up left and right, but the future, Martin told them, lay up in the sky – in apartment houses and family hotels, in grand multiple dwellings. And as he spoke, the park, the river, the trembling spots of sun and shade, the three women, all fell away; and he saw, rising up along the avenues between the Central Park and the river, into the blue air, high buildings, shining and many-windowed, serene and imperious.

He learned one evening that they had never ridden on an El train. The next Sunday Martin led them up a flight of roofed iron stairs toward the station high above the street. With its peaked gables and its gingerbread trim, the station looked like a country cottage raised on iron columns. Martin bought four tickets in the station agent's office and led the three women through the two waiting rooms, one for men and one for women, each with its pine benches and black walnut paneling. Sunlight poured through the blue stained-glass windows and lay in long blue parallelograms on the floor. Outside on the roofed platform they looked down at rows of striped awnings over the shop windows of Columbus Avenue, each with its patch of shade, and watched the black roofs of passing hacks. Suddenly there was a throbbing in the platform, a growing roar – people stepped back. Mrs. Vernon gripped Martin's arm, white smoke mixed with fiery ashes streamed backward as the engine neared, and with a hiss of steam and a grinding sound like the clashing of many pairs of scissors, the train halted at the platform. There was a sting of coalsmoke in the air. The cars were apple green. Martin looked at his three women defiantly, as if to say: Isn't it a fine color! Isn't it grand! Inside he gestured proudly toward the oak-paneled ceilings, as if he had designed them himself, pointed out the mahogany-trimmed walls painted with plants and flowers, the tapestry curtains over the wide, arched windows; and guiding the three women past the long seats that ran parallel to the walls, he led them to the center of the car, where a group of red leather seats were set at right angles to the wall and faced each other, and where Mrs. Vernon, holding onto her hat, insisted on having a seat by the window.

He tried to show them the city stretching away to the north and south, from the northernmost station with its shady beer garden to the South Ferry terminal with its view of the bay: the thicket of masts and yardarms tilted in every direction, the slow-moving tugs hauling barges, ferries crossing to the Jersey shore. From shaking clattering cars he made them look for signs painted on the sides of rushing-away buildings: New York Belting and Packing Company, Vulcanized Rubber, Knox the Hatter, Street Brass, Oyster House, Men's Fine Clothes. From trains rushing north and south he pointed at the tops of horsecars and brewer's wagons, at wharves and square-riggers and barrel-heaped barges, at awnings stained rust-red from showers of iron particles ground off by El train brake shoes. He pointed at open windows through which they could see women bent over sewing machines and coatless men in vests playing cards around a table, pointed at intersecting avenues and distant high hotels – and there in the sky, a miracle of steel-frame construction, the American Surety building, twenty stories high, dwarfing old Trinity's brown-stone tower.

But from the carpeted cars, steaming along at the height of third-story windows, the city seemed to evade him, to be always ducking out of sight around a corner. Irked at himself, Martin led the Vernon women down clattering station stairways to look at details: strips of sun and shadow rippling across a cabhorse's back under a curving El track, old steel rails glinting in cobble-stones. He bought them bags of hot peanuts from a peanut wagon with a steam whistle. He showed them Mott Street pushcarts heaped with goats' cheese and green olives and sweet fennel, took them along East River docks where bowsprits and jib booms reached halfway across the street. He walked them through an open market down by Pier 19, where horses in blankets stood hitched to wagons loaded with baskets of cab-bages and turnips. 'Look at that!' he cried, pointing to an old-clothes seller wearing a swaying stack of twelve hats, a gigantic pair of wooden scissors over a cutter's shop. Down a narrow sidestreet in a bright crack between warehouses, an East River scow filled with cobblestones slipped by. But the images seemed scattered and disconnected; and Martin felt a disappointment, a restlessness, as if he needed to go about it another way, a way that eluded him.

Although Martin liked having the three Vernon women with him on weekend excursions and on evenings in the lamplit parlor, he also enjoyed the combinations that arose when one or another of them was absent. Some evenings Caroline would excuse herself before the others, pleading tiredness, urging them to stay – and the sense that he was alone with Mrs. Vernon and Emmeline made Martin experience an exhilarating peacefulness, which puzzled and even disturbed him, for it was as if Caroline had in some way constrained him. At the same time his awareness of her absence, sharp as an odor, made him realize the intensity of her presence, when she was actually there, despite the fact that her actual presence resembled nothing so much as absence. Even Mrs. Vernon and Emmeline seemed to relax a little when Caroline was absent, to become slightly more playful – and leaning toward him with shining eyes, Mrs. Vernon tapped him lightly on the wrist with the tip of her black silk fan.

From the beginning he had noticed that Mrs. Vernon had a girlishness, even a flirtatiousness, that seemed to expand and flourish at certain times, such as when her older daughter was absent. She would place the flat of her hand on her breastbone and roll her eyes upward to express exasperation with the chambermaid; she would open her fan and, leaning toward Martin, whisper behind the outspread black silk with its pattern of gold peacocks and fruit trees, about the evening dress of a woman passing in the lobby; she would refer to herself as an old dinosaur and look merrily at Martin, who would immediately compliment her and be rewarded by a tap of the fan on the knee. She demanded that he call her Margaret, which after all was her name, and it was true enough that Mrs. Margaret Vernon, seated beside Emmeline, was the handsomer woman, with her large dark eyes and her thick lustrous dark hair pulled straight up at the sides and arranged in a soft mass at the top, stuck through with glinting tortoiseshell combs. She had passed on to Emmeline her eyes and her hair, but in Emmeline the hair had become thicker and more tangled and lay across her forehead in small tense ringlets, and her dark intelligent eyes looked out from under thick brownish-black eyebrows with small black visible hairs between them. On her cheeks, dusky beside her mother's whiteness, he saw faint traces of dark down. It struck Martin that Emmeline, however playful and quick-witted she was, kept a watchful eye on her mother, as she did on Caroline – as if, to the degree that Margaret Vernon relinquished motherliness, Emmeline herself assumed the burden. Martin, hearing the creak of a corset as Margaret Vernon turned gaily in her chair, remembered suddenly Louise Hamilton in the dusky parlor, the sound of her dress, the lifting of her elbows as she reached to unbind her hair – and in the lamplit parlor he felt a sensual confusion, as if he were courting Mrs. Margaret Vernon. Then he turned his face abruptly to Emmeline Vernon, who looked at him and said, 'Yes?' In the lamplight her black hair and lustrous eyebrows seemed charged with energy, her cheeks glowed, a warmth seemed to penetrate the skin of his face; and turning his eyes to the empty chair, with a directness that would have been impossible had Caroline Vernon actually been sitting there, he studied the faint impression in the dark red cushion and the pattern of raised gold lines in the padded arms. And all the while he felt pleasurably penetrated by the gaze, playful and intense, by the deep inner attention, of Margaret and Emmeline Vernon.

One evening after a late supper with his mother and father in the kitchen over the cigar store, Martin returned to the Bellingham and was surprised to find Margaret Vernon alone. She explained that Caroline had been feeling unwell all day, as she sometimes did after a poor night's sleep. Emmeline had gone out alone in the afternoon and returned just in time for supper; she had accompanied Caroline upstairs to play two-hand euchre and would come down later. Martin sat down in his armchair, struck by the double absence, by the novel sensation of being alone with Margaret Vernon. She herself seemed a little constrained, and after a few light passages of conversation turned the talk to the subject of her daughters. She was concerned about them – two young women in a strange city. She was less concerned about Emmeline, who had always been a rock, than about Caroline, who – to speak frankly – might easily have been the center of an admiring circle of marriage-able young gentlemen had she not so dreadfully discour-aged all social efforts on her behalf. It sometimes seemed that Caroline wanted nothing better than to sit through life – simply sit there, without lifting a finger on her own behalf, though with her beauty it would take little more than an ever so slightly lifted finger: like that. Martin watched as the index finger of Margaret Vernon's left hand rose very slightly from the dark red chairarm and returned to its place. Of course there was no reasoning with her. There was no talking to her. She did what she wanted to do and that was that. There had been a young man or two, one from a good Boston family, but Caroline – well, Caroline had simply acted as if he wasn't there. She had barely looked at him. And yet she wasn't cold by nature, she was a warm-hearted trusting girl once you got to know her. Of course she was difficult to get to know. She could be trying at times. He knew that, of course. But he also knew, he was getting to know, how warm and trusting she really was. Caroline was a treasure, really. But oh my. Mrs. Vernon hoped she wasn't presuming on their friendship by going on and on. It was just that a mother's patience had its limits. It was good to know she could rely on Martin. And she gave him a searching look.

Martin assured her that she could rely on him. Her look of relief was so visible, so immense and unexpected, that he suddenly wondered whether she had been asking obliquely about his intentions toward her daughter. Immediately he wondered whether he had answered.

The theme of Caroline returned a week later, when Caroline rose from her chair in the parlor and, pleading tiredness, retired to her room. Martin, alone with

Margaret Vernon and Emmeline, asked whether Caroline had been sleeping poorly again; he hoped she wasn't coming down with a cold. 'Caroline has never been sick a day in her life,' Margaret Vernon declared, drawing back her shoulders and lifting her chin, as if to defy a challenge – except of course for little indispositions, headaches and such, all of which could be traced to her trouble falling asleep. Emmeline looked at her mother wryly and asked how a daily indisposition differed from an illness. At this Mrs. Vernon said that Caroline was healthy as a horse and had never had anything the matter with her that a ten-minute nap couldn't cure – and she might add that it was unbecoming of Emmeline to paint so black a picture of her sister, whose only fault was a certain nervousness of disposition that prevented her from sleeping like an ox. Emmeline, who had drawn back at her mother's reply, seemed about to answer but said nothing. When Margaret Vernon rose to leave a half hour later, Emmeline said she would follow in a few minutes.

As soon as she was alone she said to Martin that she hoped she hadn't painted a black picture of anyone; sometimes her mother, with the best of intentions, spoke more heatedly than perhaps she ought. In fact Caroline's health was a mystery to both of them, for though it was true she was almost never sick in the ordinary sense – colds and fevers and what have you – it was also true that she was almost never free of some disturbing symptom or other, such as the headaches that often drove her to her bed. Oh, they had taken her

96

to doctors, who had scratched their heads and pulled at their whiskers and prescribed mysterious tinctures and syrups that might as well have been sugar-water for all the good they did her. What Caroline needed, Emmeline believed, was more exercise; she had been pleased to see her sister's pleasure in their Sunday excursions. In one sense her mother was right: Caroline was strong, despite her apparent frailty, and she could outwalk anyone when she wanted to. It was just that she so seldom wanted to.

'Then I'm glad she comes along on our little outings,' Martin said.

'Oh,' Emmeline said, with an impatient shrug of one shoulder, 'she wouldn't miss those for anything.'

'I've noticed she never complains.'

'Not to you,' Emmeline said sharply.

The idea that he was perhaps courting Caroline Vernon without quite knowing it, that his attentions to the Vernons were imagined by them to be a courtship of one of them, that his sense of deepening friendship against a sunlit background of vigorous family outings concealed more complex intimacies, all this did not disturb Martin, who found it perfectly reasonable that he should be assumed to have an interest in the older and prettier daughter, and who did not in any sense wish to deny an interest in her, though he was content to let such interest as he had remain pleasantly undefined.

One summer evening when he entered the lobby and saw all three women look up from their chairs in the parlor with an alertness, an air of pleasurable anticipation, that precisely matched his own, he felt so generously welcomed, even by Caroline, who slowly lowered her eyes, that he could not imagine any deeper happiness than just this nightly surrender to the spiritual embrace of the three Vernon women. He would have liked to keep them like that indefinitely: Margaret Vernon looking at him with frank pleasure as she waved at her chest with her black silk fan, Emmeline Vernon looking up at him intently from under her brownish-black eyebrows, Caroline Vernon gazing at him from half-closed eyes, her head resting back against the dark-red gold-flowered shimmer of the armchair, the pale hair pulled so tightly back that it seemed to tug painfully against the skin of her temples, the long pale-green sleeves buttoned tightly at the wrist.

For several months now, if not precisely for Caroline's sake, then for the sake of all three women, Martin had stopped his visits to the room with rattling windows off Sixth Avenue, visits from which he had returned to the lamplit parlor of the Bellingham feeling furtive and unclean.

One hot summer night at about half-past nine Martin suggested that they all take a little walk. Caroline seemed to hesitate, but then decided to join them, and walking two by two, Martin and Margaret Vernon in front of Emmeline and Caroline, they made their way east to the Central Park, skirted by a low wall of cut stone. They turned in at an entrance and walked along a winding path through sharp scents of unknown blossoms and dark green leaves and distant riverwater.

Through the thick-leaved trees Martin could see bits of yellow from the windows in the dark buildings facing the Park. Over the buildings the night sky was a deep purplish blue. Now and then they passed shadowy well-dressed couples strolling arm in arm and Martin overheard bits of murmured conversation: 'No, of course, I understand what you . . .' On nearby paths he heard footsteps and light laughter. Pieces of laughter seemed to float through the branches and get tangled in the leaves. For some reason he remembered a story that Gerda the Swede had told him. One summer night when she was fourteen and still living with her mother she had gone walking with an older boy in the Park. He had led her off the path into a dark clump of trees and begun kissing her, but not in the way she had expected: he had stood behind her, kissing the back of her neck and her cheek over and over and rubbing his hands slowly up and down on her breasts and pressing against her from behind. He had suddenly stopped without doing anything else at all, even though she had just stood there with her eyes closed, waiting for whatever was going to happen. Martin, who had been struck by the slight perversity of that half-seduction, was suddenly disturbed by the tenderness of those kisses. The vivid memory of Gerda's story, the sharp smell of the leaves, the dim rattle of carriage wheels, the scratchy sound of Emmeline's and Caroline's shoes behind him on the gravel path, wisps of light laughter hanging in the branches, the glint of Margaret Vernon's combs, all this irritated Martin, who turned and said harshly: 'Well! Let's turn back, shall we? It's getting late!'

'Oh,' said Margaret Vernon, 'it's such a lovely . . .'

Emmeline looked at him sharply.

Caroline, glancing at him and looking away, murmured, 'I suppose . . . it is getting a little . . .'

14

THE EIGHTH DAY
OF THE WEEK

On Sunday mornings the Vernons never came down to the lobby before ten o'clock. Martin, who always woke early, left the hotel at half-past five in the morning with the sense of seizing for himself a small and private day within the larger day, a kind of eighth day situated between Saturday and Sunday. In his private morning, before the official part of the day that he spent with the Vernons, he would walk down to the railroad yards and watch freight cars being loaded onto a barge destined for one of the Jersey rail docks, or go up along the Boulevard where shanties still stood in the high weeds of unsold lots, or walk up and down blocks of small shops on Amsterdam and Columbus. About eight o'clock he would stop at a restaurant and have a breakfast of eggs and steak, folding a newspaper under the side of his plate and glancing out the plate-glass window at the avenue. Dundee had agreed in principle to putting money in an uptown lunchroom and it was important to choose the location with care. After breakfast Martin liked to walk along the Central Park, admiring the handful of hotels among the undeveloped lots on the other side of the street, and then he would take a crosstown car to Eleventh Avenue and walk down to the park by the river. From time to time he would consult his pocket watch, and a little before ten he would return to the lobby of the Bellingham.

One Sunday morning when Martin returned to his hotel he saw that the women had not yet come down. Instead of sitting in the lobby with his newspaper he decided to go up to his rooms and change his shirt, for the August morning had grown hot. The door in the corridor stood partway open and in the lock was a big key with an oval piece of stamped metal hanging from it. As he entered the sunny parlor he saw through the open door of his bedroom part of a tin bucket with a mop-handle slanting up. 'It's all right, Marie,' he called out, sitting down in his flowered easy chair beside the sofa. 'I'll wait.' He had spoken a few times with Marie Haskova, a serious heavy-shouldered girl of sixteen or seventeen in a drab black uniform with a white apron, who wore a foolish-looking dustcap on her thick black hair. She had a room in the attic at the top of the hotel, where most of the maids lived. Once or twice from her stubborn face he had wrested a sudden swift smile, which had quickly faded, leaving her with her habitual look of faint bitterness about the mouth, of heavy melancholy in her eyes. Once she had told him that her father was a stonecutter who lived in a room over a saloon near the Brooklyn shipyards. She had been born in Bohemia but could not remember it. In his flowered armchair Martin tried to imagine Bohemia, which his mother had visited as a child, but he could see only vague forests and misty darkness. Irked at his ignorance, and feeling a touch of pity for the girl, Martin walked over to the doorway and leaned a shoulder against the jamb. 'I walked down by the river,' he said, 'and I tried to imagine what this city will look like in twenty years. I like to do that, and I'm good at it. But today something happened: I couldn't do it. Everything stayed just the way it was. I thought: this is how it is for most people. Things just being there.' His words irritated him, as if he had meant to say something quite different, which he could no longer remember. Marie Haskova had looked up as he stood in the doorway and then returned to her work, smoothing down a sheet and tucking it tightly under the mattress. She looked tired and hot in her black dress and slightly soiled white apron, with its drooping bow in back, one of whose loops was much bigger than the other; a hank of black hair hung along one cheek. 'It was peaceful down there,' Martin said, suddenly exasperated at this dull block of a girl with her busy hands and expressionless face, at himself, at the red-and-black feather duster lying across the edge of the dresser and the tin bucket with the slanting mop. He took a step into the room with a strange feeling of exhilaration – light poured through the open window. Marie Haskova stopped moving, as if she were listening very hard. In the sudden stillness Martin felt a change in the atmosphere, as sharp and definite as a darkening of sunlit air, and he knew with utter certainty that he could walk across the room to Marie Haskova and place his hand on her arm, her warm upper arm, and draw her to the bed, that in the stillness she was simply waiting for him to complete his walk across the room to her. Even as his thigh muscles tightened in preparation for the walk across the room, where there was a girl waiting for him, a big-hipped girl with a soft-looking back and hair like black fire, Martin felt a hesitation. What surprised him wasn't the hesitation, already hardening into a refusal, but his sense that the refusal was a burst of loyalty – not to his future bride, closed in her long dream, but to his bride's sister, with her intelligent, watchful eyes. In the stillness that at any moment would dissolve, that even now was changing, Martin felt an outstreaming of tenderness toward Marie Haskova, with her large pale hands and bitten-down nails. It was all strange, as strange as the sun slanting across Marie Haskova's broad shoulders, the glitter of black-beaded pins in her hair, the startling blackness of her hair, the red and black feathers of the duster, the reddish light coming through the edge of the heavy red curtains. Then there was only the slow, heavy movement of her body as she resumed her work, the clank of the bucket, the sound of a steamboat from the river.

When Martin rode down in the elevator and entered the lobby, he saw the three Vernon women sitting in chairs by a window. They looked up at him one after the other: first Margaret Vernon, with her merry dark eyes, then Emmeline, with a slight frown, then Caroline, brushing his face with her drooping glance.

'What shall it be today, ladies? The Boulevard? The river? The Battery? The Park? Excursions on the half hour to points of interest historical, geographical –'

'My, but aren't you the energetic one today,' Emmeline remarked.

'That sounds like a criticism,' Martin said, thrusting his hands into his pockets and breaking into a laugh.

15

Mr. Westerhoven
Makes a
Proposal

On the first of September Martin and Walter Dundee took over the lease of a restaurant on Columbus Avenue near the corner of Eighty-fourth Street, between a greengrocer's shop and a bakery. By mid-October the new lunchroom was ready for business. The Uptown Metropolitan Lunchroom was carefully designed to bring to mind the original Metropolitan, without imitating it exactly. The facade was painted the same cheerful shade of blue, with yellow trim, the awning was dark blue fringed with white, and on the sidewalk near the door stood another wooden Pilgrim: a man in breeches and buckle shoes, holding in his hands a horn of plenty. On his tall hat was a sign announcing a breakfast special of buckwheat cakes and sausage. The establishment was on a single floor, without a billiard parlor, and sought the patronage of women as well as men. One week before opening day, heralded by posters, billboards, and streetcar ads, a red-painted delivery wagon trimmed with gold, drawn by a white horse with a red-and-gold saddle, and driven by a man dressed like a Pilgrim, made its way up and down the six long avenues of the West End, from Fifty-ninth to 110th streets, bearing on its sides in large gold letters the name of the new lunchroom and the date of the opening day.

At dinner a week after the successful opening of the Uptown Metropolitan, Martin said to Dundee, 'I was wondering whether I ought to get married. What do you think?'

Dundee looked at him in surprise. 'I didn't know you'd met someone. Keeping her secret, were you?'

'No, not secret, exactly. Her name is Caroline Vernon and she lives with her mother and sister up at the Bellingham. I wonder whether I ought to marry her.'

Dundee laughed. 'And you want me to make up your mind for you?'

'It's this way, Walter. I haven't thought much about it, but they all seem to expect it.'

'They do, do they?' Dundee put down his knife. 'Look here, Martin. A good woman who loves you right is the greatest gift a man can have on God's earth. Let me ask you something. Do you love her?'

'That's what I was wondering about.'

Dundee looked at him. 'By George if you're wondering about it.' He shrugged. 'And the young lady? What does she think?'

'I have no idea. I've never spoken to her alone.' Martin paused. 'It's complicated.'

Dundee appeared to wait for him to continue, then picked up his knife. 'I wouldn't jump into it,' he said.

The leasing of the Columbus Avenue restaurant in September, the preparation of the advertising campaign, the lunch hours spent at the developing lunchroom, the long evenings with Dundee, all this had returned Martin to his familiar world, so that at times it seemed to him that he had had a summer dream of women. He still saw the Vernons in the evenings and went out with them on short Sunday excursions, but Saturday afternoons and most of his Sundays were devoted to the Uptown Metropolitan. With Marie Haskova he had fallen into an ambiguous kind of friendship. After Sunday breakfast at the Uptown Metropolitan, he would return to his rooms to wait for the Vernons, but also in the hope of seeing Marie Haskova, who timed her work to coincide with his return. He liked the quiet girl with her sudden questioning glances, felt an interest in her, liked to hear her talk about things. And he was curious about her arrangement with the Bellingham: he questioned her closely about her hours, her room duties, the staff dining room in the basement, the maids' quarters at the top of the building. She told him that she cleaned fourteen apartments on her floor, starting at seven in the morning. She was so tired by the end of the day that after dinner in the overheated basement she went up to her room and fell asleep, though it was hard to stay asleep for long, what with doors slamming and girls arguing and giggling and making a racket – the laundry girls were the worst, the head housekeeper was always giving them a warning. One morning she took him up in the service elevator to the attic floor. In the stuffy half-dark lit by two dim gas brackets with murky globes, rows of brown doors stood close together. A big girl in a doorway, wearing the gray uniform of a laundress, looked at Marie with a leer. Martin glanced in at Marie's room, number 7, a dark box with a bed and a wooden chair and a small window giving a view of chimney pots and water tanks on the roofs of row houses. The girls weren't allowed to eat in their rooms, Marie said, but they all did; she showed him a tin of oyster biscuits. When he and Marie returned down the hall, Martin heard a sudden burst of laughter; a door slammed; and the brown doors, the half-darkness, the muffled laughter, all was strangely familiar to Martin, as if, behind a suddenly opened door, he might find Dora or Gerda the Swede.

His little Sunday morning friendship with Marie Haskova, with its air of faint ambiguity, as if he were concealing from the Vernons a secret mistress, in one sense simplified his relation to them, for whatever he felt for the three Vernon women had nothing to do with secret liaisons. The Vernons, all three of them in a kind of lump, could be imagined only as a wife. And yet in another sense Marie Haskova confused his feelings for them, for it was as if the vague desire aroused by the Vernon women were seeking an outlet in young Marie Haskova. But there were deeper confusions, elusive connections that he could barely sense. There was something unspoken between him and Marie Haskova, something secretive and unacknowledged – but weren't the secretive and the unacknowledged the very sign of his union with Caroline Vernon? Then the two women, so rigorously set apart, would grow confused in his mind, so that speaking with Marie Haskova he would suddenly think of Caroline Vernon's pale tight-bound hair and small straight shoulders, her brown eyebrows darker than her hair, the half-closed indolent eyes, and he would be startled to see, there before him, Marie Haskova with her strong cheekbones, her broad shoulders, her trace of bitterness about the mouth. And once, stepping into the lobby of the Bellingham after his Sunday morning walk and seeing Caroline sitting with her mother and sister, Caroline with her half-closed eyes and fine-cut nose, he suddenly imagined Marie Haskova with her swift, quickly fading smile, her melancholy eyes, her dark box of a room with its view of chimney pots and water tanks on the tops of row houses, and so intense was his vision of Marie Haskova that even as he walked toward Caroline Vernon in the sunny lobby with her head reclined on a garnet-and-green armchair, a few strands of pale hair escaping from the side of her neck, he was walking along the half-dark corridor with Marie Haskova to sounds of muffled laughter, while Emmeline looked at him with her air of alertness and Mrs. Vernon fiddled with the lace collar of her blue silk dress.

From this tangle of women Martin was glad to escape into the world of leases and ads and plate glass and cast iron, a hard-edged world of carefully defined problems demanding precise solutions. And Martin was restless again. The new lunchroom had barely been launched when he began searching for a third location on another uptown avenue. He felt stung into activity by the sharp autumn days. Dundee wanted to wait, Dundee always wanted to wait, but Martin thought it was wrongheaded not to strike quickly while people were still talking about the Uptown Metropolitan. Success was in the air.

He had his eye on the Boulevard, which below Seventy-second Street held stretches of four-story brick or frame buildings with shops at street level and modest apartments above. On one block he found a saloon, a grocery, a vacant store, a butcher shop, an undertaker's, and a vacant lot. The vacant store interested him – he imagined it with a coat of skyblue paint and a dark blue awning fringed with white – but so did the vacant lot: speculators were clinging to their Boulevard properties as prices rose year by year. Rumors had sprung up again that the city was going underground, that trains would run below the Boulevard, with stations along the way. Martin imagined a city with trains in the air and trains under the ground, a fierce and magical city of moving iron, while along the trembling avenues there rose, in the clashing air, higher and higher, still buildings.

He was beginning to feel impatient with his long hours at the Vanderlyn. Not only was he reading and thinking through the daily correspondence, but he was drafting and typing up replies, which Mr. Westerhoven merely glanced at before unscrewing the cap of his shiny black fountain pen with the gold point, pressing it over the bottom of the pen with squeaky sounds, and signing his name in gleaming black ink, with many loops and swirls and a final flourish that reminded Martin of tying a shoelace. He would hold the typed letter at arm's length, stare for a moment as if he were looking at a picture in a museum, and pass it suddenly to Martin with a rush of sound, half flutter and half crackle, for Martin to insert in an envelope and drop into a basket of envelopes, which a desk clerk would later carry over to the bellboys for stamping. Martin didn't object to writing letters for Mr. Westerhoven, nor did he mind when Mr. Westerhoven, checking a draft, changed blunt phrases to more elaborate and circumspect locutions – no, what he kept coming up against was the knowledge that only small changes would ever be made in the operation of the hotel, and those only after the overcoming of an immense resistance on the part of Mr. Westerhoven, who liked to call himself a 'preserver' and a 'reconciler.' 'You know, Martin,' he would say, pacing in his office with his coat open and his thumbs stuck in the pockets of his checkered vest, 'what's necessary in this business is to reconcile the best of the old with the best of the new.' By this he meant that although he had yielded in the matter of the new incandescent lights, he would be damned if he'd replace his fine old steam elevators with new-fangled electric ones, at tremendous cost – and to what end? To what end? He asked Martin: to what end?

In Mr. Westerhoven's arguments there was always a ground of the solid and practical, but Martin knew that they were arguing less about elevators or telephones or expenditures than about something else: they were arguing about the manager's secret desire to stop the city from its rush into the new century, his desire to return to his childhood parlor with its soft dark rug, its heavy curtains and vases of heavy-headed flowers, its mother with her bag of knitting in an easy chair by the window. Mr. Westerhoven had taken to sighing at the thought of the new department stores with their big plate-glass display windows full of fancy merchandise and had begun shopping in small out-of-the-way places, from which he would return with a hand-woven rug for his office, an old-fashioned snuffbox with hand-painted porcelain Cupids on the boxlid, a walking stick with an ivory head carved in the shape of a monkey. In his office hung a gilt-framed engraving that showed a bareheaded young woman with a flower in her hair, standing in a bower with a dreamy look on her sunny-and-shady face; at her feet lay a letter that she had just dropped.

Perhaps it was Mr. Westerhoven's accumulation of knickknacks, perhaps it was the sense of stepping from the street into the old-fashioned lobby and from the lobby into the dark-paneled warm office with its thick-piled rug and glints of lamplit dark wood, in any case Martin sometimes had the sensation that he was stepping each day out of a world of excavations, scaffolding, and steam cranes lifted against the sky, into Mr. Westerhoven's childhood parlor, with its heavy curtains looped back from the tall window, its odor of furniture polish and velvet, its dark softness of rug and sofa and tasseled pillow.

One rainy morning Martin was sitting at his desk in Mr. Westerhoven's office, going over the housekeeper's accounts and trying to decide whether the recent rash of torn bedsheets meant it was time to order a complete new set of bed linen, perhaps with the miniature image of the Vanderlyn in one corner, sewn in blue thread. Or was red thread better? The door opened and Mr. Westerhoven entered in his rubbers and ulster, holding a dripping umbrella. He plunged the umbrella into a stand that he had picked up in an antique shop near Washington Square, then hung his coat on a peg of the hat rack. He hooked his fedora over a second peg, pulled off his rubbers and hung each one on a separate peg, undid the buttons of his suit jacket, let out his breath once with a great whooshing sound, and, hooking his thumbs in the pockets of his vest, began walking up and down in the space between Martin's desk and his own.

'A splendid day, my boy, wouldn't you say? Well, but what I meant to say was: wretched, of course. A wretched day! Splendid in its own way, of course, but wretched nonetheless. Were it not for my umbrella – but why speak of that? I have something to say to you and I find myself a little . . . well of course, yes. And yet I have never been one to beat about the proverbial bush. Suffice to say that your services here – but of course you know all that. Great things are afoot, Martin. Our Mr. Henning – don't breathe a word of this, my boy – our own Mr. Henning has been offered a managerial position at the Breresley – the Breresley, forsooth – and the good man has seen fit to inform me that it is his wish and desire to terminate his inestimable services and in short to leave us in the um proverbial lurch. To put it in a nutshell: as assistant manager of the Vanderlyn, you will report to me on a regular – but we can discuss the details later. Well? What do you say?'

Later that morning Martin paid a visit to George

Henning in his office. Mr. Henning said that because of certain drawbacks in his present position he had started putting out feelers a year ago, hoping to find an assistant manager's position at a good hotel; the offer from the Breresley had come as a complete surprise. The drawbacks, to be frank, concerned his prospects of advancement. In the normal course of things he would expect to become manager of the Vanderlyn, upon Mr. Westerhoven's retirement in five or six years, but the special favor Mr. Westerhoven had shown Martin had made his own prospects less certain. In any case it was a splendid chance for Martin, whose line to the managership would now be secure; and during the next three weeks, before his move to the Breresley, he would be glad to be of help to Martin in the transition to assistant manager. Mr. Henning's words were friendly, but something cool in his manner, something tight about the mouth, reminded Martin that the assistant manager saw in him only someone who stood in the way.

At lunch with Walter Dundee that afternoon, where he had planned to discuss his ideas for turning the billiard parlor on the second floor into a second-floor lunchroom, Martin opened his mouth to speak of Mr. Westerhoven's offer, suddenly hesitated, and closed his mouth over a piece of rye bread and liverwurst. The hesitation puzzled him, but by the end of lunch, during which Dundee had advised waiting another six months before plunging recklessly into additional expense, Martin felt an odd exhilaration. That night in the parlor of the Bellingham he announced his decision to Margaret,

Emmeline, and Caroline Vernon: he would leave the Vanderlyn.

Margaret Vernon, who at the news of Mr. Westerhoven's offer had clasped her hands at her throat and looked at him with a kind of eager delight, continued to clasp her hands while her look changed to the polite blankness with which she had been taught to conceal disapproval or confusion; Caroline glanced away; Emmeline leaned forward and said fiercely, 'Good for you, Martin. Now you'll show them.'

'Show them what, dear?' asked Margaret Vernon, and cleared her throat.

'Oh, mother,' Emmeline said.

'Not a bad question, actually,' Martin said.

'Show them what he can do,' Emmeline said. 'Without them.'

'I understand, Emmy, of course I do, but I was wondering . . .'

'Does this mean . . .,' Caroline said.

'Yes?' asked Martin sharply.

'Oh, nothing,' Caroline said.

'I think what Caroline means,' began Mrs. Vernon, bursting into a cough.

16

Business and Pleasure

A slanting rain drove against the awning, rushed in black rivulets along the curbs, glistened on the backs of cabhorses and flew from rattling wheels, worked its way down behind the awning and trickled along the restaurant window.

'You can say what you like,' Martin said at the window table, 'but my mind is made up. Are you coming in with me or aren't you?'

'Now hold on, Martin,' Dundee said. 'One thing at a time. Are you sure you've thought this thing through? Do you know what you want?'

'I know what I damn well don't want,' Martin said. 'I don't want to become Mr. George Henning.'

'Slim chance of that, Martin.' Dundee slapped the table with the flat of his hand. 'Don't you see what it is? They're grooming you for manager. Six years at a bet, maybe five. You could take this hotel –'

'I don't want to take it. I want to leave it.' Martin heard something harsh and contemptuous in his tone and made an effort to speak evenly. 'I'm cut out for something else.'

'And what may that be?'

'Something' – Martin shrugged impatiently – 'larger. It'll come to me. But right now: are you in with me or not?'

'I'm a hotel man, Martin. I don't aim to set up in a new line of work at this stage of the game. But this scheme of yours – I won't stand in your way.'

'Then I can borrow against the business –'

'For one more lunchroom. After that I plan to sit tight, keep my money safe in the bank. Pick up a little railroad stock, maybe.'

'Suit yourself.' Martin looked out the window at dark streetcar rails glistening in the rain. 'I was thinking of Westerhoven's rubbers. He hung them on the hat rack to dry. They dripped a puddle onto his rug. I suppose I'll miss the old place once I'm out of it for good.'

'Martin!' cried Dundee. 'Take the job. It's the chance of a lifetime.'

Martin turned to him with a look of surprise.

As he threw himself into the adventure of his new life, Martin realized how hungry he had been for time, sheer time. Now he rose at five in the morning to walk the still-dark avenues, observing the early morning El stations, the streetcars, the opening of newsstands and streetcorner cafes, the movement of people on the sidewalks. He stood on corners of cross streets and avenues, counting the number of people who passed in ten-minute intervals, recording the numbers in a note-book, studying them over breakfast at restaurants up and down the West End, trying to work out a system. The original idea for converting the Paradise Musée into a lunchroom and billiard parlor had come out of nowhere – it had been an impulse, a whim – but he was convinced that he could now go about things in a clear-headed orderly way. Martin knew that what attracted him wasn't the actual lunchroom, for he had no passion for lunchrooms, no special fondness for them, in a sense no interest in them; his passion was for working things out, bringing things together, arranging the unarrange-able, making combinations. Even the idea for a second lunchroom resembling the first had been a kind of lucky intuition, but the advantages of a string of separate yet related establishments now struck him as immense: an ad for one was an ad for all, so that advertising costs would be far less than if it were a question of three different businesses, and the risks of newness would be diminished by the air of familiarity lent to the newest member through deliberate association with the others. At the same time, larger food orders from a combination of lunchrooms meant discounts from suppliers. Money saved in purchasing and advertising meant increased profits – and increased profits meant another lunch-room.

But first it was necessary to look more closely at the operation of the two Metropolitans. The downtown manager was a business friend of Dundee's, who had been the purchasing agent for the Vanderlyn dining rooms and had managed a lunch counter in one of the big department stores, and was grateful for the chance to manage a small business at a generous salary; he was a scrupulous and good-natured man who had the respect of his workers and provided detailed financial reports. He agreed with Martin that the two floors of billiard tables, though they turned a small profit, could be used to better purpose. The uptown manager had been recommended by a friend of Dundee's and had struck Martin as being a little too fond of bay rum hair oil and heavy gold rings with raised initials. His reports were always late and included questionable expenses, he had already fired the cashier and two waiters, and he was often absent on unexplained business. Martin asked to see the books, noticed a few suspicious figures, and discovered that the new cashier, who turned out to be the manager's brother, had been stealing fifty dollars a day. He fired both of them and threatened them with jail unless they returned the missing money. Fortunately the downtown manager knew someone who was perfect for the job and came with sterling references, but the incident impressed on Martin the importance of managers and the necessity for tight control of the business.

Of such things he spoke to the Vernons in the evenings, in the soft armchair in the quiet parlor, by the dark table with its dome-shaded porcelain lamp hand-painted with Nile-green sailboats, its gleam of slender glasses holding amber and emerald and ruby liquids. At times he wondered a little what they made of it all. Margaret Vernon listened with a dutiful and effortful attention, interrupted by fits of distraction during which she followed someone moving through the lobby, while Caroline listened without impatience but without any expression on her face. Only Emmeline asked questions. They were sharp, good questions, the questions of someone who knew what Martin was talking about and wanted to know more. It was she who grasped quickly the advantages of linked stores, the crucial role of managers, the need for strong central control. 'If you sent out letters to your managers,' she said, leaning forward with a frown of concentration and one hand clenched in a fist on her knee, 'say every month or so, stating your policy and making suggestions – some kind of monthly statement or letter, a reminder – then it seems to me –' and he saw it clearly, saw that it could be made to work. And he felt a flow of gratitude toward this energetic woman with the plain features and the too-thick eyebrows, a flow of brotherly affection, as if he had been married for some time to silent Caroline and had formed, with his sister-in-law, an intellectual friendship. Sometimes, when he tried to imagine his future life, a life in which he was the husband of Caroline, he saw himself seated in an armchair in the high-ceilinged bedroom of a grand hotel, talking pleasantly to Emmeline in the chair beside him, while a few feet away, on the edge of the polished brass bed, wearing a green silk dress, her pale hair pulled back tight, her hands interlaced in her lap and her eyelids half-closed, sat Caroline, silent, expressionless, inaccessible.

The thought of Caroline's remoteness, her enclosure in a private dream, a secret room, stirred Martin to a kind of irritable desire, and in the lamplit parlor he would turn sharply to her, as if to surprise her in some furtive act. He would see her sitting quietly there, not looking at him, with one arm resting on the dark red chairarm, the sleeve tight at the wrist, the fingers of her hand slightly curved, in a motionlessness that seemed at once tense and languorous.

And he would try to enter her dream, there in the chair beside him, no more than a foot away – so close that if he wished he could have reached out and placed his hand on the back of her curved hand; and as he imagined the palm of his hand slowly covering her hand, suddenly he imagined her naked body, he saw the ribs expanding and contracting as she breathed, the tendon taut at the side of her bent knee, the nipples stiffening, the tiny pale hairs on her stomach glittering, but he could not imagine the expression on her face.

He took to inviting the Vernons to accompany him on occasional late-morning or afternoon business expeditions, eager for Emmeline's impressions. She argued in favor of the Boulevard over Amsterdam, despite higher rents, but urged him to consider Riverside as well, since there he could take advantage of the streams of Sunday cyclists who liked to ride up the winding avenue all the way to the Claremont Inn. Martin argued that he wanted a lunchroom in an established neighborhood, that Sunday cyclists were a weak foundation on which to erect a business, but that perhaps in two or three years, when the Drive had made its choice between the private châteaux of soda-water merchants or glove-hook heiresses and the new apartment houses and family hotels that were becoming visible in the West End –

along old Eighth Avenue facing the Central Park, on the Boulevard, on the avenue corners of Seventy-second Street – perhaps then a Riverside Metropolitan would be possible. He showed her his figures, which she studied carefully, and she announced that the figures spoke in favor of an older and half-commercial Boulevard location near the bottom of the Park. He proposed the merits of two or three locations farther north, but Emmeline had become fanatical in defense of the block with the saloon and grocery and butcher shop.

He needed a place from which to conduct business. It was all very well to study figures and plan advertising campaigns in the parlor of a bachelor suite, but he needed a place in which he might hold interviews with prospective managers, a place of business uncompromised by flowered armchairs and a paneled door concealing a bedroom. He found a brown room with a window on the fourth floor of an old commercial building on Chambers Street, off lower Broadway, which he furnished with an old desk full of pigeonholes, a creaking swivel-chair, two parlor lamps, and a serviceable armchair for visitors. Mrs. Vernon wondered whether it wasn't rather gloomy, but Emmeline declared that a pair of muslin curtains, not falsely cheery, would give it exactly the touch it needed.

After that, things moved quickly: Martin leased the vacant store on the Boulevard, advertised for managers, and conducted half a dozen interviews before choosing an energetic man named Henry McFarlane, who had hotel and restaurant experience and displayed an immediate grasp of the linked-store system. Then he called in all three managers to discuss policy, and threw himself into a vigorous advertising campaign, during which he made the decision to change the name of his group of restaurants from the Metropolitan Lunchroom to the Metropolitan Cafe. Dundee was skeptical, but offered no objection; he appeared to be losing interest in lunchrooms. Emmeline's eager interest in all phases of the business, her confessed dissatisfaction with her idle way of life, and his desire to keep a close watch over the operation of the new restaurant led him one day to offer her the job of cashier, which she passionately accepted despite the murmured objections of Mrs. Vernon, who felt it dimly unbecoming to the family name. The next day Martin took Emmeline down to the cafe, where workmen were setting up pedestal tables along one wall, and showed her how to operate a cash register.

She was seated behind it on the day of the Grand Opening, announced by the largest publicity campaign that Martin had yet mounted on behalf of his expanding business. Martin cut the ribbon that stretched between the posts of the awning of the new Metropolitan Cafe, with its large plate-glass windows set in brick painted skyblue and its wooden Pilgrim on the sidewalk – and as the two halves of the ribbon fluttered down, the chief cook and the waiters and the dishwashers and Emmeline released into the sky hundreds of blue balloons, while the crowd on the sidewalk cheered. Martin was given to amused skepticism on the occasion of opening days, but he was surprised by the size of the turnout, by the sheer success of the posters and newspaper ads and the skyblue advertising wagons with brightly painted signs that he had hired to roll up and down the avenues two weeks in advance of opening day. As he sat at a window table with Margaret Vernon and Caroline and Walter Dundee, eating two eggs with fried steak and glancing at Emmeline in her striped percale shirtwaist on the stool behind the cash register and at the sidewalk spectators clustered at the window, he felt, even as he turned over the idea of a fourth cafe in Brooklyn, a little sharp burst of restlessness, of dissatisfaction, as if he were supposed to be doing something else, something grander, higher, more difficult, more dangerous, more daring.

17

COURTSHIP

The sense that a different future awaited him, a future that, once he saw it rising in the distance, would be as deeply familiar to him as his own childhood, remained strong in Martin even as the success of the new cafe became a certainty. It was a certainty measurable by the nightly and weekly and monthly accounts that Martin carefully kept in his brown office with the green muslin curtains, behind a door with M. DRESSLER lettered in gold paint on the panel. On a shiny black typewriter with round black keys rimmed in nickel, Martin typed bi-weekly directions to all three managers, reminding them to keep the plate-glass windows clean at all times, proposing that they advertise daily specials on sign-boards set up on the sidewalk, and suggesting ways to draw in customers during slow hours. One of Martin's experiments that proved popular was the Five-Minute Breakfast: a reduced-rate breakfast of fried eggs and hamsteak guaranteed to be served within five minutes, for people in a hurry. But the main purpose of the letters was to remind the managers that the three cafes were not independent businesses but members of a single enterprise, in which the successful operation of one member contributed to the success of the whole.

In the window of Emmeline's cafe he installed a movable display powered by a toy steam engine. Before the puckered lips of a wooden face in profile, a flat wooden cup of coffee slowly rose and fell, rose and fell; each time it touched the lips, the head tipped back as if to drink. When Emmeline reported that people on the sidewalk were stopping to watch the moving cup of coffee, Martin installed the same display in his two other Metropolitans.

As revenues poured in, Martin continued to advertise, leasing space on billboards and in streetcars; and he began to search for a fourth location, taking the cable cars over the bridge to Brooklyn and walking the streets of neighborhoods once glimpsed from the horsecars of his childhood.

The question of a new location was one he liked to discuss with Emmeline, when he stopped in at the Boulevard cafe once or twice a week during her lunch break and whisked her off to a different restaurant, or when he accompanied her back to the hotel now and then at the end of her shift. Her brave plunge into the world of work, her quick grasp of day-to-day business and the larger design, her sharp insistent questions, all this made Martin seek her company as he had never sought the company of George Henning or Mr. Wester-hoven. She seemed to have thrown herself into his business as into a romance. She listened carefully to customers, reported their occasional complaints, proposed the idea, which Martin quickly adopted, of a Metropolitan dessert: a special pastry filled with chopped apples and shaped like a Pilgrim, available to the Metropolitan through the same bakery that supplied their pies. And Emmeline listened to Martin – listened with a faint frown of attention, with a stillness of concentration, that inspired in him stricter efforts at clarity. She took sides with his ambition and kept in step with his boldest designs. One day as they were discussing the expansion of the business to Brooklyn she said to him, 'But what do you want, Martin? What is it you actually want?'

'Oh, everything,' he said, lightly but without a smile.

'But I don't think you do, not in the usual way. In a way you don't want anything. You don't care if you're rich. Suppose you were rich, really rich. What would you do then?'

'Oh, then,' Martin said. He thought of himself as a child standing in the waves at West Brighton, feeling the world rushing away in every direction. 'Anyway, what makes you think I don't want to be rich?'

He saw that he had offended her, that he had taken the wrong tone. 'Listen, Em. I don't know what I want. But I want – more than this.' He swept out his arm lightly, gracefully, in a gesture that seemed to include the restaurant in which they were seated, but that might have included, for all he knew, the whole world.

Sometimes, when he looked across a table at Emmeline, he had the sense that he and she had been married for a long time. It was a comfortable companionable sort of marriage, calm and peaceful as cozy furniture in a firelit room. And at once he would think of Caroline, tense and languorous in her armchair in the hotel parlor, waiting for something, something that was bound to happen or perhaps would never happen – Caroline with her half-closed eyes and motionless fingers and pale hair pulled back tight on both sides. For it was Caroline after all whom he had married, or was about to marry, or had somehow forgotten to marry. And when on Sunday mornings he stood against the doorjamb talking with Marie Haskova and watching her bend this way and that, Marie Haskova with her heavy body and sudden swift questioning glances, then too he would think of Caroline, waiting in her chair for something to happen. Perhaps they were all waiting for something to happen – waiting for him to make up his mind. For it was as if he had three wives, and was married to all of them, or none of them, or some of them, or now one and now another of them. Of the three wives, Emmeline and Marie Haskova were the most vividly present to him, the most solidly there, whereas Caroline seemed a ghost-wife, a dream-wife – though he wondered whether it wasn't precisely her lack of substance that allowed her to haunt and hover, to invade the edges of other women.

In any case in being with Emmeline he was always with Caroline, as if she rose up most vividly in relation to others. One day he asked Emmeline a question about her sister, and after that he asked others – he had many questions about Caroline, as if he had seen a hand-painted photograph of Emmeline's sister and were working his way up to an introduction. What did she like? What did she do? What did she think about? To all his questions Emmeline listened carefully and gave thoughtful, meticulous answers, which somehow didn't clarify anything and tended to float out of his mind the moment he was alone. Caroline then was a mystery: the mystery irritated and attracted him, he would have to let it go at that.

Sometimes, speaking to Emmeline about cafe business, he would feel a sudden gratitude to Caroline, for having a sister who understood everything. Then a tenderness would come over him for Caroline, alone with her mother in the big hotel, waiting for something to happen, and he would long to see her in her dark red armchair with her white fingers and heavy-lidded eyes.

One day at lunch Martin said to Emmeline, 'Do you think Caroline would like to marry me?'

Emmeline looked at him. 'That's a strange question for you to ask me.'

'But you're the only one I *can* ask.'

'There's always Caroline, you know. Let's not forget Caroline.'

'Oh, Caroline,' he said impatiently.

The truth was that Caroline often irked him, even as she became fixed in his mind as a white bride. It struck him that the pleasure he felt in the presence of Marie Haskova was in part a pleasure directed against Caroline, as if by enjoying the company of Marie Haskova he were warning Caroline not to push him too far. For

Marie liked him, there was no question about that; and when he thought of Marie Haskova with her slow body, her melancholy eyes, and her sudden questioning glances, he would become angry at Caroline, for invading his time with Marie, for harming her in some way.

But when he walked along the cold streets toward the Bellingham at night, taking deep breaths of clear cold air, then he looked about with pleasure at the yellow windows of the dark row houses; and when he entered the Bellingham and felt his cheeks tingle and tighten in the steam-heated air, when he saw the three Vernon women waiting for him about the little table, then he felt a great surge of pleasure, and sank down gratefully into his armchair in the circle of his dark-haired sister, his adoring mother, and his sister's sister, his tense, languorous, floating, ungraspable bride.

'She's willing,' Emmeline said a few days later, a little breathlessly, as she leaned forward over a corner table.

'Willing?'

'To marry you.' She paused. 'It's what you wanted me to find out.'

'And you asked her? Flat out?'

'Well no. You're angry.'

'I'm surprised. You asked her?'

'I talked to her. We talked about things. Caroline trusts me, she knows I understand her. I didn't ask her, for heaven's sake, but I found out.' She picked up her cup of tea and held it in both hands without drinking it. 'Now you can decide.'

'Decide what?'

'Whether to marry her.'

'And you think I should?'

She lifted the cup to her mouth but did not drink. From behind the cup, as from behind a curtain, she said, so quietly that he could barely hear her: 'It would be so good for Caroline.'

'And me? Would it be good for me?'

'Oh, everything's good for you,' Emmeline said harshly.

In the evening he felt a slight awkwardness as he entered the lamplit parlor and sank into the familiar armchair, but nothing had changed: Margaret Vernon greeted him with the same girlish effusiveness, Emmeline began describing a jammed cash-register key that she had managed to fix, and Caroline sat dreamily in her chair, glancing at him in greeting and letting her eyes slide away. He tried to find a hint in her, a secret sign, perhaps a faint flush in the skin over her cheekbone or a barely visible tightening of the tendons in the back of her hand, but he couldn't be certain, and only when he was alone in his room did it strike him that the change was in him, as he watched her secretly, searching for a sign.

He thought about his new secret bride in his brown office with the green muslin curtains, and at dinner in the kitchen over the cigar store as his mother placed before him a heap of stewmeat and boiled onions, and in the parlor of his bachelor suite as he stood against the doorjamb watching Marie Haskova with her red-and-black feather duster; and it seemed to him that Caroline's power of invasion had increased, that she was hovering behind his heavy red curtains, seeping into the edges of things, rippling in the swish of other women's dresses, glimmering up at him from rainslick streets.

At night, instead of falling asleep at once, he lay in the dark imagining Caroline Vernon. She sat in her chair, in the dark of the deserted parlor, and suddenly she rose and came toward him at the other end of the room, but when she reached him she passed through him and came out the other side – and from the chair she rose again and came toward him, and passed through him, while from the chair she rose and came toward him, rose and came toward him, rose and rose and rose.

As the weather grew warm a restlessness came over Martin. He would hover close to Marie Haskova on Sunday mornings, watching her move about in her black uniform and speaking to her about his cafes, his life in the cigar store, the Irish maids in the Vanderlyn; and as he watched the black cloth tighten against her bending back, as he watched her rough-palmed hands with their faint odor of lye and furniture polish, he wondered whether he hovered around her not because she was a temptation that he continually enjoyed overcoming, but because she was a peaceful place he could go to, away from Caroline.

In the warm-cool evenings he again walked out with the Vernon women. He would stroll along the lamplit sidewalks with Margaret Vernon, a few steps in front of Emmeline and Caroline, and at the street crossing he would continue with Emmeline, behind Margaret and Caroline, and at the next crossing he would continue with Margaret, behind Emmeline and Caroline. One night in the park he was surprised to find himself walking beside Caroline, through spaces of lamplight and spaces of dark. A sharp moist smell of green was in the air, heavy and bitter, mixed with the sweet decay of brown oak leaves. In the glare of the lamps her cape was very black, her coat very red, her hair very yellow. She looked like a new painting, all wet and shiny, but already she was fading into the darkness between lamps. Something crackled in the black trees. From beyond a turn in the path a stick struck the ground at regular intervals. 'Do you know what I was thinking,' Martin heard himself say, startled by the sound of his voice, as if he had reached out and touched her mouth. Somewhere a man and woman laughed together and suddenly stopped. Around the bend came an old man in a silk hat, striking the ground with his stick, striking the ground with his stick.

All night long the sharp stick struck the ground as Martin lay in a restless half-sleep, and now the old man was thrusting his pointed walking stick into Caroline's foot: blood ran from her shoe. Martin rose in the dark, washed in cold water, put on his suit, and went down to the lobby. It was half past three. The lobby was empty except for the night clerk. Martin sat in a lobby chair with a view of the elevator corridor and waited for the graying of the dark lobby windows. She was closed in dream, a princess in a tower, scarcely a flesh-and-blood woman at all. Did he then desire her not for herself but for all that was unawakened in her, all that had not yet come into being? His mother had read him that story: at the Prince's kiss, Dornröschen opened her eyes. Then the fire leaped in the fireplace, the horses in the stable stirred, the pigeons on the roof took their heads from under their wings. And a mournful desire moved in him, for the princess in her chamber, as he imagined her young body stirring, the ribs moving under the skin, the wrists turning, the eyes, dark with dream, slowly opening after their hundred years' sleep.

At five minutes before six, Emmeline appeared around the corner of the elevator corridor and gave a start. She was wearing a coat and hat and carried an umbrella. She came swiftly toward him but Martin did not rise.

'Tell her –' he said. 'Tell her –' His eyes hurt, his eyelids trembled, there was a muffled buzzing deep in his brain.

'You don't look well,' Emmeline said, bending toward him with a frown.

'Tell her,' he said. 'Tell her I –' In his throbbing ears his voice sounded faint and thin, and he was reminded of a child he had once seen on a calendar, kneeling and looking up with pleading moist dark eyes. He tried to recall where he had seen that calendar, and in the gray dawn of the lobby, where elevator grilles were already rattling open, his eyes burned, his nose stung, a bell rang.

18

THE BLUE VELVET
BOX

Two nights later when Caroline rose from her chair in the parlor and Margaret rose after her, Emmeline said that she had some business to discuss with Martin and would be along in just a few minutes.

Her mother looked at her doubtfully. 'Don't be too long, dear. You know you need your rest, what with this job of yours that makes you get up in the middle of the night like a – like a rooster.'

'I'll be along directly,' Emmeline said.

She and Martin sat silently across from each other as they watched Caroline and Margaret walk from the parlor. They remained silent as they listened to the sound of the closing elevator door.

Martin leaned forward. 'You've spoken to her?'

'I have.'

'And she's – receptive?'

'She's not unreceptive. With Caroline it isn't always

possible to be definite. So much depends on how she's slept the night before.'

'Still, you feel –'

'I do.'

Martin reached into the pocket of his coat and removed a small blue velvet box, which he placed on the table. He watched Emmeline look at the box.

'Here,' Martin said. 'Let me show you.'

He bent over and quickly pulled up the lid, which was attached to the box by a hinge on one side. Emmeline leaned forward, resting one palm on the arm of her chair.

'Oh, she'll like that,' Emmeline said, and leaned back.

'Good. The real question is whether she'll accept it. You say it all depends on how well she sleeps?'

'Not entirely, of course. I was exaggerating. Caroline does what she wants to: always. But there are worse times and better times at which to speak to her.'

'It's asking a great deal of you, I know.'

'I can promise only one thing: to find the most propitious time.'

'But that one thing is everything. I can't thank you enough. But would you mind' – he bent over the box – 'for just a moment? I'd like to see –'

'If it's absolutely necessary.'

'Just for one half second. Here. Let me do it for you.'

Martin rose quickly from his chair and bent over Emmeline, who held out her hand stiffly.

Martin straightened up and walked behind her chair, where he stood looking down at her hand. The hand turned slightly in one direction, then in the other. On

137

the table the inside of the blue velvet box was violent black. The fingers contracted into a loose fist and slowly spread out again.

Martin began walking around the circle of armchairs to his seat, watching Emmeline's hand as he went.

As he sank back into his chair he said, 'I can't begin to tell you –'

'Don't,' Emmeline said.

19

WEDDING NIGHT

In the warm May evenings the strolls continued, but now Martin always walked beside Caroline, a few steps in front of Margaret and Emmeline. They walked past the sudden sharp scents of window boxes heavy with purple and yellow flowers, under branches of leaves green-glowing and translucent in the light of street-lamps, into the darkening Park. They had never spoken directly of their engagement, although the night after his talk with Emmeline he had walked into the lamplit parlor where the three women were sitting about the little table, and drawing closer he had seen something flash up from the back of Caroline's hand outspread on the dark-red gold-flowered chairarm. Margaret Vernon, glancing quickly from Emmeline to Caroline, had congratulated him with a kind of muted effusiveness, while Caroline, raising her eyelids abruptly, had looked at him with large dark eyes that immediately vanished under lowered lashes. After that she walked by his side in the warm evenings, holding herself very straight. Sometimes he would bend his head slightly to say something meant for her alone, such as 'These spring nights are the best time of year, don't you think, Caroline?' and the sound of her name, issuing from his mouth, seemed to him so intimate, so much like a hand stroking her face, that he could scarcely attend to her murmured reply, which in any case was so soft that he could barely hear it, a reply that sounded like 'Oh, that's all right,' as if she hadn't quite heard him correctly. The constraint between them, the sharp edge of formality that thrust at him from every movement of Caroline's body, seemed quite proper to Martin, since easy-going camaraderie was the note of his friendship with Emmeline – a friendship that flourished precisely to the extent that the sexual wasn't in question. His ambiguous friendship with Marie Haskova was another matter, for his sense of ease with her, his pleasure in watching her, his playfulness, his laughter, all this was made possible by the existence of something unsettled and secretive between them, which lent to their casual meetings an air of intimacy, of adventure. Therefore the slight awkwardness that he felt in the presence of Caroline, his sometimes exasperated sense of a resistance, an inviolable propriety, struck Martin as entirely correct, since in the absence of such constraints there would have been nothing for her to be except a friend or a mistress. Had she flirted with him, had she invited secret, forbidden caresses, she would have seemed commonplace to him, a mere step away from Gerda the

Swede. It was as if her perplexing, irritating coolness, her difficulty, were a sign of her high value.

Nevertheless it was always a relief to be seated again in the familiar circle of the hotel parlor, where he could talk easily with Emmeline and Margaret while watching Caroline out of the corner of his eye. The wedding had been set for early September, and Margaret Vernon threw herself into a flurry of meticulous planning. This too struck Martin as entirely proper, though the plans themselves held little interest for him. Sometimes it all seemed to him a grotesque sham, as if what everyone was really talking about was the night when Caroline would be alone in a room with him, naked and defenseless, with no way out – and at this thought, which filled him with remorse and desire, he would shift uneasily in his seat and glance at Caroline, who sat staring quietly before her with half-closed eyes.

The knowledge that he was going to marry Caroline Vernon, that he would be moving from his two rooms to a larger apartment on a different floor, made him fear that his friendship with Marie Haskova would undergo a change or even vanish entirely. Already it seemed to Martin that she was changing, as if she herself were going to be married; and a jealousy would come over him, at the thought that Marie was leaving him, that Caroline would soon be taking her away. It was cruel of Caroline to do that, even if he and Marie Haskova sometimes exchanged ambiguous glances, glances that, however harmless and playful they might be, nevertheless contained something forbidden. He hadn't yet told Marie that he was going to be married. The slight

deception disturbed him, for he wanted to be frank with
Marie Haskova; and his faint, continual sense of wrong-
ing her made him hover close, as if he were trying to set
things right.

In the hot days of August, Martin prepared to open
two new cafes: one on the other side of town, on Second
Avenue, and one in Brooklyn, on a shady side street off
Fulton Street, a few blocks from City Hall Park. Dundee
had been willing, even eager, to let Martin buy his share
of the partnership, as if he'd gotten in over his head and
were relieved to have his money safe in the bank at last.
Martin planned to introduce a new kind of cookie into
his five cafes, a modern gingerbread or sugar cookie in
four shapes: a Broadway cable car, an El train engine, a
Napoleon bicycle, and a Hudson River Day Line
steamer. The head chef of the bakery had already
ordered the tin molds. Martin next turned to the
question of managers. Since the manager of the Boulevard Metropolitan lived in Flatbush, Martin transferred
him to the Brooklyn Metropolitan – against the strong
protest of Emmeline, who liked McFarlane and argued
that the move would harm the cafe. She stared at
Martin with a flash of fear when he promptly offered her
the vacated post.

'But I can't –'

'Of course you can,' Martin said. 'Believe me. You
already know everything about the business.'

'I don't know. People will say you're playing favor-
ites.'

'What people? I'll fire them. Look, Em. I want
someone in there who knows the business, someone I

can trust. You know I count on you. You're my right-hand man.'

'I'm not a man.'

'Right-hand woman, then.' He paused to see whether he had hurt her. 'Let me tell you something. You already practically manage that cafe. So do it in public. Go ahead and do it. You can do it. Do it.'

She laughed. 'Maybe I just will. But keep your voice down. People are staring.'

For the new Second Avenue cafe Martin approached the thirty-year-old manager of a nearby lunchroom that he had discovered during his search for a new location, and offered a ten percent increase in salary. The young manager, who knew Martin, hesitated, folded his arms across his chest, worked a muscle in his cheek, and suddenly thrust out a strong hand. Martin reported the development to Walter Dundee at dinner the next night, and Dundee in return reported that the Vanderlyn was in trouble: the hotel was losing money, the owners were becoming impatient, old Mr. Westerhoven's days were numbered. Poor Westerhoven seemed unable to make up his mind about anything important, but as if to show that he was a man of iron will he had become fanatical about trivial matters – a bad business, however you looked at it. What the hotel needed was thorough renovation, but Alexander Westerhoven wasn't the man to see it that way, and even if he'd seen it that way he no longer had the confidence of the owners, who were unwilling to sink more money into a failing business and were said to be divided over what course to pursue.

Dundee frowned suddenly and began rapping his forehead with the tip of a finger. His face cleared. 'I've got it now. A message for you. That Hamilton woman was in last week, asked to be remembered to you. You remember Louise Hamilton.' A sharp regret came over Martin: nearly ten years had passed since his little adventure in Room 411. He wondered whether he had been happy then. 'She used to send me out to buy cough syrup,' Martin said. He remembered the dusky parlor, her head resting on two pillows on the sofa, the skin below her eyes waxy and blue, the surprising silk-smoothness of her skin. He had entered her fever-dream: she had dreamed him. A big-boned woman. Marie Haskova: he wondered whether he had known it all along.

'We'll be moving into a larger suite at the Bellingham,' Martin was saying.

'You like it up there, do you?' Without waiting for an answer Dundee continued: 'Mother and sister staying on?'

'Yes.' He paused. 'We get on well. What's wrong with that?'

'Nothing,' Dundee said. 'Not a thing.'

The two new cafes opened on consecutive Saturdays in early August, to the strains of German band music and the release of a thousand balloons. All children under twelve received a free prize: a little tin bank shaped like a slice of apple pie, with a coin slot at the top. Martin began taking the cable cars daily over the bridge to Brooklyn, where he was quickly satisfied that the new blue cafe had caught on nicely, and on his return he would stop first at the Second Avenue cafe, where the efficient young manager already spoke of expanding the premises by leasing the basement, and then at the Columbus Avenue cafe, and finally at the Boulevard cafe. Emmeline had taken command at the Boulevard, whose brick facade had received a fresh coat of skyblue paint and whose plate-glass windows glistened, but Martin saw that she needed continual reassurance about small matters, such as whether she had the authority to order new sets of salt and pepper shakers without first consulting him. She had had to speak to one of the waiters about his careless appearance and was worried about her tone, but Martin assured her that the staff liked and respected her. He saw that they did. He noticed small improvements about the place – green plants in the windows, a dish of free raspberry candies wrapped in cellophane beside the cash register – and decided to introduce them immediately into his four other cafes. 'People like it here, Martin,' she confided with a worried look. 'I can see that they do. But it makes them want to linger. The people waiting get annoyed. We lose customers.' She suggested a session for training waiters in the delicate art of moving customers gently along. 'Mother is dashing around like mad,' she added, and for a moment Martin imagined Margaret Vernon running in and out of the restaurant with advice for Emmeline, before he realized that of course she was speaking of the wedding arrangements.

He noticed the arrangements out of the corner of his eye as he hurled himself into fifteen- and sixteen-hour days, typing letters, visiting his five cafes, studying managerial reports, keeping accounts. Sometimes he had the sense that, just outside the door of his office, a crowd of wedding guests was gathering – at any moment a great burst of music would sound, champagne would run down the sides of bottles, bouquets of flowers would spring up from empty vases. He had talked vaguely to Caroline of a wedding trip in the late winter or early spring, since it was out of the question for him to leave town now. The five-room suite, directly across the hall from Margaret and Emmeline, would be ready for occupancy a week before the wedding. Martin imagined Marie Haskova cleaning on the floor above, with her red-and-black feather duster. He had told her he was going to be married, but had not said when. In the summer evenings, he walked with the Vernon women to the Park and sat with them for a while in the lamplit parlor off the lobby, as if no one wanted anything to change. Caroline sat in her red chair. From beyond the parlor came muffled sounds of opening elevator doors, dim laughter, a noise in the street. Martin was tired.

And the wedding came, the wedding that he had been hearing about for a long time; it was soon over. Martin smiled and waved his hand and stepped into a waiting carriage. He was very tired. And after all he was relieved to find himself sitting beside Caroline in the carriage he had hired, rolling now through the great Park. The carriage had been decorated with wreaths of flowers, and through one window he could see a purple blossom bouncing in and out of view as it struck the side of the carriage over and over again. He wondered what kind of flower it actually was. 'Look at that flower, Caroline,' he said. She sat by the window and he sat beside her, with a space between. In her white wedding dress she struck him as younger than ever – she looked like a young girl dressed up in a play about a queen. His father in his handsome rented clothes, with his thick brown mustache streaked with gray, with his pulled-back shoulders and large melancholy eyes, had looked like a gallant army officer. His mother had worn fresh flowers in her hat; when he bent to kiss her, she turned her cheek in a gesture he remembered from childhood bedtimes. It was three o'clock in the afternoon, and it occurred to Martin, leaning his head back in the soothing carriage, that there was quite a bit of day to get through. He had instructed the driver to take a few turns around the Park and then go up and down the great avenues. Then a light supper and a return to the Bellingham, where their five newly furnished rooms awaited them. It was warm in the carriage: sunlight and leafshade rippled across the dark leather seats, across Martin's legs and Caroline's white dress. Her hand, rippling with sun and shade, lay in her white lap. Caroline's face was turned toward the window. Martin reached out a hand, hesitated, and then gently placed his hand on hers. Caroline stiffened and withdrew her hand as she turned to him with a startled look. 'I'm sorry,' Martin said. 'I didn't mean –' 'You startled me,' Caroline said, and he in turn was startled: he thought she was going to cry. But she gave an odd, childish pout and suddenly reached over and patted the back of his hand twice. Then she withdrew her hand and placed it in her lap. Martin, holding his breath, looked at her hand in her lap. He looked at her arm, at her cheekbone, at her black eyelashes and brown eyebrows and pale yellow hair. Then he let out his breath and in the warm carriage closed his eyes.

It was late dusk when they returned to the Bellingham, the time of day when the eastern sky has already turned to night and the west looks pale, almost white, so that if you turn your head back and forth – and Martin stopped, in order to show Caroline how to turn her head back and forth, but also because he had been seized by the memory of doing exactly this head-turning, at exactly this time of day, but for the life of him he couldn't remember when. Caroline turned her head from side to side without saying anything and went with him into the lobby of the Bellingham Hotel. In the lamplit parlor he saw them, Margaret and Emmeline, sitting at the familiar table. And Martin felt a motion of irritation – why didn't they leave him alone, why were they always surrounding him? But as he sank into the familiar chair he felt deeply soothed, it was as if all his muscles ached and now, in the soft chair in the light of the familiar lamp, among the well-known voices, he were being stroked by gentle hands. And Caroline in her chair seemed less strange to him, though he would have liked to shift her hand slightly on the red chairarm, where it had assumed an unfamiliar position, with three fingers curled under and one outstretched: a horrible, grotesque position, really, as if her hand had come to rest in a painful way from which she was unable to release it. And so he turned his face away and began to settle in, but just then Emmeline rose up before him, and beside her Margaret Vernon: they were leaving. For of course it had to be this way, on a night that was unlike other nights, however much it might look the same. And as he wondered what was going to happen next, Caroline rose, with a little stifled yawn.

All four walked over to the elevator and waited for the door to open. Together they rose in the elevator, standing in silence behind the elevator man in his maroon jacket and green pants, together they stepped out onto the fifth-floor landing. Martin held open a door with a glass window in it. Two by two they walked along the corridor, Martin and Caroline behind Emmeline and Margaret, and two by two they turned left into the next corridor. Emmeline stopped before her door and inserted the key while Mrs. Vernon said what a lovely wedding it had been and Caroline stood with lowered eyes beside Martin as he opened his own door, across the corridor from the Vernon door and five feet farther along.

'Good night,' Mrs. Vernon said.

'Good night,' said Martin.

'Good night,' Emmeline said.

'Good night,' said Caroline.

Martin held open his door for Caroline and followed her in, and as he closed the door he heard the deadbolt catch in the lock across the way.

'I'm tired,' murmured Caroline in the parlor, and rustled away through a door as Martin entered from the front hall and sank down in his flowered armchair. The chair had been moved to the new parlor from Martin's bachelor suite on the sixth floor, and it sat uneasily amidst the new sofa, the loveseat, the stiff upholstered chairs, the mahogany rocker with its tasseled cushion. Against one wall stood a dark, shiny piano with framed photographs of Margaret with a bearded stranger, Caroline in an unfamiliar dress, Emmeline and Caroline at the age of twelve; Martin had bought the piano, even though Caroline had said she played 'only a little.' One door led to a small library, with a rolltop desk, a tufted reading chair upholstered in silk damask, and mahogany bookcases with glass doors. Three shelves contained Caroline's collection of books, mostly novels and sets of poets, and one shelf held Martin's books: *Brown's Business Correspondence*, *Book-keeping at a Glance*, *Science for the Citizen*, *The Home Mechanic*, *Famous Battles in History*, *Business Pointers*, and a scattering of boyhood books given to him by his mother and various aunts. The remaining shelves held Caroline's favorite possessions: a music box with a turning ballerina, a large oyster shell, a little glass deer, and above all her many elegant dolls, seated side by side, row after row of them, princesses and soldiers and washerwomen and milkmaids and fine ladies with parasols. Martin had never seen so many dolls; something about their faces disturbed him, as if they had been caught in a moment of sadness from which they could never escape.

But he could no longer hear Caroline moving in the far rooms and rose to find her. He turned out the lamp in the parlor and passed into a room that looked like another parlor, a room whose purpose was not entirely clear to him: Caroline had called it a sitting room. From here one reached a small hall that led to the remaining rooms: the guest chamber, the bathroom, and the master bedroom.

When Martin entered the bedroom it was entirely dark, illuminated only by the dim light that entered through the door he held open. In the near-blackness he saw the dark glimmer of the wardrobe mirror and a big block of darkness that was the marriage bed. Caroline lay on the far side with the covers up to her chin and one arm on the dark coverlet. As he drew closer he saw that the arm was concealed to the frilled wrist by the white sleeve of her wedding dress – but no, coming closer he saw that it was the sleeve of some other garment, a nightdress, probably. She lay on her back with her eyes closed, her head slightly turned, her hair covering her cheek and lying bunched and shadowy on the pillow. She was asleep. And an irritation seized him, to see that she had undone her hair alone, that she had slipped into sleep as into a narrow space where he could not follow her, that of all possible solutions to the problem of the wedding night, a problem he now recognized in all its gravity, she had chosen this one. 'Caroline,' he whispered, 'Caroline,' and sitting down on the edge of the bed he shook her by the shoulder, which through the bedcovers he could feel in its sharpness of bone and roundness of flesh, a sharp-roundness, a contradiction. Beyond the bed sat an armchair with something hunched over the back, something that looked like a big crab – her corset in a tangle of strings. He shook her harder and her eyes opened. She sat up abruptly, pulling the covers up to her neck, but carelessly, so that a part hung down and exposed a piece of her naked white nightdress. 'Caroline,' he said, struck by the note of reproach in his voice, of injury, 'you didn't say good night.'

Now two lines appeared between her dark eyebrows, she looked at him with sleepy reproachful eyes. 'I fell asleep,' she said. In her white nightdress, with her sleepy pouting gaze and her hair falling over one shoulder, she looked to him like a little girl, a sullen mischievous little girl who was trying to tease him and make him lose his temper. But it was all a game, and in the spirit of the game he reached out and put his hand on her hair-covered sharp-round shoulder. The shoulder pulled away. 'I'm tired,' she said irritably and slid down under the covers. Turning away, she pulled the covers tightly about her. Martin sat on the edge of the bed, staring at the mirrored doors of the wardrobe. The Vernons had traveled with their wardrobes, even though the Bellingham had built-in closets. After a while he rose to prepare for bed. But at the dresser a new problem confronted him, for he did not know whether the stylish new pajamas he had purchased for the occasion might strike her as immodest, might perhaps alarm her by thrusting before her gaze the outline of a pair of legs, and after standing in doubt before the open drawer with the folded pajamas in his hands, he replaced them in a corner of the drawer and removed his new striped nightshirt, with its embroidered collar and cuffs.

When he returned from the bathroom he lay down on his side of the bed and listened to the angry thudding of his heart, which reminded him of the sound of heavy rain on the awning of his father's store, when he stood under it on rainy mornings. And a desolation seized him: she was not treating him right, she was slipping away into the sleep of girlhood and leaving him out in the rain. Under the covers he slipped toward her until his leg touched hers. All along his leg he felt a sharp burning, his head felt hot, he was about to burst, and rolling heavily against her he began shaking her shoulder, but struggling into half-waking she pushed away his hand, she pushed at him and pressed the side of her face into the pillow as if he were burning a light in her eyes.

Angrily Martin got up and went out of the room.

He walked up and down the unfamiliar parlor in his morocco slippers, he threw himself into his armchair and tried to remember his first sight of Caroline, but it was no use, nothing was any use, and for some reason he thought of the corridor in the Vanderlyn, the actors and actresses, the naked foot on the bed seen through the half-opened door. He rose from the chair, for he needed to walk, to move about; and making his way to the entrance hall, he took down his black overcoat from the hall tree and put it on. Then a remorse came over him, for after all it was his wedding night, and with his coat still on he returned to the bedroom and stopped in the doorway. 'I'm going out, Caroline,' he said, in a whisper so soft that it was as if he had only thought the words, while he stared at shadowy Caroline lying in the bed, lying so motionless that one might have thought he had plunged a knife deep into her chest. 'I'm going out, Caroline,' he said again, but she lay silent in the coffin-bed. Then he turned and made his way from the too-still room into a small hall that led him astray, for he found himself in the library, where glints of dark glass concealed dolls bowed down with sadness, and passing through a door he saw that he was in the dark parlor, of all places, which led to another hall, and seeing his hat on a hook he placed it on his head, opened a door, and stepped into the dim-lit corridor.

He walked briskly past neighboring doors and turned into the longer corridor. At the end he pushed open a door that gave onto the landing. Martin began to climb the stairs, pulling himself up faster by holding onto the rail. At the eighth floor he looked down over the railing and saw the sharp-turning stair-flights dropping away in smaller and smaller rectangles, as if the stair-flights were parts of a swiftly unfolding telescope. He pushed open a door and climbed a final flight of stairs, pushed open another door, and found himself in a narrow dark corridor lit by two gas brackets with murky globes. Some of the doors were without numbers, he could barely see, suddenly he was standing before number 7. He knocked lightly and then sharply, not caring, but looking around anyway to see whether any doors were opening, inside he heard a noise, and then the door opened. Marie looked at him with weary startled eyes. Gently she took his arm and led him into the small black room, where he knocked his foot against a wooden chair that scraped on the floor. In blackness she drew him to the bed, in silence she waited while he removed his coat and hat, in silence and blackness he lay down with Marie Haskova and celebrated his wedding night, thinking for a moment of Louise Hamilton on her fever-couch and then of Caroline's unbound hair, her sharp-round shoulder, her sullen sleepy look, the white sleeve of her nightdress, so that it seemed to him, as he lay back on the black bed beside Marie, whom he could hear breathing as if she had already fallen asleep, that if he had been unfaithful to Caroline by coming here on his wedding night, he had also been unfaithful to Marie, who had taken him in without a word, without a reproach, only to find herself secretly replaced, in her own bed, by Caroline.

It was still dark when Martin returned a little while later to his apartment. He hung his hat on the hall tree and stepped into the parlor, where the mantel clock showed that it was not yet three in the morning. When he pushed open the door of the bedroom he saw Caroline sitting up in bed in the dark. 'Where were you?' she said. 'I was frightened.' And a tenderness came over him: she wasn't angry, he had abandoned her, he longed to ask her to forgive him. 'I couldn't sleep,' Martin said. 'I can't sleep either,' Caroline said, in a tone so forlorn that Martin sat down beside her and put an arm around her stiffening shoulders, as if to comfort a child. 'It will be all right,' Martin said, stroking her hair, and now there came to him, looming out of nowhere, the face of little Alice Bell, with her yellow hair and serious eyes, her trembling shoulders. But already he could feel desire rising in him, a scent of blossoms streamed from her hair or her nightdress, he noticed that he was still wearing his coat, and dropping his hand to the front of her nightdress he touched her breast. Caroline stiffened and pushed away his hand. 'Don't do that,' she said. Rage flamed in him. 'Damn it,' he said, and struck the bed with his fist. Then he stood up and strode from the room, strode through room after room, until it seemed to him that he was rushing through hundreds of rooms, until he came to a door that he jerked open.

He strode across the corridor and knocked loudly on the door across the way. 'I'll knock it down if they don't open,' he said to himself, or maybe aloud, the words sounded very clear and distinct, so perhaps he had spoken them. It was Emmeline who opened the door.

'What is it? God! Are you all right?'

'Get your mother,' Martin said as he stalked into the parlor, barely able to see Emmeline for the rage in his heart. He could feel blood beating in his temples and in his eyes. Emmeline returned with Margaret Vernon, in a flowery dressing gown that she clasped at the throat; she looked up at him in fearful bewilderment, as if she were about to cry. Martin felt like slapping her face; his arm was trembling, he wanted to lie down.

'Tell her,' he said in a kind of hushed shout.

'I don't understand,' wailed Mrs. Vernon.

Martin took a deep breath. 'Instruct your daughter. Tell her about marriage. Tell her. Tell her.' He pointed to the door.

A confused, pained look crossed Margaret Vernon's face, as if he had struck her, but to Martin's surprise she said nothing and, lowering her eyes, obediently opened the door and went out. Martin sat in a chair and closed his eyes; when he opened them he was puzzled to see Emmeline sitting across from him. He had been dreaming of his old room over the cigar store. Behind him the door opened. 'It's all right now,' Mrs. Vernon said, with dignity. 'You can go back.'

Martin nodded stiffly and strode back into his apartment, shutting the door hard behind him. He hung his coat on a peg of the hall tree, then turned out the lamp in the parlor and made his way through the dark, till passing through a door he found himself suddenly surrounded by dim dolls in glass cases. He groped his way back into the parlor and made his way to another door, and stepping through he saw again the glimmering glass cases, the shadowy sad dolls, and stumbling away he passed through another dark room, and again it seemed to him that he was passing through many rooms, through all the rooms of the city, in order to reach his wife. After a while he came to a door, a door that was partly open, as if he had already come through it the other way. He pushed at it uncertainly. Caroline was sitting up in bed, in the dark. 'Mother spoke to me,' she said. Martin wondered what the devil Mrs. Vernon had told her. He went over to the bed and lay down, and as he did so a heavy weight seemed to roll through his skull and press against the top of his head. He felt something soft and dry and cool on his forehead, and for a moment he was startled, almost frightened: what could it be? Then he realized that it was Caroline's hand. He raised a hand and patted the back of her hand.

'Everything's going to be all right, Caroline.' The words soothed him, an immense, crushing peace came over him, in the dark he patted her hand again, and at once he began dreaming: he was sitting on a sunny-and-shady bench beside his mother, she was wearing a hat with black ostrich feathers, and beyond the edges of the hat, which seemed far above his head, he could see tall buildings against the brilliant blue sky.

20

THE FATE OF THE VANDERLYN

For the Christmas season Martin directed his managers to trim their windows with holly wreaths and cotton snow. They were to make room inside for a Christmas tree trimmed with colored glass balls and clearly visible from the street. He instructed each female employee to wear green and red ribbons in her hair and each male employee to wear a green and red silk flower in his buttonhole. Special Christmas napkins were to be used, beginning on the first of December, and each table was to have a red or green wax candle. Free red and green candy suckers, wrapped in red and green waxed paper twisted at the ends, were to sit in baskets beside each cash register. Martin had found a small candy shop and manufactory on Broome Street willing to supply his cafes with hard candy at the low price of twenty cents a pound, if he ordered one hundred pounds, and he instructed the managers to divide the remaining candy evenly among all employees on the day after Christmas.

Holiday profits from the five Metropolitans were so high that Martin immediately began to lay plans for another cafe in Brooklyn; and in the new year he received from the owner of a big department store an offer to purchase his chain of cafes for a remarkable sum.

His life outside the business had returned to its accustomed round. In the morning Martin rose early, long before Caroline, and took breakfast with Emmeline at a corner table in the restaurant of the Bellingham. In the evening he returned to the hotel at eight or nine to find Caroline and Emmeline and Margaret sitting in the lamplit parlor. For nothing had changed, nothing would ever change, throughout eternity he would step from the lobby into the lamplit parlor where three women sat waiting, while somewhere in another life a marriage took place: her hand in her sunny lap, the carriage creaking, fresh flowers in his mother's hat. And approaching the women Martin would bend over Caroline and kiss her lightly on her uplifted cheek, while a carriage full of sunlight disappeared into the long afternoon, and sinking into his armchair he felt himself sinking down into deep cool subterranean vaults. There he found himself talking with Emmeline and Margaret, while Caroline sat with half-closed eyes. After a while Emmeline would rise, explaining that she had to get up early, urging the others to stay. And at once Margaret would rise, and slowly Caroline would rise, and then Martin himself would rise, out of the cool vaults into steamheated lamplit air. Together all four would walk to the elevators, together they would ride to the fifth floor. And two by two they would walk down the corridor, two by two they would turn left, and at their doors they would pause and say good night, two by two.

Caroline was tired, always tired. She had begun to complain of pains in her back; and although in the days after their wedding night she had obediently performed her nightly duty, Martin had taken to slipping less and less often over to her side of the bed, for she seemed to take no pleasure in his attentions, lying motionless and silent beneath him, and turning abruptly onto her side, without a word, as soon as he was through.

Sometimes, when she was fully clothed, Caroline would fall into a playful affection. She would ruffle his hair, and rub his shoulder, and give him little hugs, and call him her little pet; and sometimes she would sit on his lap. In these moods she would allow him to hug her and stroke her hair, but at the first sign of desire she would stand up quickly, with an odd, disturbed look, as if he had spoiled something, as if he had failed to understand.

She complained of a heaviness, a tiredness, of pains in her legs, of a sensation of pressure in her temples, of headaches branching out like pictures of lightning in chromos of storms, of flutters in her eyelids, of a vague malaise, as if something were not right, not really right at all; and stretching out on the blue-green damask sofa in her mother's parlor, beneath a heavy comforter, with one arm thrown over her eyes, she would lie for hours in the dusk of long winter afternoons.

One morning when Martin stepped out of the apartment he saw Marie Haskova with her mop and bucket, walking slowly and heavily down the hall. Even as his muscles tightened he realized that it was the fifth-floor maid, a heavyset fiftyish woman with thick hams and very pale smooth skin, who put him in mind of a stern nun. It occurred to him that just above his head Marie Haskova was making her rounds, confined forever to her floor as if she had disappeared into the forests of Bohemia. Secretly she moved through the building by service elevator, silently she took her meals in the basement, unseen she lay down in her attic bed – a ghost of the Bellingham, fluttering in the dark, ungraspable.

Often at night Martin lay thinking of Marie Haskova in her ghostly attic chamber, of Louise Hamilton in her dusky parlor, of Dora and Gerda in the house with rattling windows, of the actresses in the hallway, of women in long dresses, of women who smiled at him in lobbies and elevators, who looked at him in a certain way. Then it seemed to him that he was surrounded by swarms of floating whispering women who brushed against him and bent over him, offering their breasts and tongues, while only Caroline, with her pale hair pulled back tight, stood with her face turned a little to one side, staring dreamily at something in the distance.

To his surprise he felt no anger at Caroline, whose remoteness seemed as fixed and unalterable as the paleness of her hair or the half-closing of her dark, unseeing eyes. He felt that he ought instead to be angry at Caroline's mother, for hadn't Margaret Vernon

brought up her daughter in utter ignorance of everything, hadn't she watched over and in a sense encouraged her illnesses, her weariness, her unawakened
existence, her dream-in-life? Yet he wasn't angry at
Margaret Vernon either. Rather he had fallen into a kind
of lassitude, in relation to Caroline, a slumber almost
like that of Caroline herself. There were times when he
marveled at the strength of her languor, which lapped
against him in slow warm waves, soothing away his
desire, filling him with a sweet, melting melancholy, a
dissolving shadowy sweetness of vague regret and dim
longing.

Such was the ghost-world into which he sank each
night and from which he rose each morning in darkness
to set forth in a world of definite things. It was a world
in which he could feel his senses waking even as he
walked in cold dawns to the iron stairs of the El, a hard
sharp exhilarating world – an Emmeline-world, as he
had come to think of it, bright and flashing, charged
with energy. Business was flourishing. In March he
leased a vacant store and basement in Brooklyn, not far
from his Metropolitan near City Hall Park, and planned
to turn it into a two-floor cafe. Daily he traveled by
cable car over the Brooklyn Bridge to check on the
progress of the new restaurant, and during the week he
continued his habit of stopping in unannounced at any
of his five cafes for a quick inspection of the tables and
kitchen and a talk with the manager. Always he looked
forward to his visit to Emmeline's Boulevard cafe,
where there would be some little change he liked to
discover, some small improvement in decor or service.

Under her management, business had nearly doubled. There was a sharp feeling of friendliness in the air of the place, and Emmeline had about her a relaxed self-assurance, a radiant ease, that seemed to seep into the folds of the curtains and the gleam of the glass saltshakers.

At dinner one night in March he learned from Walter Dundee that the affairs of the Vanderlyn had reached a crisis. Dundee had it on good authority that rather than dipping into their pockets the owners were planning to turn their backs on the Vanderlyn, to get out altogether – in short, to sell. No telling what might happen now – it all depended on who the devil they sold it to. But Dundee, who had fought for change all along, felt it was a bad affair whatever way you looked at it; things would never be the same. 'But I thought you didn't want them to be the same,' Martin said, struck by the contradiction. Did Dundee secretly want things to stay the same after all, was the shrewd engineer finally ready to sink into the shadows with old Mr. Westerhoven? But Dundee, as if sensing something disdainful in Martin's words, sharply rejected any suggestion of contradiction. If he worried about the change of ownership, it wasn't from fear that the Vanderlyn would become modern and efficient and workable, since a well-intentioned push into the modern world was exactly what was necessary. No, what troubled him was that in carrying out the necessary change, the spirit of the place would some-how be harmed, since a hotel was more than the sum of its electric wires and varnish – he had worked in his share of hotels before settling at the Vanderlyn, and he knew. Westerhoven's error was to confuse the spirit of the place with the out-of-date, the technologically antiquated. But there was a benevolence about the Vanderlyn, a sense of good will, which affected visitors like an atmosphere, an atmosphere of well-being, and this atmosphere had nothing to do with old-fashioned creaking elevators and faulty heating systems but rather with the will of the owners as expressed in the will of the manager and his staff – and it was the possible corruption of this will that troubled his sleep. Martin, who had suspected Dundee of a secret wavering, felt a rush of affection for the man, who had defended himself well and now looked at Martin sternly with his sharp blue eyes. With his close-cropped gray hair, his clean-shaven chin, his long nose and shrewd blue eyes, Dundee reminded Martin of a ship's captain or a preacher.

'Very much the captain,' Emmeline remarked at lunch the next day, 'though I'm not sure about the preacher. More the Sunday-school teacher, I'd say: he has that air of clean-smelling cloth and moral upright-ness, though really he's more worldly than that. He's right about the spirit of a hotel, too – you can feel it right away, almost before you step into the lobby – but I'd say he underestimates things like rugs, armchairs, paint, all these material things. They're part of the spirit too, if you see what I mean, a sort of, well, material way of expressing something that isn't material at all. So if you look at things a certain way, you could say that a good old mahogany armchair isn't really there at all –

it's sheer spirit! Oh, I'm kidding, but I'm not kidding. I like your friend. He's a good man.'

As often when talking to Emmeline, Martin had the sense that he had leaped into a comfortable steam train and was off in an exhilarating rush.

'Does it bother you,' Emmeline said, 'that Dundee thinks you should have stayed at the Vanderlyn?'

'No.' The question took him by surprise. 'No, it isn't that. But there's something about this whole Vanderlyn business. I can't put my finger on it.'

'Well, when you do –'

'When I do?'

She laughed. 'Then you can stop thinking about it.'

He thought about it as he orchestrated the advertising campaign for the opening of the sixth Metropolitan, though it wasn't so much thinking as a kind of puzzled brooding. The Vanderlyn had threatened to smother him, and he had gone his own way: it was as simple as that. But was it really as simple as that? He remembered his excitement when, in the early days of his secretary-ship, he had had the sense of penetrating secrets, of seeing connections and combinations, of holding in his mind the complex system of forces that constituted the world of the Vanderlyn. In comparison to the gorgeous interwoven design of a hotel, a cafe was bare white cloth. The interest lay in the multiplication of cafes, in the complex management of an expanding business. And business was booming: he was a success, people with money had begun to take notice, they were offering large sums for his multiplying chain of blue cafes, which need never stop expanding, which grew, in a sense, with only the slightest help from him: and he saw a line of blue cafes stretching side by side clear across the country. And a restlessness came over him, at the thought of all those blue cafes, repeating themselves across the plains and mountains.

The cafe opened at the end of March, to the music of a fourteen-piece German band. Receipts for the first day more than doubled those of previous opening days, and customers continued to pour into the blue cafe through the double glass doors at street level and the blue wooden door at the bottom of the blue-painted steps. In the sunken area before the basement level there was space for three white metal tables, which proved highly popular on warm days. Martin imagined a great court, filled with white metal tables, under high trees. Already he had begun to plan a seventh cafe, in Coney Island, perhaps in West Brighton. In mid-April the crisis of the Vanderlyn seemed to have passed, the owners were hesitating, but at the end of the month Dundee suddenly reported that the decision to sell was near: there was now talk that the building would be demolished and replaced by a twelve-story commercial building, although this was little more than a rumor. At about this time Martin stopped at the Vanderlyn one sunny afternoon, for he felt a desire to sit in the lobby. He hadn't entered the building since refusing Mr. Westerhoven's offer nearly two years ago.

John Babcock was behind the desk, and nodded rather stiffly to Martin. Beside him was a new clerk, who looked up at Martin as if prepared to offer him a room. On the bench sat two bellboys whom Martin had never

167

seen before. He sat down in a familiar armchair in the sunny lobby, with a view of the cigar stand, which was now a cigar-and-candy stand run by a plump man with round eyeglasses. He had heard that Bill Baer had a cigar store of his own on Amsterdam Avenue. The door to Mr. Westerhoven's office was just out of sight. A man in a checked vest sat in an armchair reading a newspaper, a gray-haired man and a gray-haired woman sat silently in two chairs side by side, a handsome woman wearing a black hat with blood-red roses strode purposefully across the lobby, a bent-over old woman stood motionless beside a chair, balanced on her shiny dark cane. It was unusually quiet for a Wednesday afternoon. Martin still liked the high old lobby, which had about it a kind of small grandeur – the carved woodwork around the arched windows was pleasing, the sort of thing you didn't see in newer, bigger hotels, and the tall, slightly absurd marble pillars, which led the eye up to a ceiling carved with gilt hexagons, filled him with a kind of anxious tenderness, as if he wished to protect them from a harsher judgment – but everywhere he saw signs of decline. The marble floor had little broken, rough places, on the arm of his chair was a small but very visible burn from cigar or cigarette ash, the curtains looped up beside the arched windows were mottled with fading – it was all beginning to look like the parlor of someone's grandmother, a comfortable old-fashioned place quietly fading. Perhaps, after all, that was Mr. Westerhoven's vision of a hotel: an old parlor, with many pleasant places for hiding, presided over by an aproned grandmother smelling of apples and pie dough.

Martin imagined many empty rooms above. The lobby was very quiet. Even the sunlight that came through the high windows was transformed into a quiet version of itself, a browner and more faded light, like the light that enters a deep forest – the forest in the tissue-paper-covered picture of Hansel and Gretel in a dimly remembered childhood book. Perhaps that was Mr. Westerhoven's deeper plan: to turn the lobby of the Vanderlyn into a deep, peaceful forest, penetrated by shafts of dim light. In the warm, faded light, in a stillness made deeper by dim sounds sifting through, Martin closed his eyes.

And at once he saw: deep under the earth, in darkness impenetrable, an immense dynamo was humming. Above the dynamo was an underground hive of shops, with electric lights and steam heat, and above the shops an underground park or garden with what seemed to be a theater of some kind. Above the ground a great lobby stretched away: elevator doors opened and closed, people strode in and out, bells rang, the squeak of valises mingled with the rattle of many keys and the ringing of many telephones, alcove opened into alcove as far as the eye could see. Above the lobby rose two floors of public rooms and then the private rooms began, floor after floor of rooms, higher and higher, a vertical city, a white tower, a steel flower – and always elevators rising and falling, from the cloud-piercing top to the darkness where the great dynamo hummed. Martin had less the sense of observing the building than of inhabiting it at every point: he rose and fell in the many elevators, he strolled through the parlor of an upper room and walked in the underground park or garden – and then it was as if the structure were his own body, his head piercing the clouds, his feet buried deep in the earth, and in his blood the plunge and rise of elevators.

Martin's eyes opened. He was sitting in the lobby of the old Vanderlyn Hotel. He was feeling a little tired, his heart was beating rapidly – and from his heart there beat, in wave after wave, a wild, sweet exhilaration.

21

NEW LIFE

'And yet you've always said you weren't cut out for hotel life,' Emmeline said. 'So it can't be that, unless it was really that all along. But I don't think so. You'd have stayed at the Vanderlyn in the first place.'

'Choking to death on the rope handed to me by Alexander Westerhoven? No thank you.'

'Anyway you've answered my question.'

'Which one was that?'

'You know: the one about what you'd do if you were ever rich. Now I know.'

'I'm not rich,' Martin said quickly, bending over his soup.

Nearly four weeks had passed since his vision in the lobby of the Vanderlyn, and the feeling of exhilaration, the sense of a sweet adventure, of a beckoning, was still with him. In a month that seemed both feverish and very calm, he had sold his chain of cafes lock, stock, and barrel to a real estate millionaire grown rich in West End land speculation, and without a moment's hesitation he had purchased the Vanderlyn. Dundee had grasped his arm warmly at the news, his eyes stern with pleasure, but Emmeline had thrown him a stricken look. To give it all up, all of it, just like that! It was too sudden, too strange, too, well, impulsive and unsettling and confusing. At the very least he ought to incorporate and raise the money for his scheme by selling shares of stock. That way, if he decided – but Martin wouldn't hear of it. He had gone off in a useful and profitable but finally boring direction and wanted no distractions. With the help of a quarter-million-dollar bank loan he planned to undertake a major renovation. Emmeline had resisted his plan that she leave the small world of the cafe to become the new food and beverage manager of the Vanderlyn; he had begged Dundee to speak to her. After a week of hesitation she had come round, though not without conditions of her own: she was willing to leave the cafe, but insisted on starting in a humbler position, perhaps as a kitchen helper. Martin countered by offering her the position of part-time day clerk and part-time secretarial assistant.

The morning after the purchase, Martin stepped into Mr. Westerhoven's office, closed the door, and offered him the newly created position of consultant to the manager, at a handsome salary. To his surprise Mr. Westerhoven held up a hand to silence him, closed his eyes, and tendered a flowery resignation. He would not impede the stream of progress, not he; no no, not he; it was time to step aside, to make room for young blood, for the new generation. In the brown room, cluttered with bronze statuettes and shelves of knickknacks, it struck Martin that Mr. Westerhoven looked like a large, bewildered boy. His thin coppery hair was combed neatly to one side, his old-fashioned morning coat had a fresh white carnation in the buttonhole, but his gaze kept drifting about the room, and he had a new habit of tugging at an earlobe and pulling at the end of his nose.

The next morning Martin introduced to the front-office staff and to the chief members of housekeeping, engineering, food services, and accounting the youthful new manager, Mr. James Osborne, whom he had hired away from a small but fashionable uptown hotel that two years earlier had undergone a successful renovation which included the transformation of the top floor into artists' studios. Martin had no plans to introduce artists' studios into the Vanderlyn, but he wanted a man who, while understanding what was charming in a somewhat antiquated hotel, wasn't afraid of change. Osborne, who was thirty-two, had an air of vigorous confidence that was only enhanced by the touch of gravity in his manner. He put Martin in mind of a successful young banker.

'Anyway,' Martin said, 'it's something I understand from the inside. And it's fresh air – fresh air. I couldn't breathe any more in the cafe business.'

'You talk a lot about that,' Emmeline said.

'About breathing?'

'About not being able to breathe.'

'Do I? That's what it comes down to, I guess. Being able to breathe.'

'That sounds like an epigram, Martin. But we'd better get back to the lobby and check up on those carpenters.'

Martin, who counted on Emmeline's advice, was throwing himself into every detail of the renovation. He planned with Osborne the strategy for closing off a block of rooms while keeping the hotel open, conducted the team of interior decorators through the entire building from basement to roof, and approved the replacement of steam engines by electric motors to drive the elevator drums. He visited furniture whole-salers with an eye to selecting beds and dressers, discussed with Dundee the wiring of the entire building for electricity, studied the plan for the installation of telephones, talked with the wood-finishers in the lobby who were repairing the carved window-moldings and the upholsterers in the basement who were recovering parlor chairs. He visited plumbing supply companies and examined porcelain bathtubs with brass fittings, polished brass tumbler-holders and cigar rests, copper-lined ash and cherry water-tanks with nickel-plated chain and pull. From years of listening to the complaints of hotel guests, Martin knew that the bathroom loomed large in the imagination of Americans. And it was precisely here, as he wandered among displays of veined marble sinks and brass towel racks, that he was struck again by a contradiction in the architecture of hotels, a contradiction that was nothing but the outward expression of a nation's inner desire. For here the technologically modern and up-to-date clashed with a certain nostalgia of decor: bathrooms with ingenious American flush toilets and needle showers were given a suggestion of the European palace by decorations such as pilasters of Siena marble and shower hoods of carved mahogany. The modern luxury bathroom mirrored the modern hotel lobby, with its combination of electric lighting and old-fashioned carved ceilings, but it was also cousin to the modern department store, where terra-cotta scrollwork and grand marble stairways clashed with electric elevators and brand-new plate-glass windows that displayed the latest folding cameras with rack-and-pinion focusing movement, waterproof overcoats with patent ventilators, and self-threading sewing machines in drop cabinets. Far from deploring such contradictions, Martin felt deeply drawn to them, as if they permitted people to live in two worlds at once, a new world of steel and dynamos and an older world of stone arches and hand-carved wood.

In addition to the cigar stand, florist's shop, news-stand, and railway-ticket office in the lobby, Martin wanted to install a barbershop and a beauty parlor. He was persuaded by the team of decorators to preserve the classic lines of the lobby and locate the new shops in the basement, in an area that could be made easily accessible by a new stairway. In the dim-lit basement passages, not yet wired for electric light, Martin imagined a subterranean street of small shops, stretching into the distance. The plan for a row of shops was opposed by Dundee as impractical, but in addition to the barbershop and beauty parlor Martin insisted on having space for a small pharmacy to supply the needs of guests, as well as for a notions shop filled with the buttons and shoelaces and ribbons that were perpetually in demand. By leasing the four shops he would quickly get back his investment; and he began to wonder whether he might be able to open a small gift shop, with sepia postcards showing views of El stations and East River ferries, sets of porcelain salt-and-pepper shakers shaped like bellboys and maids, cast-iron Broadway cable-car banks, tin wind-up express wagons drawn by two horses, toy wooden barges loaded with little barrels and sacks, and optical fountain pens that revealed, when you unscrewed the cap and held it to your eye, a tiny color transparency of the Brooklyn Bridge against a brilliant blue sky.

As carpenters began hammering in the basement, as plumbers and wallpaper hangers set to work in the first block of sealed-off rooms, Martin devoted a few hours each day to wandering the floors of the great department stores that had enchanted his boyhood. The attraction of the great emporiums, though it remained in some sense obscure to him, in another was luminously clear: he admired the stores as immense solutions to problems of organizing space, of bringing together in a complex harmony an astonishing number of often clashing notes. What struck him wasn't so much the mingling of diverse merchandise in a great flow of departments as the ingenious inclusion of elements that ought to have clashed but didn't: the tearooms and cafeterias where customers refreshed themselves in order to gain more energy for buying, the organ in the rotunda, the odd services – a bank, a barbershop – that seemed to make of each grand emporium a little enclosed city, a roofed city with an intricate system of elevators and stairs moving shoppers vertically through a world of attractions. One department store contained a dentist's office, another a small theater. The idea was to lure customers in by means of skillfully arranged display windows and then to persuade them that they never had to leave, since everything they desired was immediately at hand. It struck him that what the stores really ought to do, if they wanted to keep customers there for as long as possible, was add several hundred parlor-and-bedroom suites. And as Martin pursued such thoughts, again he was struck by the kinship between the hotel and the department store, for each sought to attract and hold customers, each sought to be a little world in itself, each brought into a single large structure an immense number of juxtaposed objects serving a single idea. The department store and the hotel were little cities within the city, but they were also experimental cities, cities in advance of the city, for they represented in different forms the thrust toward vertical community that seemed to Martin the great fact of the modern city. That thrust was now being expressed in new forms, based on steel-frame construction, which allowed newspaper offices and insurance buildings to rise above the towering spire of Trinity Church; and Martin imagined great structures hundreds of stories high, each a city in itself, rising across the land.

From such imaginings he returned to the renovation of his six-story hotel, a small affair after all, though on the spot it loomed large enough. The operation was going to take longer than he had thought, some six months at least, as teams of workers moved by service elevator through carefully isolated portions of the hotel. Plumbing, Osborne explained, posed the trickiest problem. Since plumbing systems were vertical, it was difficult to leave access along all corridors while delivering materials to the bathrooms; the solution was a system of hoists erected outside the hotel, which permitted pipes and sinks to be brought in through the windows. Osborne showed himself to be expert at meeting complaints about noise and inconvenience, though even he proved helpless before the fury of guests when one of the new electric elevators stopped for six hours because of an electrician's blunder. Martin followed closely the remodeling of rooms, sometimes with the exasperated sense that what was really needed was the utter annihilation of all the rooms in the hotel and their rebuilding in new patterns. One day, struck suddenly by the dullness of the etchings that hung in every room, etchings that showed the Grand Canal in Venice, or the Tower of London, or the Arc de Triomphe, he ordered them replaced by contemporary chromos: skaters in the Central Park, tugs and barges passing under the Brooklyn Bridge, fashionable women strolling along Ladies' Mile, the yellow Moorish tower on Madison Square Garden with the gilded statue of Diana on top. Meanwhile he followed the expansion into the basement with sharp interest. He urged the carpenters to find room for another shop, and another, and he began to think of his basement shops as the Vanderlyn Bazaar, an attraction he planned to advertise.

The meticulously planned ad campaign had already begun in the daily papers and a handful of weeklies, where the New Vanderlyn was said to combine the amenities of a vanished way of life with every up-to-date convenience, but Martin planned to intensify the campaign as the renovation went forward. He needed some striking angle, some catchy device, and in moments of exuberance imagined painting the facade blue or erecting on the roof a fifteen-foot statue of George Washington or Pocahontas. A new hotel on Central Park West had advertised a croquet court on its roof – surely he could find something of the kind for the poor old Vanderlyn. But the poor old Vanderlyn resisted the showy and flamboyant, and Martin confined himself to a continual pressure of newspaper and magazine advertisement and a specially printed brochure that he distributed to the new travel agencies and made available in neat piles on the front desk. Extravagance would be confined to the official opening day, when he planned to release ten thousand balloons into the sky, hire an orchestra to play in the lobby, and invite journalists to a special dinner where he would pass out sealed envelopes, twenty of which contained a ticket allowing a free visit to the new barbershop.

Martin had fallen into the habit of discussing every detail of the business with Emmeline, who in turn reported the reactions of guests to the long renovation. 'You're going to make a success of it,' she said, 'though of course you know that. You can tell they like it, like being in on big goings-on, even if they complain about little things. And the questions about the basement! A woman told me the other day she'd heard you were building a department store under the hotel.'

'Now there's an idea,' Martin said. 'I wish I'd thought of it myself.'

'Oh you have,' said Emmeline, 'you have.'

She had thrown herself into her new job at the front desk with splendid zest. Martin saw that she was taken with the life of the lobby, with the sense of many lines of energy converging toward her from the elevators and the street, with her responsibility for providing comfort for strangers – and at the same time she revealed a gift for sympathy, for swift intelligent response, entirely lacking in an otherwise highly competent clerk like John Babcock. Her duties as part-time assistant consisted in accompanying him to wholesale furniture dealers and plumbing supply companies, making herself familiar with the working of all departments of the hotel, and reviewing accounts submitted to the Chambers Street office. And she was teaching herself how to type. She confessed to Martin that she had slipped his old book out from under Caroline's radiator and replaced it with a block of wood.

One morning as Martin was riding up to the fifth floor to inspect a newly decorated parlor-and-bedroom suite, the elevator boy stopped at the fourth floor and opened the car for a handsome woman in a black coat and black hat who asked the boy if the car was going down. When she learned it was going up, she entered with a look of such irritation and impatience that Martin said, 'Take us down, Howard. I'm in no hurry.' He was in fact in a hurry. The woman glanced at him sharply and said nothing, but at the ground floor she turned to him and said, 'I appreciate your consideration,' and gave him a

searching look before striding out of the car. He had
seen her once or twice in the lobby, sitting in a straight-
backed chair and glancing at the lobby clock. The next
day he saw her at a desk in a writing room, and the day
after that he met her on the stairs, which he was
climbing two at a time. 'If you have a minute, Mr.
Dressler,' she said, 'I need to discuss something with
you. Kindly follow me.' He wondered, as he followed,
whether she had known who he was all along or
whether she had made it her business to find out. In her
parlor she turned to give him the same searching look
he remembered from the elevator, a penetrating and
almost imperious look that seemed to be asking a
question and making a demand. A sense of marvelous
danger hung in the air. Martin, tense with energy,
followed her into the bedroom, where she turned with a
look of challenge. He was surprised by the length of her
forearms, by the matting of blond hairs on her stomach,
and by a kind of cool, wary ardor; she kept her combs in
her hair and scarcely moved under him, though he
noticed a line of dampness by the hair of her temple.
Her long satiny body reminded him of a splendid bridge
or a high, glittering steel beam swinging through the air.
When he saw her later that day, sitting upright in the
lobby, in a dark blue dress and small hat with a half veil,
she gave him a quick hard smile and averted her eyes.
The veil made it seem as if the upper part of her face
were dissolving. He became aware that he had stopped
and was looking at her, and immediately he continued
across the lobby to the front desk, where Emmeline
said, 'I hope you're not falling in love with her too.'

'I like that "too,"' Martin said.

'Oh, we're all in love with her, aren't we, John. She looks like some wonderful sort of panther.'

'Yes ma'am,' said John Babcock with a tight smile.

An odd shame came over Martin, who suddenly disliked the thought of himself and the woman, her long forearms, the line of dampness at her temple; he disliked having to conceal these details from Emmeline. He glanced over at the lobby, but the woman was no longer there.

'She vanishes,' Emmeline was saying. She lowered her voice melodramatically. 'The ghost of the Vanderlyn.' Martin saw her staring at him, her eyes shining with innocent mischief, with pleasure; some instinct in her had penetrated his secret, though she herself knew nothing about it. And an irritation came over him at her ferreting out his secret and not knowing it, at his many wives, all sliding into one another, at the vanishing woman who now reminded him a little of Caroline, despite the broad shoulders, for the pale hair at the temples was Caroline's hair and the look of slight strain between the eyes was Caroline's look. Then she was an emissary of Caroline's, sent by her to trap him on the stairs.

'So long as she doesn't vanish without paying for her room,' he said.

That night he felt a slight awkwardness on seeing Caroline, an awkwardness immediately replaced by irritation as she failed to ask him about his day, for he thought he might have confessed to her what he had done. But she was tired, a tiredness came over him at her tiredness, and he slipped as if comfortably into his marriage tiredness, waking for only a moment to notice a faint change, a little hairline fracture in the smooth surface of his marriage, through which other women might now enter, even if they were only emissaries of Caroline, ghost-Carolines who lured you into a room and turned to place both hands on your shoulders as they began to dissolve under the blue mist of their veils.

As the official date for the completion of the New Vanderlyn and the opening of the Vanderlyn Bazaar drew near, Martin was seized with restlessness. The New Vanderlyn gave every promise of success. The last block of rooms had been reserved far in advance, the new bathroom fixtures were praised by every guest, the grand old lobby had been skillfully remodeled with period furniture meant to summon up the amenities of a vanished past and with new steam radiators hidden behind Japanese screens, people in the street stopped in to inquire about the Vanderlyn Bazaar, and though Martin had no doubt of the success of his venture, he was aware of a sense of impediment, of dissatisfaction. His feeling reminded him of something, and one morning as he walked from the El station to the Vanderlyn and passed a cigar store it came to him: he recalled standing in the window of his father's store, stepping among the neat wooden boxes of cigars. What the window had needed was a dramatic new treatment, an eye-striking all-new display, but hampered by the heaviness of his father's disapproval, by the sheer weight of things-as-they-were, he had produced his inadequate cigar tree. Now he had created the New Vanderlyn, a far better cigar tree, a successful cigar tree that was going to make a success of the old hotel – but in truth he was still stepping carefully among the neat cigar boxes.

One afternoon not long after the official opening of the New Vanderlyn, in October 1897 – it had been a success, as he had known it would be, and the shops of the Vanderlyn Bazaar were bursting with business – Martin rode uptown on the Sixth Avenue Elevated, which above Fifty-third Street continued along the double track it shared with the Ninth Avenue line. He did not get off until the station at Ninety-third Street. It was a clear cold blue day. He walked toward the river and then turned uptown along the winding avenue that ran along the park. It was rumored that an apartment house would soon rise among the stone mansions of the avenue, but blocks of vacant lots and high rocky outcroppings still gave a touch of wildness that invigorated him. On a sloping side street he stopped at a hoarding and looked over the rough boards at an excavation in progress. A yellow steam shovel sat at the bottom of a pit of blasted rock and hard-looking chalky dirt. The dipper handle of the shovel swung slowly and stopped over a truck heaped with dirt and rocks. Dirt poured from the dipper and slid down the sides of the heap in the truck. A dark horse with a dirty white mane that looked like thick pieces of yarn snorted as it lifted and lowered a hoof. A workman in a blue wool cap sat on a rock eating an apple. Perhaps because of the cold clear air and the clear blue sky, Martin had the sense that he could see things very clearly: the woolly yellowish-white hairs in the horse's mane, the work-man's reddish hand matted with yellow hairs, wheel ruts in the dirt ramp leading down to the pit, the shadowed hole drilled in a boulder for a stick of dynamite, the glistening black letters of the company name on the yellow cab of the steam shovel, the smokelike rippling shadow cast on the rocky dirt by bursts of steam from the shovel's stack. He felt clear and clean and calm. You dug into the ground and made a hole, and from that hole a building grew – or a wondrous bridge. In his childhood, workmen had been lowered to the bottom of the East River in two great wooden caissons, and from there they had dug down through mud and clay and sand and boulders to a depth of more than forty feet. From those two holes under the river the towers of the great bridge had slowly risen up, block by granite block. Now buildings with frames of steel were rising above the height of the mighty bridgetowers. All across the city steam shovels were digging, truck horses pulling, boom derricks swinging. The edge of a pink poster flapped on the fence. Steam poured from the shovel, the truck horses snorted and stamped, a small bird lit on the hoarding and at once rose up, flying higher and higher into the bright clear sky.

22

RUDOLF ARLING

Rudolf Arling had come to America from Austria at the age of twenty-six with a reputation for bold and original creations and a fanatical attention to detail. In Vienna he had begun as a designer of stage sets but was soon creating theaters as well. At twenty-three he was commissioned to design a large pleasure garden on the outskirts of the city, with carousels, dance pavilions, and a beer garden under a grove of lindens; in the center of the park he placed a colossal building that he called a Pleasure Dome, a cylindrical white structure six stories high with hydraulic elevators that carried enchanted visitors to a wide upper walk from which they had a view of the entire park and, on clear days, the city by the Danube and the famous woods. The pleasure dome made his reputation. The six floors contained pleasures of every kind, including a panorama of Vienna with more than five hundred feet of slowly unwinding scenes, a puppet theater, a room of magical paintings that moved in their frames, an automaton chess player called Kressler who was said to be the offspring of Maelzel's chess player and the Lorelei, a theater for magic-lantern shows with clever dissolves and sophisticated effects of motion, an indoor carousel of winged horses suspended from steel cables that swung out as the center pole turned, a wax museum, a haunted chamber, and a roof garden with plenty of beer and wurst. It was noted that the young architect's passion for the colossal went hand in hand with a love for the minute, for he had designed every detail of the interior, from the wooden wings of the carousel horses to the porcelain salt and pepper shakers, shaped like elves, of the popular roof garden. In America, which he called the country of the future, Rudolf Arling traveled across the land designing grain elevators, railroad bridges, steel mills, ice plants, hydroelectric generating stations, and a steel-frame department store in Chicago with plate-glass windows as large as entire rooms. At the end of his travels he spent six months in Coney Island, designing a block-long shooting gallery with dozens of ingenious targets, including a miniature river steamboat with turning sidewheel paddles, a train of fourteen cars pulled by a steam engine, a covered wagon pursued by Indians, and a skyscraper containing a working elevator that rose and fell through twenty-four floors of lighted windows. In Manhattan he was invited to join a firm that built apartment houses, but Arling soon quarreled with his partners and set up his own office, in an old commercial building off lower Broadway, where he designed a double set of row houses facing each other across a street and connected by a subterranean walkway and an ornate stone bridge. Arling next designed a new kind of department store, shaped like a gigantic cylinder with a hollow center crisscrossed by steel bridges leading to circular aisles of merchandise. The design was rejected by the business partners who had commissioned it and who preferred an up-to-date but familiar kind of store, and it was the rejected plan, which Rudolf Arling showed to Martin toward the end of their first meeting, that convinced Martin that here was the man he was looking for.

Rudolf Arling was thirty-four years old, fair-haired and big-boned, with a short trim blond beard and piercing gray eyes. He agreed to listen seriously to Martin's ideas, which by this time were abundant and precise, and to apply them whenever possible, but he insisted on absolute freedom in the design of the floor plans, which he defined as the sum of solutions to precise technical problems. Martin hesitated, irked by the imperious tone but attracted by the air of supreme confidence, and hired him after their second meeting, during which Rudolf Arling introduced the idea of inner eclecticism.

It was an age, Arling said, of outward eclecticism, as everyone knew – witness the confections of cast iron and marble covered with Renaissance scrolls and brackets that greeted the eye on every New York street. But far more than this it was an age of inner or enclosed eclecticism, by which he meant not the familiar combination of antiquated styles with modern technological devices like elevators and telephones, but rather the tendency of modern structures to embrace and enclose as many different elements as possible. Consider the modern apartment building with its hairdresser and tailor's shop, the Pullman train with its dining tables and parlor chairs and beds, the transatlantic steamer, the department store with its tearoom and glove counter and string orchestra, the hotel lobby, the drugstore window, the knickknack shelf, the dime museum, the Iron Pier at Coney Island with its food stands and bath lockers and dance platform, and that marvel of the modern world, that model of ingenuity and know-how, the American sales catalogue, with its grab bag of detachable collars and steel plows, tin toys and buggies and sacks of nuts, all enclosed within the covers of a single book – a book far more wide-reaching than any epic. This striving after the enclosed eclectic was a note he had heard in Martin's ideas for a large family hotel, and more than anything else it made him think that the two of them saw things in somewhat the same way. He had been struck by Martin's idea for several basement levels, devoted to shops and a subterranean courtyard; it was the sort of thing he liked to work out.

After all, Martin thought, I can always fire him if he doesn't stick to my plan.

The success of the New Vanderlyn was gratifying no matter how Martin looked at it: revenues were up, vacancies were practically unheard of, guests paid their compliments to the manager and then repeated their praises to cousins and neighbors in Philadelphia and Boston. Within three months half a dozen more shops were leased in the Vanderlyn Bazaar. The new telephones rang on the polished front desk, electric lights flashed out the floor numbers above the bronze doors of elevators, dresses swished across the lobby – and always, in a careful gesture of the young manager, in the sweep of heavy drapes along the high windows, in the tapestry-upholstered armchairs beside their reading lamps, in the open doors leading to softly lit reading rooms or private lounges, always there was an invitation to put oneself at ease, to escape from the harshness of the world into a pleasant haven that was itself a little world, with carefully controlled excitements of its own. People came in from the street, to buy a cigar or newspaper, to sit for a while in the great public lobby, perhaps to have lunch in the public restaurant or get a haircut in the Vanderlyn Bazaar. And guests stayed on, soothed by glints of lamplight on rich brown wood, excited by the promise of something they could not name.

Even as Martin hired workers to increase the shop space in the Vanderlyn Bazaar, he pursued his walks north of the Bellingham, along the mansions and vacant lots of Riverside Drive. He had in mind a certain stretch in the nineties, where whole blocks of vacant lots with rocky outcrops gave the city a wild and stubborn air. Some of the lots and blocks were owned by private speculators, but others were in the hands of Lellyveld and White, a real estate firm that sold lots to builders and provided them with building loans. One day Martin visited Lellyveld and White, whose offices were in Bank Street, not far from his own small office. Lellyveld was a jovial man with glittering eyeglasses and thinning black hair, combed back over the shining knobs of his temples. He told Martin that a block of lots was indeed available on Riverside, up in the mid-nineties. A week later Martin had the first of his meetings with Rudolf Arling, and only then did he reveal his plan to Emmeline.

It was to be eighteen stories high, with turrets and cupolas and a broad central tower rising another six stories: a fever-dream of stone, an extravaganza in the wilderness, awaiting the advance of civilization that had already been set in motion by the announcement of the plan for a subway under the Boulevard. The Dressler, soaring into the sky like a great forest of stone, would also throw down deep roots: three underground levels and a basement, including a subterranean courtyard illuminated by electric lights twenty-four hours a day and a level of shops arranged in a labyrinthine arcade. The ground floor was to be a vast system of interconnected lobbies, ladies' parlors, smoking rooms, reading rooms, and arcaded walkways, above which would rise more than two thousand rooms, arranged in seductive combinations and divided into suites or apartments ranging from a single room with bath to twenty rooms with six baths. Roughly half the apartments would be provided with kitchens and dining rooms, so that guests could choose between the pleasure of private meals in their own suites or public meals in any of several hotel dining rooms. Monotonous regularity, he had told Rudolf Arling, was to be avoided like the plague: the note to strike was pleasurable diversity, a sense of spaces opening out endlessly, of turnings and twistings, of new discoveries beyond the next door.

'It reminds me of something,' Emmeline said. 'It's a hotel, an apartment hotel, but it reminds me of something else. It's like something strange you come across in a dream.'

It wasn't exactly what he had hoped to hear; he considered it. 'You mean a nightmare?'

'No, not that. I'm just trying to see it. There's a strangeness, Martin, like a picture of a castle in an old book.'

'A castle with elevators and electric lights and a parking space for motorcars. You think it's bound to fail.'

'I think it might do anything.' She paused. 'It's a leap.'

'In the dark?'

'Or straight into the light. I don't know which.'

He drummed his fingers. 'Well, I'll find out soon enough. Meanwhile you can get a nice safe job with Bill Baer in the family cigar store.'

Emmeline's cheeks flared. 'That was cruel. Why do you take that cruel tone?'

'Since you're leaving me –'

'I'll never leave you,' she said coldly.

Though his mind was made up, Emmeline's hesitation, her failure to embrace his plan at once, set him wondering, and when a few weeks later he stood beside Rudolf Arling and bent over a great sheet of paper covered with meticulously drawn small strokes of black ink, indicating the structure of the grand ground floor, after which the architect spread out for his inspection an India-ink wash of the building itself, with its prickly roofline of turrets and gables, it struck Martin that she had been right: it was something you might come across in a dream. It was precisely what excited him about the drawing, and about the venture itself. Through the great arch of the entranceway, which rose to the height of two stories, Martin could see shadowy figures standing about, and bending closer he saw or seemed to see, through one of the scores of little windows, a woman's face. 'You appreciate my little joke, then,' Rudolf Arling said, and Martin saw that the architect was watching him closely. The fierce gray eyes had the shimmer of mercury. Martin saw that here and there in the windows of the hotel, little hands were clutching curtains. He had the sense that Arling had imagined, in precise detail, the furnishings of the more than two thousand invisible rooms, including the designs of the brass handles on bureau drawers and the contents of jewel-boxes.

From a window in Arling's small office, crowded with carved parlor stands heaped with statuettes and little ivory animals, there was a view of the East River and part of the Brooklyn tower of the great bridge. The view of the bridge made an impression on Martin, it seemed a secret bond between him and the architect, for hadn't he as a child looked up at the great tower as the ferry approached the Brooklyn shore? But he was struck still more by the framed engraving that Arling had hung beside the window. The engraving showed a bearded, brooding Washington Roebling seated at his window in Brooklyn Heights with his hands folded tensely on the broad windowsill. Through Roebling's window was a view of the Manhattan tower of the great bridge, its two Gothic arches crisscrossed by a pattern of cables and suspenders. On the windowsill beyond Roebling's folded hands stood a pair of large binoculars. On a table beneath the window curtain lay a violin.

'Well I must say,' Margaret Vernon said, frowning down at the fan of cards in her left hand, 'I don't understand why there's all this talk about going underground when there are already trains in the air and trains on the streets. It makes me wonder what the world is coming to. I think . . . yes.' She played the ten of diamonds.

'But mother,' Emmeline said, 'you've always said the El roads were dirty and noisy and scared the horses to death. Your turn, Martin.'

Martin played the queen of diamonds.

'Well I might have known,' Margaret Vernon said, staring forlornly at her hand. She placed the cards face down on the table and heaved a sigh. 'Mrs. Wallace told me that when she was a little girl she saw a live coal fall right through the track onto a butcher's awning. It burned a hole clean through.'

'Well there you are,' said Emmeline. 'Lucky it didn't catch fire.'

'I don't know whether it caught fire. I wouldn't be at all surprised if it did. Your turn, Caroline. Don't forget that diamonds are trumps, dear. It's just like Martin to have a queen of diamonds. Lucky in cards, unlucky in love, my father always used to say. Imagine those poor men working outside in this hot weather. How are things coming along up there?'

'Martin,' Emmeline said, 'mother asked you a question.'

'Is it my turn?' Martin asked, looking up in surprise.

One winter day Martin picked Emmeline up at the Vanderlyn after work and took a long ride uptown in a hansom cab. It was already dark, snow glittered under the lamps in Madison Square Park. As a child he had always stopped at the park with his mother, so that the places beyond seemed to him not simply inaccessible but imaginary, like pictures of igloos or cactus flowers. Adulthood therefore was sheer magic: with a wave of the wand you summoned a cab and ventured into the imaginary world. He directed the cabby to go up Fifth Avenue and cut across the Park at Seventy-second Street. On one side the great palaces rose from the shadowy snow like presences glimpsed in mirrors. In the light of a streetlamp a bearded man in a shiny silk hat and a long coat with a black fur collar stood knocking his stick against the side of his snowy shoe. It occurred to Martin that Emmeline must be hungry, that he had forgotten about dinner. They turned into the Park; lights seemed to blink or tremble through faintly shaking black branches. Martin remembered riding in the Park on his wedding day, the purple flower, leaf-shade rippling on her white dress. On the other side of the Park the cab continued across town and turned up Riverside. Through the trees the river showed white and black: black water, white snow on ice. One by one the mansions behind their walls would melt away, they were nothing but palaces of snow and ice. Through the side window he could see up ahead a faint glow from the building site.

The building had not yet risen above the ground; the hoarding rose higher than Martin's head. He led Emmeline through a gate behind which a guard with a kerosene lantern sat in a wooden shack. At the edge of the great pit two big arc lights gave off a harsh white light. Below, sharp black shadows lay crisscrossed over a sunken world of steel columns and snowy wooden planks, through which openings gave glimpses of lower depths. Here and there men worked beside glowing lanterns.

Martin led Emmeline along the grassy side of the pit to a place where the columns and floors came up to ground level. He picked up a lantern and stepped out onto the snow-streaked planks. 'It's safe,' he said. 'Are you willing?' Holding out the lantern by the handle, he took her hand and led her onto the temporary floor. The floor ended ten feet later; a ladder led down to the next level, which stretched halfway across the excavation. Holding out his lantern, he made his way down. At the bottom he stamped. 'It's safe,' he called up, but Emmeline had already started down. When she stood beside him she looked up and said, 'It's like a canyon.' 'A poured concrete canyon,' Martin said, pointing to a half-finished wall behind scaffolding. A face looked down from above. 'You want to be careful down there, Mr. Dressler. Slippery as all get-out.' 'We're fine,' Martin called, and gave a wave. At a black opening he shone the lantern at a ladder going down. 'I think we'll be better off down there. Are you game?' He climbed down first, then held the lantern up for Emmeline, startled to see one of her button boots reaching down from shadowy shaking skirts. 'Careful,' he called up. At the bottom she stamped snow from her boot and said, 'Where now?' The darkness was broken here and there by patches of light from openings in the floor above. Shadowy steel columns rose up before them and in every direction. He led her along, holding up his lantern, past ladders and piles of lumber and a solitary black glove. 'This will be the main shopping arcade,' Martin said, 'with smaller branches running off. Watch it.' They were nearing an open end of the building. 'Look!' cried Emmeline. She stepped to the last column and pointed down to moonlit rockpiles, swept her arm out at the shadowy moon-glittering far wall of the pit. 'Come back!' Martin said. She turned and walked with him past dark columns glinting with lantern-light. Martin stopped and held up the lantern to Emmeline's face. 'Well? What do you think?' Her face in the light was so bright it looked wet. 'I was right,' she whispered. 'I was right, I was right.' He looked at her, not understanding. 'What I said that time: it's something you come across in a dream. It's a castle in a forest.' He stared at her fiercely; she burst out laughing. 'Oh come on,' she cried, 'I want to keep going forever. Come on!' Her face was so bright that he had to lower the lantern.

23

HARWINTON

'Imagine two stones,' Harwinton said. 'Gray, smooth, flattish: small enough to hold comfortably in your hand. There is nothing interesting about these stones. Now, imagine that I single out one of them. Either one will do. I describe the pleasing feel of the stone in my hand. I compare its color to the color of an exotic animal. I admire its remarkable shape. I say that this stone fills me with well-being and confidence. Then I tell you that you may have either of the two stones. Which one are you more likely to choose? That's advertising.'

'But suppose one stone is really superior to the other?' Martin said.

'That's an interesting fact. It may even be a useful fact, a fact we can use. But it has nothing to do with the art of advertising.'

As Harwinton spoke, Martin was struck again by his extreme youthfulness: with his short sandy hair combed neatly to one side in the manner of a schoolboy, his light-blue blond-lashed eyes, and his small neat teeth, he looked no older than seventeen. In fact he was twenty-eight and reputed to be one of the best in the business. Harwinton had grown up in Indiana and attended the University of Minnesota, where a popular professor of psychology had given a series of lectures on the psychology of advertising, with special emphasis on the role of association in making ads memorable. He had made them read *The Principles of Psychology* by William James. Did Martin know the book? As Harwinton put it, his eyes were opened: advertising was a science, a system of measurable strategies for awaking and securing the attention of buyers. A study conducted by a professor at Northwestern University in Evanston, Illinois, had demonstrated that the right-hand pages of a magazine held the attention of readers more than the left-hand pages. Experiments aimed at gathering information about the attention value of particular kinds of space had shown that a full-page ad was more than twice as effective as a half-page ad. But size alone was only part of it: there was also the question of seizing the attention forcibly by an imaginative but experimentally verifiable use of words and pictures. One test showed that of fifty people who were asked to look through a magazine, immediately close it, and name all advertisements remembered, twenty-three mentioned In-er-Seal, but only sixteen of those twenty-three knew that In-er-Seal was used for wrapping a biscuit, whereas all twenty of the people who remembered the Pears advertisement knew that Pears was a kind of soap. Harwinton had come to New York to work in one of the new ad agencies, where he had devised a successful campaign for a new kind of pink soap powder produced by a company determined to seize a portion of the market controlled by cleansers in cake form. A year later he had begun his own agency, with a staff of artists and copywriters and a specially trained band of researchers who prepared questionnaires, conducted scientifically controlled tests, and studied the effectiveness of particular ads on particular social and economic groups.

'At least you admit,' Martin said, 'that there's a difference between a cake of soap and an eighteen-story hotel.'

'Only a very small one. Let me explain something, Mr. Dressler. The world sits there. It may have a meaning. As a private citizen, I am entitled to believe that it does. But as an advertiser, I train myself to experience the world as an immense blankness. It's my job to provide that blankness with meaning.'

'I'll grant you the point. Still, you have to admit –'

'A man comes to me with a cake of scouring soap. He wants me to sell it for him. I see a white lump. It's my job to make this white lump, which has no meaning, except in the most limited and practical sense, the most important thing in the world. I create a meaning for it. I create desire. To have this soap is to have what Aristotle says all men desire: happiness.'

When Harwinton spoke, in his cool and precise way, he looked directly at Martin with his light-blue eyes, never once averting his gaze; and Martin noticed that when he spoke he never moved his long, well-manicured hands or his erect body.

'And you yourself don't believe a word of it?'

'Belief has nothing to do with it. I present it. I create an illusion. We are speaking of art, Mr. Dressler. Let me ask you something. Do you believe that the actor on the stage is really a villain? Let me ask you something else. If he isn't a villain, then is he a liar?'

Harwinton bent suddenly and removed from a drawer in his desk a thin black folder, which he passed across the desk to Martin. The folder contained a full-page magazine ad that Harwinton had designed for a new fountain pen with a hard rubber barrel – a pen no different, he assured Martin, from a dozen other fountain pens on the market. A frowning clerk was seated at a rolltop desk cluttered with pen nibs, his face and hands covered with black splotches of ink, his hair wild. Beside him, at a second desk, a handsome clerk with a mustache and a smile sat holding a fountain pen. He was speaking to a well-dressed woman with masses of dark hair pinned up under her ribboned hat, who was standing beside him and leaning over so that her elbows rested on the high back of his desk. What struck Martin was the tight corseting of the woman, her look of dreamy adoration, her full bosom and well-defined rump, the slightly rakish look of the clerk with the fountain pen.

'I'll order one of these,' Martin said, laughing and pointing to the woman. And at once he felt that he had said something crude, that Harwinton's light smile was the smile an adult might give to a child who had said something forgivable but wrong. As if to escape judgment Martin looked away and glanced about the office, which seemed to contain nothing but Harwinton's large flat-topped mahogany desk with its many drawers and, on the bare walls, a black-framed diploma from the University of Minnesota. The room made Martin think of a smooth-shaven face. The big bare desk stood across from an armchair for visitors, in which Martin sat, and it was only here that any concession had been made toward pleasure, for really it was a remarkably satisfying chair, upholstered in red silk plush and richly fringed, with a first-rate spring seat and spring back. Harwinton's own chair was high-backed, straight, and wooden. The impression of bareness and sharp angles, the high hard chair, Harwinton's close-trimmed hair and smooth upper lip, his tight-buttoned jacket and thin, almost bony fingers, all this made Martin think of a young monk or priest.

'You may be interested in other examples of our work,' Harwinton said, and bending over swiftly and precisely he removed from another drawer a heavy black folder. He opened it to reveal a collection of newspaper ads: ads for a blacking brush, an electric insole, a stick of graphite for bicycle chains, a wire rat trap with a coppered steel spring, a cherrywood stereographoscope mounted on a folding rosewood frame on a polished nickel stand, a brick-lined heating stove with a sheet-iron ash pan and mica door, a double-door hardwood refrigerator with a porcelain-enameled water cooler and an extra-large ice chamber, a sewing machine with an automatic bobbin winder in a drop cabinet with carved

202

panel doors. From another drawer Harwinton drew out a four-color poster showing an ad for a new carpet sweeper with a spring-action dumper and a rubber furniture protector – and now from drawer after drawer came bursts of color, a riot of bright designs, showing a copper-lined bathtub, a jar of brilliantine, a spring-wagon harness of oak-tanned leather, a cake of lemon-juice complexion soap, as if the secret life of the room were this hidden profusion of images, sprouting in the dark, multiplying, unstoppable, like scarlet secrets whispered in the darkness of the confessional. Martin lingered over one poster advertising a rubberized protective blanket for horses. It showed a rearing black horse under an Elevated track, with a bright red coal burning on its back. The horse's nostrils were flared, its brilliant white teeth bared, its eyes wild with terror. Its head was twisted back, as if it were straining to bite the blazing coal. The delivery wagon was on two wheels and a barrel was about to topple into the street.

The two images – the crazed horse, the full-bosomed dreamy woman – stayed with Martin, mingling with a third: the light-blue blond-lashed eyes of Harwinton, under the smooth forehead with its sandy schoolboy's hair.

'He reminds me of something very up-to-date and efficient,' Martin said to Emmeline that evening, 'like a typewriter or an electric circuit.'

'You don't like him.'

'I don't dislike him. He interests me. Harwinton is the future.'

'But I don't have a sense of him. I don't know what he's like.'

'But that's just the point. He isn't "like" anything. He reminds me of a boy I knew in third grade, William Harris was his name. He was a quiet boy, wrote very neatly, and kept to himself. I remember he wore very tight knee socks. No one disliked him, but no one really liked him either. He moved away the next summer, and when I tried to remember him in fourth grade, I couldn't remember his face. I couldn't remember anything he did. I could only remember that he was there.'

'At least he was there. That's something. I'll cling to that. Well then. Do you think you'll hire this Mr. Harwinton?'

'I've already hired him.'

'Then you do like him!'

'I don't dislike him. And one other thing: he takes you in. Those baby-blue eyes never stopped looking at me for a second.'

'Well don't forget, you interest him. You're a native, a kid from New York, and he's from – you said Indiana?'

'That's what he said: Indiana. Imagine being from Indiana. Where is Indiana?'

'It's near Alaska,' Emmeline said.

24

THE DRESSLER

The Hotel Dressler opened on August 31, 1899, on Martin's twenty-seventh birthday. Long articles in the major city papers praised the building's boldness of vision, its structural ingenuity, its ability to overcome sheer massiveness by means of an elegant design that led the eye upward through three major groupings to the two-story mansard roof with its tower, and if one journalist chose to complain that the building was 'wasteful,' that the facade was so heavily ornamented that it put him in mind of a gigantic wedding cake, even he felt compelled to acknowledge the exuberance of the Dressler, its sheer delight in itself. Crowds came to stare at the block-long building on Riverside Drive that rose eighteen stories into the air, with a central tower that soared to the height of another six stories; and the management received scores of requests for apartments, requests that were carefully entered on a large waiting list, for all apartments had been rented six months before opening day.

Harwinton had devised a shrewd ad campaign. It was aimed broadly at the middle class, but sought in particular to attract what Harwinton called the expanding middle of the middle class – those people who, having reached a comfortable level of existence, aspired to the trappings of wealth without being wealthy. His central theme was 'luxury for the non-luxurious income,' an idea repeated in countless newspaper and magazine ads and in a handsome promotional brochure. But Harwinton also emphasized a second and far more dramatic theme: the location of the Dressler. In doing so he drew on two contradictory ideas. The Dressler, he argued, was a rural retreat, a peaceful outpost far from the clamor of downtown Manhattan, but at the same time the Dressler was located in a new and thriving part of the city, only a short distance from a convenient Elevated station, and even closer to the projected subway station on the Boulevard – was located, in short, in the very path of progress. For it was Harwinton's belief that every city dweller harbored a double desire: the desire to be in the thick of things, and the equal and opposite desire to escape from the horrible thick of things to some peaceful rural place with shady paths, murmuring streams, and the hum of bumblebees over vaguely imagined flowers. It was the good fortune of the Dressler to be able to attach to itself both these desires, for while on the one hand it could offer to the prospective long-term resident a park and a river, a veritable vision of pastoral retreat, on the other it could offer the thrilling sense of being in the forefront of the city's relentless northward advance. It simply sat there, waiting for the rest of the city to catch up.

The Dressler itself, as the doubting journalist had pointed out and as Martin readily acknowledged, was a massive contradiction: a modern steel-frame building sheathed in heavily ornamented masonry-walls meant to summon up a dream of châteaux and palaces. Every effort had been made to draw the eye away from the monotony of vertical repetition to interruptive or irregular features, such as the two-story arched entranceways and the group of gigantic statues on the fourth-floor cornice, representing Pilgrims and Indians. Above all the eye was drawn to the elaborate roof, with its corner cupolas, its high chimneys, and its central openwork stone tower supplied with a circular observation platform and topped by an eight-foot finial. But the real battle against symmetry took place inside, where no two apartments were alike and where every public room was designed in a different period style. Even more striking, as several journalists remarked, were a number of odd features never seen before in an apartment hotel. It was noted that among the public rooms of the first two floors – the restaurants, the smoking rooms, the reading rooms, the ladies' parlors – was a scattering of peculiar rooms that seemed to be there to amuse or instruct. Thus there was a circular theater in which a panorama of the entire Manhattan shoreline continually unwound; a room containing a wigwam, a wax squaw gathering sticks, a young brave hacking a rock with a sharpened stone tool, and a seated chief smoking a long pipe, set against a painted background depicting a riverbank; and a hall called the Pageant of Industry and Invention, which contained working scale models of an Otis elevator, a steam train on an Elevated track, a Broadway cable car, and a steam crane lifting an I-beam, as well as full-scale models of a steam turbine, an internal combustion engine, and an electric generator with a drive pulley. These rooms seemed to some commentators a puzzling intrusion of the museum into the world of the hotel, although most acknowledged the rooms' festive and instructional nature.

No less puzzling to the journalists were a number of curious developments on the upper floors. At the end of a corridor on the sixth floor a four-room apartment had been transformed into an artificial cave, with narrow dim-lit passageways and a real waterfall. On the fourteenth floor a five-room apartment had become a forest, with thick trunks manufactured to resemble pine and oak, greenish light falling through a roof of thick-leaved branches, and a sudden bright-lit glade of real-looking grass and yellow silk wild-flowers. These playful rooms, which Harwinton had named Relaxation Rooms, gave to the hotel a slightly theatrical flavor, a note reinforced by the Riverview Lobby on the tenth floor. Reserved for the exclusive use of hotel guests, the Riverview Lobby was notable not only for its dramatic view of the Hudson and the cliffs of Jersey, but for its meticulous design in the style of an old-fashioned Victorian parlor, with plenty of fringed and tasseled armchairs and couches, statues of coyly bending nymphs, flower arrangements under belljars, majolica vases, an ormolu clock on the marble mantel shelf, and sepia photographs of unsmiling grandfathers in oval frames.

Martin followed the newspaper reports with close interest, puzzled himself by an occasional note of bewilderment or blame, for didn't they understand that it had all been thought out carefully, didn't they understand that in any case it had been given to him by the friendly powers, who had led him to the Vanderlyn Hotel at the age of fourteen? But he was pleased by the sheer weight of attention given to the Hotel Dressler, attention that, even if it was sometimes perplexed or disapproving, suggested that he had struck a nerve. He was above all pleased by the interest shown in the first three underground levels, for it was here that he had permitted himself to develop certain ideas that gave him a deep, almost guilty pleasure, as if the sunken world beneath the hotel had encouraged a freedom forbidden by the clear light of upper floors. On the first level, not open to the general public, was the courtyard, with its gardens and gravel paths and wooden benches, its shady bowers, its central three-tiered fountain – a place where hotel guests and invited friends might walk at all hours of the day and night, untroubled by changes in weather. On the second level was the Shopping Arcade, composed of scores of shops and booths on intersecting corridors, interrupted by well-lit plazas with fountains and benches. And on the third level, advertised by Harwinton as one of the wonders of the West End, you came to the Theater District, where Rudolf Arling had designed a series of paved streets illuminated by electric streetlamps and lined with theaters in flamboyant styles with alluring names (the Chinese Garden, the New Lyceum, the Little Theater, the Black Rose), including, in addition to dramatic theaters, a vaudeville theater, a concert hall, an opera house, and a nickelodeon.

Beneath the three levels, and entirely ignored by the journalists, lay the basement, the true bottom of the Dressler, which housed the electric plant, the steam plant, and a warren of workrooms for the maintenance staff.

From the artful rooms and subterranean paths of his high hotel Martin sometimes liked to remove himself in order to look up at the great mass of the building, pierced on each of its facades by an exterior court. It was as if he wanted to hold it all in his eye in a single glance. But what he saw in that glance gave way with a rush to all that he couldn't see, so that the unseen courts became filled with flowerbeds and gravel walks, the high-arched main entrances on the side streets were immediately connected by a block-long gallery leading to the elevator lobby, each room revealed its furniture, and below the ground, invisible but seen, people walked in the paths of the courtyard and the aisles of the Shopping Arcade and the streets of the Theater District until Martin seemed to hold in his mind the entire contents of the building – and almost reeling under the weight of images he would return inside with a sense of seeking relief from an attack of dizziness.

Martin had taken a modest apartment for himself and Caroline on the sixteenth floor, facing the river, and a second apartment, adjoining theirs, for Emmeline and

Margaret. It was Emmeline who understood: the move from the Bellingham to the Dressler had nothing to do with a desire for luxurious living and everything to do with being on the spot. Martin needed to take possession of his creation, to feel it working all around him and through him. He had given the actual job of management to James Osborne, whom he hired away from the Vanderlyn; at first Emmeline had refused the offer of assistant manager, but after a week of brooding she accepted with the understanding that it was only a trial. Daily Martin consulted with Osborne and Emmeline, weekly he attended the meeting of the manager and the department heads, but his passion was to inhabit the Dressler as fully as possible. He ate meals at each of the seven restaurants and tearooms, spoke to the linen-room attendants and seamstresses and chambermaids, sat in the main lobby and listened to guests from behind his newspaper. He examined the steam plant and electric plant in the massive basement beneath the theaters. He strolled in the underground courtyard, bought neckties and umbrellas in the Shopping Arcade, took Caroline and Emmeline and Margaret to a melodrama at the Black Rose. Emmeline had quickly become ardent in her loyalty to the Dressler and often accompanied Martin on his rounds; once, stopping abruptly on a street in the Theater District, she seemed about to say something and then to change her mind. 'A penny for your thoughts,' Martin lightly said. Emmeline hesitated a moment before answering. 'I was thinking,' she said, 'about the castle in the forest, that night,' and Martin was cast suddenly back to the lantern-lit columns, the ladders going down, the moon-glittering edge of the pit.

Although all three underground levels were a striking success, the Theater District in particular was attracting enthusiastic audiences, who after the performances liked to stroll along the cut-stone sidewalks of the six underground streets lit by electric streetlamps and lined by theaters glowing with electric signs. People liked to drink coffee and wine at the two outdoor cafes, or to sit on the slatted wooden benches of a small lamplit park beneath artificial elms, where they could admire the handsome views at the end of each street – views that were in fact large murals painted onto the foundation walls by a commercial artist named Clement Ward who was noted for his skill in depicting urban scenes, especially night scenes showing meticulously drawn cast-iron streetlamps, El stanchions rising to overhead tracks, and the windows of crowded, smoky saloons. Emmeline agreed with Martin that two more cafes were necessary, for many theater-goers preferred to linger in the artificial streets rather than return to the Empire Bar on the first floor or ride to the roof garden under the stars; and Martin discussed with one of the hotel engineers the possibility of fitting the ceiling of the Theater District with very small, very dim electric lights, to create an effect of starlight.

The roof garden was itself a popular spot, with its railed promenade, its flower gardens and small orchard of fruit trees, its scattering of gazebos and Swiss chalets, its red and blue and green Japanese lanterns, and its open-air restaurant of small round tables and canework chairs beneath a roof supported by white wooden posts joined by scrollwork. One rainy summer night when Martin stepped under the roof with Emmeline he saw that the wind was blowing the rain across the floor, so that customers were huddling in one corner. The next morning he arranged for the installation of protective metal screens on spring rollers, which could be lowered during storms.

A few days later Martin asked Emmeline to walk with him from the roof garden down to the boiler room, located in one of the basement divisions beneath the underground theaters. As they descended from landing to landing, Martin was struck by the monotony of the descent: each major stairway landing faced a row of elevator doors and had on each side a door with a window that led to a corridor, while between the elevator landings the stairway turned once to form a secondary landing with a potted plant. The plants exasperated Martin. By the time he reached the main lobby he had decided to have them replaced by varied arrangements of couches, lamps, and bookshelves, so that those who chose to walk would be able to rest along the way. The neat, boring elevator landings posed a more difficult problem. Emmeline suggested artwork of some kind, perhaps framed paintings, and it was Rudolf Arling who took it up, turning over the idea and shaping it into a plan that seized Martin's interest: in keeping with the theatrical nature of the roof garden and the third underground level, each landing would be designed to convey a different atmosphere. The walls of one landing would be hung with fishing nets and starfish and illuminated by green-blue light, another landing would be supplied with an Ionic column and wall murals of ruined temples and blue sea, a third would have a papier-mâché Indian in authentic garb against a background of thick pine trunks and winding forest paths, the whole bathed in a dark green woodland light.

Although Martin spent a good part of his day inspecting his hotel, talking with workers, and in general considering ways to improve the operation of the Dressler and the well-being of his guests, he also continued his habit of taking long walks in the neighborhood. He liked to follow the progress of excavations, to examine the facades of half-built apartment houses sheathed in scaffolding. Often he would pause thoughtfully before vacant lots. A great burst of building was taking place on the Boulevard, recently re-named Broadway, in anticipation of the new subway that would run under its entire length, but Martin had his eye on a stretch of empty land on Riverside Drive, some ten blocks north of the Dressler. He had reached an understanding with Lellyveld and White, who owned the land and were pleased with the financial reports from the Dressler, and one day after lunch he began meeting again with Rudolf Arling.

All such matters Martin discussed with Emmeline – at lunch, in her office during the day, and at dinner in the main dining room with Caroline and Margaret. Often the four of them took a stroll in the underground courtyard after dinner, after which Caroline would return to her rooms. Margaret was concerned about

Caroline. She had seemed so happy in her new apartment with its lovely view, she had looked forward to exploring the new hotel, which she referred to as the Castle – and really, if you thought about it, she was just like a princess in a castle, married to a powerful prince – but she had gradually returned to her old habits, more and more she had confined herself to her apartment, and now you could scarcely coax her to take an after-dinner stroll in the courtyard. And Margaret Vernon, who had been fiddling with her dress collar, would look sharply at Martin, as if to surprise in him the secret of Caroline's behavior, while Martin, who had grown skeptical about Caroline's capacity for pleasure, but who at the same time wondered irritably whether he was to blame for not loving her enough, would answer with a touch of impatience that Caroline was welcome to do as she liked.

'Of course it's all very well to let Caroline go her own way,' Margaret said one night, while brushing something from the sleeve of her dress. 'Especially when her own husband and sister prefer each other's company.'

Martin felt something burst in his neck. 'What the devil is that supposed to mean? Em and I have business to discuss – lots of it. If Caroline showed a second's worth of interest in all this –'

'Well I just think it's a shame, that's all,' Mrs. Vernon said, giving a sigh in the manner of an actress on the melodrama stage as she rose from her seat; and turning to Emmeline she said, 'Now don't stay up late, dear. It's very bad for your health.'

Martin watched Margaret Vernon walk away and then

turned to Emmeline. 'What the devil was that all about?'

'I suppose I do monopolize you,' Emmeline said.

'Oh, wonderful. Caroline has no interest in anything that concerns me, but because I'm her husband I'm supposed to prefer her company to yours.'

'It would seem reasonable. Please keep your voice down.'

Martin lowered his voice. 'It's not reasonable. It's unreasonable. Your mother is being unreasonable. What does she expect me to do? Sit in my parlor all day playing euchre with her and Caroline?'

'Still, I don't like it when you speak to her like that.'

'And the way she speaks to me? Do you like that? "Of course it's all very well." Who the deuce does she think she's speaking to?'

'Shall we walk?'

A few nights later Margaret Vernon returned to the subject of Caroline. Martin, stiffening, stared straight ahead while he prepared to tamp down his anger, but Margaret Vernon made no effort to suppress her excitement. Looking from one to the other from behind her rapidly fluttering blue-and-green silk fan, she announced that Caroline had found a friend.

'A friend!' said Martin, irritated at the sound of false heartiness in his voice. 'And who may that be?'

'You'll find out soon enough,' Mrs. Vernon somewhat mysteriously replied.

When Mrs. Vernon had left, Martin looked at Emmeline. 'What do you make of it?'

'It isn't as if Caroline doesn't make friends,' Emmeline said. 'She's actually rather good at it, when she wants to be.'

'Then why doesn't she ever want to be?'

'Well, she has you.'

Martin looked at her. 'Well yes. She does have me. And now she has a new friend.'

'So it would seem.'

'And what does that mean?'

'Oh, nothing. I've seen these little friendships of Caroline's. Shall we walk?'

25

A Fifth Chair at Dinner

Caroline's friend joined them at dinner in the main dining room the following night, and as she sat down Martin realized that he had seen her somewhere in the hotel, a tall, thirtyish woman, though for the life of him he couldn't recall where. It was Margaret who explained: Claire Moore lived on the sixteenth floor around a bend in the corridor. She was a late riser, like Caroline – or, as Claire Moore herself laughingly put it, like all widows without a guilty conscience – and she had passed Caroline several times in the corridor before introducing herself at the elevator late one morning. The next day she had invited Caroline to her apartment for a cup of tea, and after that it was luncheons, afternoon outings, a great visiting back and forth. And Martin was surprised: he had expected someone proper and boring, someone trained to talk about weather and food and to grow gradually invisible in company, and instead he found himself in the presence of a lively woman with a strong laugh in a strong throat, an air of humorous self-assurance, and a habit of sharp observation. She was handsome in a sudden, erratic way, her face with its strong bones bursting into moments of radiance as her long-fingered hands swept through the air and her eyes glistened with energy. Her hair – Caroline's hair, he saw immediately – moved when she laughed, and it struck Martin that motion was her element: she darted even as she sat, a bird in flight, a flock of birds. And always she glanced admiringly at Caroline, drew her into the circle of her anecdotes, praised her hair, a ribbon, the color of her clothes; and throwing back her handsome head, she laughed her full laugh, drawing back her lips from her very white teeth and showing the strong column of her trachea against the skin of her throat.

Now every night at dinner a fifth chair sat at Martin's table, awaiting Claire Moore, who arrived with Caroline a little late, a little breathless, glowing with health as if she had just come from a long brisk walk by the river, and who even as she began to sit was already describing the day's outing: they had gone shopping for hats, they had gone walking in the park, they had found a simply wonderful little out-of-the-way lunch place with the most imaginative sandwiches, they had braved the crowds of a tremendous tearoom that seated seven hundred. Think of it: seven hundred! Caro had been a brick – a brick, really – and she had seen the glorious humor of it: seven hundred ladies in a department store, taking tea. For the joke of it was of course that tea was an intimate occasion, which had been spread out and extended until it was like – well – as she had remarked to Caro at the time – it was like rowing in a boat the size of a barge. Here Martin begged to disagree. He himself found nothing humorous about sheer size, which on the contrary produced a sensation of power, of majesty – had anyone ever laughed at the Brooklyn Bridge? But of course he understood she wasn't referring to size alone, but to a special development that he himself had given some thought to: the expansion of small private events into large public ones. A family hotel was a perfect example. Here the guest willingly gave up certain privacies, such as that of dining alone, in exchange for the convenience of public service. And in doing so, an entirely new idea was born: the large public dining room, which wasn't a grotesque, bloated version of an intimate family dining room, but something entirely new, something massive and modern, and no more comic than an El track or a twenty-story office building or a transatlantic steamer.

Martin, surprised by his little outburst, was gratified and at the same time oddly irritated by the sudden serious attention with which Claire Moore listened to his words; and when he stopped speaking she struck her hands together, shook back her hair, and looking Martin directly in the eye said she would certainly think twice before daring to attack a tearoom again.

Martin wasn't sure what to make of this powerful, laughing woman, who had taken up with Caroline and suddenly was there, at dinner, inescapably. She whisked

Caroline from one shop to another and reported tirelessly the slightest incident of their daily adventures, suffusing every small thing with the drama of her temperament, while Caroline seemed uplifted on the waves of Claire Moore's unremitting attention.

'I don't know what to make of her,' he said to Emmeline as they strolled along a secluded path in the underground courtyard.

'I don't like it,' Emmeline said.

'It?'

'This sudden friendship. Her attachment to Caroline – her attachment to us. She herself –' Here Emmeline gave a shrug.

'She seems fond of Caroline. I can't imagine what they talk about.'

'Oh, she's probably fond of her, in a way. Caroline draws people. She doesn't need to say much. You see how they are at dinner.'

'I think I like her. She's good for Caroline. She gets her out.'

'It won't end well,' Emmeline said.

The friends, Margaret Vernon reported, had become inseparable, simply inseparable. They visited back and forth a hundred times a day, they attended afternoon performances at the Black Rose or the New Lyceum, when they weren't going off on one of Claire Moore's thousand little excursions. It was the best thing in the world for Caroline, who needed nothing but a little encouragement before she warmed to people; it was so good for her to get out of herself, to say nothing of getting out of her apartment. She simply adored the theater. And Claire was a good friend; you could tell she cared about Caroline, asking her opinion about things, admiring her, worrying when Caroline was out of sorts. Martin, watching the friendship out of the corner of his eye, was certain of only one thing: Claire Moore was most definitely there, occupying the fifth chair at dinner, a powerful and laughing woman. She was attentive to Caroline, praised her repeatedly, though not quite as often as at first, reported their little adventures, drew Caroline skillfully into the circle of her talk, which would widen suddenly to include Martin and Emmeline and Margaret, rippled with words and laughter; and from time to time, in response to a witty turn of phrase, Caroline would lightly smile.

For if it was true that Claire Moore had taken up with Caroline, watched her admiringly, seemed to dote on her, it was also true that Caroline in her quieter way was preoccupied with Claire Moore. Martin could feel her soaking up Claire Moore, absorbing her moods, taking her in. Sometimes Caroline would raise her hand in a way Claire Moore had; once, drawn for a moment into the swirl of Claire Moore's talk about a play they had seen, she began to speak and broke off to search for a word, and the precise tilt of her head, the precise manner in which she tightened her eyebrows in thought, brought Claire Moore sharply to mind. But more than this was the intensity with which Caroline listened to her friend, watched her even when she wasn't watching her, seemed to take in the talk through the tendons of her neck. She appeared impatient sometimes, as if she wished the dinner would end, and it was true enough that Claire Moore seemed to enjoy prolonging the dinners, seemed to enjoy talking to the others and especially to Martin, whom she liked to draw out on the subjects of modern living, the proposed subway system, steel-frame architecture, the future of the Upper West Side. As Martin spoke, he could feel Claire Moore listening closely to him, penetrating him with her attention. Two chairs away, Caroline sat with her eyes lowered, one hand resting tensely beside her plate.

'Caroline's jealous of you,' Emmeline said one evening after Margaret had retired upstairs.

'That's ridiculous,' Martin said, but even as he spoke he saw that it wasn't. Claire Moore was looking at Caroline a little less often, turning a little more often in his direction; without in any sense ignoring Caroline, she was shifting her very slightly from the center of her attention. Martin, who was used to being flirted with by attractive women, detected in Claire Moore no surreptitious looks, no secret signs; but he could feel in her, as she sat down to dinner, as she placed her forearms on the table, as she turned to him with a question and shook back her hair, a quickened interest.

'I'm not mistaken about these things,' Emmeline said firmly. It was plain for all to see that Caroline had a little 'crush' on Claire Moore, who was tiring of her; she'd had little crushes before, little intense friendships with women that flared up because of someone's interest in her. Take the case of Catherine Winter. At the age of twelve Caroline had taken up with Catherine Winter, a slightly older girl with jet-black hair, a sharp wit, and a passion for music, as well as a gift for drawing cruelly satirical sketches of family members. But above all Catherine Winter had the gift of bringing Caroline out of herself, of animating her, of filling her with feelings. The girls quickly became inseparable. The trouble was that whereas Catherine Winter was enough for Caroline, Caroline wasn't enough for Catherine Winter, who was drawn to Caroline's quietness but made friends easily and liked social occasions. Caroline, who wanted Catherine Winter all for herself, began making demands, but demands were precisely what one didn't make of Catherine Winter; there was an argument, tears, and then – silence. Caroline refused to talk to Catherine Winter again, who for her part threw herself into the social round. Caroline shut herself up in her room and wouldn't speak to anyone for a week – not even to Emmeline, whom she always turned to in the end. Emmeline herself had grown to be a watcher of Caroline's moods, a student of her sorrows; and while she suffered for Caroline, she had also begun to sense in these little friendships a dubious element. For if Caroline, through her friendships, was trying to achieve a kind of independence from her sister and mother, her efforts took the form always of a new dependence, a kind of desperate fanatical clinging, which was bound to end in defeat. But Caroline wasn't the only victim, for from the beginning Emmeline had sensed in those friendships an attempt, hidden perhaps from Caroline herself, to make Emmeline jealous, to hurt her by parading a rival. Oh, make no mistake about it, there was a touch of vindictiveness in Caroline's little passions.

Martin was surprised by the turn in Emmeline's analysis, which was accompanied by a slight change in her face, as of a tightening of unseen muscles. And feeling a sudden impulse to protect Caroline from a kind of passionate harshness in her sister's pursuit of hidden things, he tried to turn her attention away from Caroline to Claire Moore, who, he argued, whatever else might be said about her, couldn't really be blamed for striking up a friendship with Caroline. But Emmeline would have none of it. Claire Moore, she said, was a bored, idle woman with too much time on her hands, who had taken up Caroline as a hobby. Caroline had been glad to be taken up, but she had begun to make demands of her own, she had begun to be difficult, had begun to be Caroline – too difficult, too Caroline by far, for the likes of Claire Moore, who, to be fair to her, had seemed to like Caroline at first. Now she was tiring of her, she had used her up, she found Martin more amusing. For Claire Moore was a kind of woman that Emmeline had observed more than once – a woman empty within, hungry to be filled, a vampire woman, drinking the blood of victims.

Martin, struck by something Emmeline had said, asked suddenly: 'And do you think Caroline is too difficult for *me!*'

Emmeline considered it. 'I didn't think she would be,' she then replied.

The end came quickly: one evening when Martin sat down to dinner the fifth chair was empty. Caroline said nothing. The empty chair remained for two more nights and then disappeared.

'She's dropped her,' Emmeline said.

'You were right, then. Poor Caroline!'

Well, yes, Emmeline said, of course: poor Caroline. But had he ever considered that Caroline's suffering had an effect on those around her, an effect of which poor Caroline could not be unaware? For with her pains, her headaches, her insomnias, her suffering, poor Caroline drew on the sympathies of those who cared about her: she became the center of her family's attention. For in her quiet way, poor Caroline did like to be the center of attention. Yes, you could almost say that poor Caroline tyrannized over them through suffering, punished them with her pain.

A few nights later, Claire Moore appeared with a black-haired woman at another table, across the room, laughing and shaking back her hair. It struck Martin that if she had dropped Caroline she had dropped him too, and he had so strong a desire to be at that table that he had to force himself not to glance across the room like an injured lover. Caroline sat looking at her plate; two little lines of strain showed between her dark eyebrows. Emmeline sat looking at Caroline.

There was a sharp bang. Martin started.

'What's that?' cried Margaret Vernon.

'It's nothing,' Emmeline said.

Caroline, reaching for her glass of water, had knocked over the salt.

26

THE NEW
DRESSLER

Martin stared at the spilled salt and thought of the sharper bangs ten blocks north, where blasting had already begun; they were going down, deep down, deep enough for seven subterranean levels and a basement. Lellyveld and White had balked at the ncw plan, they had raised innumerable objections to the sketches and blue-prints, until Martin and Rudolf Arling had risen together in anger, threatening to take the sketches elsewhere – a bluff, really, though the anger had been genuine enough. And Lellyveld had backed down, as if he had only been waiting for them to rise against him before demonstrating his magnanimity. Martin in any case had gotten what he wanted: space to breathe in. The New Dressler would rise twenty-four stories and would incorporate more boldly the idea of inner eclecticism shadowed in the old. Harwinton, who was kept informed of developments, planned what he called a mystery campaign, to pique the public interest. Even as the hoarding went up, the first posters appeared: against a black background stood a large question mark, bright yellow.

After the Claire Moore episode Caroline had withdrawn to her apartment, from which she emerged only for a late breakfast in a secluded corner of the breakfast room and dinner in the main dining room with her mother and Martin and Emmeline. She refused to go shopping with her mother, refused to stroll after dinner in the courtyard, refused, despite her recent passion for the theater, to set foot in the Theater District. Margaret reported anxiously that the poor girl sat for hours over games of patience; it was bound to be bad for her back. Often when Martin returned to his rooms to dress for dinner, he would find the apartment empty: Caroline was next door, sitting in her mother's parlor. Since Caroline was always asleep when he woke early in the morning, and asleep when he went up to his bed late at night, it struck Martin that he saw her only at dinner, when she seemed faded and tired, as if she had been pulled with difficulty out of the thick, sticky sleep surrounding her on both sides of dinner, an ooze of sleep into which she would be sucked the moment she put down her fork; and as he glanced at her shadowy form in the bed at night, or her pale face staring at the brilliant white cloth of the dinner table, it seemed to him that she was gradually dissolving, like the sugar cubes he had liked to drop long ago into a glass of water and watch until there was nothing left but a slightly cloudy liquid.

Martin meanwhile had begun to spend more time away from the Dressler, for he wanted to follow closely every detail of the construction of the new building. He watched the drilling of blast holes in boulders, the arrival of the first steel beams and columns on flatbed trucks pulled by teams of big truck-horses, the making of the plank-and-steel retaining walls, the lifting of the steel by towering steam cranes, floor by subterranean floor; and as the first columns rose over the top of the excavation, Martin had the sudden sharp sense of the bones of his shoulders pressing upward against his skin.

Sometimes he seemed to hear, all up and down the West End, a great ripping or breaking, as bedrock split open to give birth to buildings. Along the Boulevard, on Amsterdam and Columbus, on lots facing the Central Park, on side streets between Sixtieth and 110th, hoardings seemed to spring up overnight. Many of the new buildings were small apartment houses under seven stories, which the housing laws did not require to be fireproofed, but ten-story and twelve-story apartment houses were also going up, and here and there a builder of hotels aspired to something grander, something that rang out like a bell. From the roof garden of the Dressler Martin looked down at a world of open pits and blasted rock, of half-finished apartments prickly with scaffolding, of steam cranes slashing their black diagonals across brownstone and brick. It was as if the West End had been raked over by a gigantic harrow and planted with seeds of steel and stone; now as the century turned, the avenues had begun to erupt in strange, immense growths: modern flowers with veins of steel, bursting out of bedrock. The rash of building had its own clear logic, based on the coming subway, just as the downtown construction of higher and higher office buildings was a direct result of the soaring cost of city real estate and the invention of the electric elevator – but Martin, looking down from the roof garden of the Dressler, wondered whether all such explanations were nothing but clever disguises meant to conceal a secret force. For what struck him was the terrible restlessness of the city, its desire to overthrow itself, to smash itself to bits and burst into new forms. The city was a fever-patient in a hospital, thrashing in its sleep, erupting in modern dreams. His own dream was to push the New Dressler beyond the limits of the old, to express in a single building what the city was expressing separately in its hotels and skyscrapers and department stores; and again he had the old dream-sense that friendly powers were leading him along, powers sympathetic to his deepest desires.

The New Dressler opened on August 31, 1902, on Martin's thirtieth birthday. The twenty-four-story building, with its seven underground levels and a massive basement, was advertised as the largest family hotel in the world, a claim immediately attacked by a journalist in the *Sun*, who asked whether it could properly be called a hotel at all. Harwinton, who had foreseen the question and secretly encouraged it, promptly flooded the city with mystery posters reading: MORE THAN A HOTEL: A WAY OF LIFE. The critics were divided over certain features, such as the three-story entrance arch decorated with twenty-four statues of

American historical and cultural figures, including Abraham Lincoln, Thomas Edison, Pocahontas, Henry Wadsworth Longfellow, Elisha Graves Otis, Washington Roebling, James Fenimore Cooper, and William Le Baron Jenney, or the arched bridges spanning the exterior courts at the level of the twelfth floor, or the profusion of ornamentation, from the small terra-cotta scenes representing American Industry on the Gothic window surrounds to the bands of painted tiles running along the base of each wrought-iron balcony and representing New York scenes both historical and contemporary, such as the director of the Dutch West India Company purchasing the isle of the Manhattoes from an Indian with one feather on his head, Washington Roebling seated at his window in Brooklyn Heights looking out at the Manhattan tower of the great bridge, and a procession of trotting rigs on a drive in the Central Park. What struck reporters most sharply, however, was the inside of the New Dressler – the secret hotel, in the phrase of one writer. Much attention was drawn by the seven underground levels, composed of a landscaped park with real squirrels and chipmunks (the first level), a complete department store (the second, third, and fourth levels), a series of Vacation Retreats (the fifth and sixth levels), and a labyrinth (the seventh level). The Vacation Retreats of the fifth and sixth levels received the most elaborate comment, for it was here that Rudolf Arling, drawing on his early days in the theater, had designed a series of six vacation spots for the use of hotel guests: a campground with tents in a brilliantly reproduced pine forest with swift-flowing streams; the deck of a transatlantic steamer, with canvas deck chairs, shuffleboard courts, and hand-tinted films of ocean scenery displayed on the walls; a wooded island with log cabins in a large lake with a ferry; a replication of the Atlantic City boardwalk, complete with roller-chair rides, as well as half a dozen streets crowded with theaters and movie houses; a health spa with mineral baths; and a national park containing a geyser, a waterfall, a glacier, a small canyon, and winding nature trails. Harwinton's ads proclaimed:

A ROOM WITH VACATION,
BEST DEAL IN THE NATION

and critics were quick to point out that a visit to a cleverly reproduced landscape underneath a hotel hardly counted as a vacation, although one reporter, after catching a trout in a campground stream and cooking it over a fire outside his tent, argued that the vacations offered by the New Dressler were superior to so-called 'real' vacations, since the Dressler vacation spots cost practically nothing (there were small charges for renting a canoe on the island lake, collecting firewood in the campground, having a drink in the bar of the trans-atlantic steamer, and so on), could be reached almost immediately and without the inconvenience and irritation of long railway journeys, and, above all, could be temporarily abandoned at night for a sound sleep in the comfort of one's own familiar bed.

But if the fifth and sixth underground levels of the New Dressler attracted strong notice, an equal amount of attention was directed at the twelfth floor, with its series of four arched bridges over the four exterior courts. For here Rudolf Arling, following Martin's careful instructions, had interrupted the pattern of apartments to devote the entire floor to what was called the Museum of Exotic Places – a series of scrupulously designed reproductions of such places as an Eskimo village, a Scottish glen, the Tuileries Gardens, the canals of Venice (with real water and gondolas), an archaeological dig in the Tigris-Euphrates valley, Shake-speare's birthplace, and the Amazon jungle, each lit by colored stage lights and inhabited by actors in authentic costumes, so that the visitor had the double sensation of entering an actual place and enjoying a clever artistic effect.

Other floors, it was noted, were not without their peculiarities, for on each floor of apartments was a suite of Culture Rooms, devoted to a wide variety of artistic, scientific, and historical subjects. There were reproduc-tions of masterpieces of American and European paint-ing by the renowned copyist Winthrop Owens, each in its precisely replicated frame; an orrery composed of transparent glass globes, illuminated from within and suspended from a starry ceiling; collections of armor, of fossils, of Egyptian artifacts; crabs and fishes in great glass aquaria; a display of Edison inventions, including the wax-cylinder phonograph, the Kinetoscope cabinet with its eyepiece and lens and its motor-turned strip of film, the carbon-filament incandescent lamp, the fluoro-scope, the quadruplex telegraph, and the electric pen with its egg-sized attached motor, all surrounding a table at which sat a lifesized waxwork of The Wizard of Menlo Park, modeled after the famous photograph of the inventor leaning his head against his half-closed hand as he sat beside his phonograph at 5 P.M. on June 16, 1888, after five days without sleep; a moving panorama called *A Steamboat Journey up the Hudson and Along the Erie Canal to Niagara*, accompanied by sound effects such as booming thunder and steamboat whistles; and a twenty-foot wooden model of Manhattan in 1850, including not only every house, farm, hotel, church, commercial building, pleasure garden, and wharf, not only automated horsecars and omnibuses running up and down the avenues, but more than 10,000 miniature people in individual dress. These displays, designed by artists and stage designers in collaboration with members of the American Museum of Natural History and the Metropolitan Museum of Art, were intended to provide hotel guests with a wide range of culture, without the considerable inconvenience of city traffic.

Such features were described, attacked, and praised in newspaper reviews that Martin read carefully and with a certain impatience, for it seemed to him that the writers were leaving something out, something that had nothing to do with hotel architecture or the suitability of cultural attractions to a family hotel, and it was not until a long article appeared in the *Architectural Record*, sharply attacking the New Dressler, that Martin felt his deeper intentions had been understood.

For the writer, after praising certain features of the design, such as the pleasing division of the massive and massively ornamented facade into three parts marked by string courses, and acknowledging certain technological advances, such as the steam-powered vacuum cleaning system and the filtered cool-air system, in which air was forced by electric blowers over iron coils submerged in icy saltwater, turned his attention to the idea represented by alien elements drawn from such modern institutions as the museum, the department store, and the world's fair. He noted the large number of theatrical elements – the actors in the twelfth-floor Museum of Exotic Places, the scenery and stage lighting in certain underground levels – which further served to remove the New Dressler from the realm of the family hotel and to give it the dubious, provisional air of a theatrical performance. The writer criticized the New Dressler as a hybrid form, a transitional form, in which the hotel had begun to lose its defining characteristics without having successfully evolved into something else, and he concluded by urging the architect to return to the problems of design posed by the modern multiple dwelling and not to succumb to the temptations of a decadent eclecticism.

Rudolf Arling was incensed by the review, which he called insolent – the corrupt hack, a lackey of the editorial board, deserved to have his neck broken – but Martin, who was uninterested in the writer's judgment, was struck by the accuracy of his description. The writer had groped his way to the center of Martin's intention and, without caring for what he found there, had revealed a shortcoming. For if the New Dressler was transitional, it wasn't, Martin insisted to Emmeline, because he had strayed from the purity of a traditional apartment hotel, but rather because he hadn't strayed far enough. He felt grateful to the attacker for revealing an error he would not make again.

'Even so,' Emmeline said, 'you've got to admit it's ungenerous. He simply doesn't take a large enough view.'

'Maybe it's the hotel that doesn't take a large enough view,' Martin countered.

Caroline had tensely refused to move to the New Dressler; she seemed alarmed at the prospect of moving anywhere. Even Emmeline had advised against it, arguing that Caroline had grown used to her rooms in the Dressler, that a change of any kind would be jarring and injurious. She and her mother couldn't of course abandon Caroline and would remain in their apartment in the Dressler, but Emmeline had agreed to join the New Dressler as assistant manager. And Martin, who needed to watch over his new hotel from the inside, took two rooms for himself on the twenty-third floor to serve as an office. Each day he rose in the old Dressler at half past five beside shadowy Caroline, who would not be up for at least another five hours. As he looked at her lying there in the graying dark, fast asleep on her back with her face turned sharply to one side, as though she were straining away from him, she seemed so heavily crushed by sleep that it was as if she could never raise her frail body against it, but must wait until sleep itself rolled from her body and lay wearily watching as, her hair hanging in damp coils about her face, she rose bruised and aching from the twisted sheets. At six

Martin walked with Emmeline along the Drive to the New Dressler. There they took breakfast in a window nook of the dining room with a view of the park and the river. Then Emmeline went to her new office in an alcove of the main lobby, while Martin took the elevator to the twenty-third floor.

Martin spent most of his day inspecting the New Dressler, speaking to staff, and mingling with guests in the seven underground levels. The atmospheric park, with its high trees, its meandering paths, and its melancholy lake, seemed to him a strong improvement over the tame courtyard of the old Dressler, although one day when he overheard a woman complaining that her children were bored he arranged for the installation of a small zoo and a carousel of wooden horses, dragons, and swans. After lunch he liked to walk along secluded paths with Emmeline, who praised the park warmly but refused to hear a word against the old courtyard of the Dressler. He was advancing, he was pushing in a direction, but he mustn't, she argued, turn his back on any of the steps along the way. For the old Dressler, just as it was, was perfect of its kind, was in fact incomparable – which wasn't in any sense meant to diminish the glory of the new. Martin tried to argue that it wasn't a matter of turning his back on anything, but rather of standing with his feet firmly planted, looking straight ahead. Yet he sensed the rightness of her reproach, for in fact he had lost interest in the Dressler as completely as he had in the Vanderlyn – and even now, as they walked in the splendid park, he had intimations of still richer scenes and adventures. Was there then something wrong with him, that he couldn't just rest content? Must he always be dreaming up improvements? And it seemed to Martin that if only he could imagine something else, something great, something greater, something as great as the whole world, then he might rest awhile.

In the meantime he made certain, after his early afternoon walks with Emmeline in the underground park, to continue his rounds. Each day he visited one or another of the Vacation Retreats on the fifth and sixth underground levels, questioning guests closely and introducing small improvements, such as maps posted on signboards along the trails of the national park. But his special pleasure was to walk along the brightly lit aisles of all three levels of his well-stocked department store and to follow closely every phase of its operation. He and Rudolf Arling had introduced into the store a number of striking features that Martin hoped would attract customers: shiny glass display cases instead of the oak counters of the old Shopping Arcade, colored lights to create dramatic moods, elaborately designed bowers and grottoes in which fashionable dresses were displayed on wax mannequins, and two electrically operated moving aisles that passed down the center of each block-long level in order to spare customers the exertion of crossing the store. The vistas of glass, the red and blue lights, the beautiful frozen mannequins, the shimmer and glitter of a world behind glass – a world that seemed to reveal itself completely while at the same time it remained tantalizingly out of reach – all this created a seductiveness, a sense of mystery, that reminded Martin of his walks with his mother past the display windows of the big Broadway stores. Unlike the other levels, which were reserved for guests, the three levels of the department store were open to the public, who were admitted through side-street entrances that led to stairways. Harwinton was conducting a separate ad campaign for the store, which he called 'Uptown's Downtown'; despite its out-of-the-way location, the department store of the New Dressler was attracting crowds of the curious, who usually returned.

In order to satisfy requests for tours of the New Dressler from journalists, prospective long-term residents, and curiosity seekers, Martin organized a staff of female guides in green uniforms with red trim. He himself liked to take people around from time to time, beginning with the roof garden and the seventh underground level, as if to draw a line around his creation. Ascending first to the roof of the New Dressler with its lush landscape of woods and streams, its cave-restaurant set in the side of a wooded hill, its peacocks and tame deer, its water tank and elevator bulkhead cleverly disguised as rustic cottages, he would descend suddenly and dramatically to the labyrinth on the seventh underground level. The labyrinth was a series of winding passages designed to meet the hotel guest's need for solitude and mystery, where one could wander for hours along dim-lit subterranean paths leading in and out of small rocky chambers supplied with benches. Black streams flowed here and there, a waterfall trickled down a sheer wall, and a number of surprises had been arranged: a narrow opening led to a library with reading lamps and couches, a winding passage went past a replicated Hindu temple, and around one bend appeared a black lake with an island, on which stood a small teahouse reachable by rowboat.

Beneath the labyrinth lay the true bottom of the New Dressler, the bottom beneath the bottom: the basement. It was a dark realm with many subdivisions, including the electric plant with its dynamos, the steam plant with its boilers, the laundry rooms with their boiling tubs and steam dryers, the ironing rooms, the storage rooms, the employee cafeteria, and the workshops for the large maintenance staff of the New Dressler: the painters, the electricians, the seamstresses, the upholsterers, the silver polishers, the carpenters. In the vast underground world of half-darkness and hissing steam, of hammer-knocks and the rumble of dynamos, Martin liked to walk for hours at a time, observing the machines that gave life to the building, watching the work of the repairmen, speaking with the laundresses, their sleeves rolled to the elbow, their forearms glistening, their faces shiny in the damp warm air.

At the end of the day, Martin walked back with Emmeline to meet Caroline and Margaret for dinner at the old Dressler. After dinner all four would take a turn in the underground courtyard, whereupon Caroline, growing tired, would retire to her rooms, and Martin would return to the New Dressler to speak with the night manager and continue his rounds.

Even as he walked through the world of the New Dressler, observing its operation, hovering, brooding over what he had built, Martin had begun to notice an alcove, a secret shadowy alcove, deep in his mind. Here images were slowly taking shape, and one day he met again with Rudolf Arling, in the small office with its view of the Brooklyn tower of the great bridge. Arling listened with interest to Martin's new idea, which kept assuming slightly different shapes, but the preliminary sketches disappointed Martin: Arling, for all his boldness, was still dreaming of a grand hotel, whereas Martin was trying to make him see something quite different. Then one day Arling simply made a leap, it was as if he had put the old way behind him forever, and now the sketches took on a startling quality, as if Martin were seeing his dream harden into shape before him. And Arling had good news. A recent commission of his, an apartment house with an all-too-familiar Beaux Arts exterior and a barrel-vault porte cochère that led to an interior courtyard, had received such favorable attention in the architectural press that he was suddenly in great demand, a fact that would serve Martin well when he approached the cautious Lellyveld. Martin reported his meetings with the architect to Emmeline after lunch as they walked on secluded paths in the subterranean park of the New Dressler, but Emmeline, who listened thoughtfully, showed signs of distraction. She confessed one afternoon that she was concerned about Caroline, whose behavior had recently taken a disturbing turn.

27

CAROLINE'S WAY

For Caroline had begun to withdraw for many hours to the sofa in her mother's parlor, where she lay with an arm thrown over her eyes. This in itself was no special cause for concern, since Caroline had often withdrawn to the family sofa, had in a sense made a career of such withdrawals, while everyone hovered about anxiously and waited for her to return to normal – although in Caroline's case it might be argued that the normal was precisely this withdrawal to the family sofa. No, what Emmeline found disturbing was Caroline's reluctance to return to her own bed at night. Margaret practically had to drag her out the door. It was a strain on poor Margaret, who worried continually about the welfare of her daughters, and especially of Caroline, who needed something to occupy her time but who unfortunately had no strong interests. During the reign of Claire Moore, Emmeline had encouraged Caroline's sudden attraction to the theater, unreasonably hoping that it would survive Claire Moore's departure. Even as a girl Caroline had had the habit of starting books and never finishing them, losing interest after the first couple of chapters, sometimes reading right up to the last chapter and then abandoning the book forever. It used to upset Emmeline terribly, all those unfinished stories lying around, like dolls with missing arms. And so in time she had come to think that Caroline's illnesses were her discovery of a way to occupy her time, although this perhaps sounded harsher than she meant it to be. She had thought that marriage – well, she had given her opinion at the time. And now Caroline was reluctant to leave her mother's parlor at all, she had even hinted that she would like to sleep on the sofa at night.

'Then let her do it,' Martin said irritably. 'For a night or two. If you think it will help.'

Emmeline was uncertain, but said that she would discuss it with her mother that very night. The next morning as they walked up Riverside to the New Dressler, Emmeline reported that perhaps it wouldn't be such a bad thing after all for Caroline to sleep on the sofa, for just a few nights, since it was something she seemed determined to do.

It was quickly arranged. Martin, who at first had been annoyed by yet another of Caroline's whims, found the new plan oddly agreeable. He no longer had to creep quietly into bed at night, for fear of waking Caroline and giving her a headache, or tiptoe about in the dark of early morning. And Caroline's absence from the apartment gave his rooms an airiness, a lightness, as if some faint disturbance in the atmosphere had cleared. But more than this, he liked the sense that the three Vernon women were together again, as if by marrying one of them he had somehow harmed the group. After dinner, walking with Caroline and Emmeline and Margaret in the underground courtyard of the Dressler, he was reminded of earlier days, when he had returned to the Bellingham and seen the three Vernon women waiting for him at the lamplit table in the parlor off the main lobby. And glancing at Caroline, who still wore her pale hair pulled back tight, so that it seemed to be tugging painfully against the skin of her temples, he felt an odd tenderness toward her, for restoring things to their original shape.

'She says she's worried about you,' Emmeline said a few nights later.

Martin laughed. 'Worried about me. I like that.'

'I don't like it.'

'That she's worried about me?'

'That she's worried about you from her sofa. She wants me to look in on you. To make sure you're all right.'

'Assure her I'm fine.'

'She's up to something,' Emmeline said.

One night about a week later Martin was sitting in his armchair in his apartment at the Dressler, looking over a sketch that Arling had given him, when there was a knock at the door. It was after eleven o'clock. Martin quickly buttoned his vest, pulled on his suit jacket, and opened the door just as he noticed irritably that he was wearing slippers.

'May I come in?' Emmeline said. 'You look angry.'

'Come in, I'm angry at my slippers.' He shut the door. 'There's something wrong?' He had said good night to her an hour ago.

'Not exactly,' Emmeline said.

Seated on the sofa facing the armchair, she explained that Caroline had insisted she come. Caroline was worried about Martin, alone in the apartment; she wanted to be assured that he was all right.

'I'm deeply touched by her concern,' Martin said.

'I wish you wouldn't sound like that. This is serious.'

'You humor her too much. You and your mother.'

'I'll tell her you're fine,' Emmeline said irritably, getting up to go.

But the next night she appeared again, looking so mortified and defiant and troubled and exhausted that Martin said, 'Look, why don't you just sit a while. I'll boil you up a cup of tea, and then you can go back. Tell Caroline I'm fine. What harm will it do?'

'Oh, I don't like it,' Emmeline said, sitting down and closing her eyes but immediately forcing them open.

After that he began to listen for Emmeline's knock, night after night, not long after eleven o'clock. The visits no longer seemed in any way irregular, but became part of the familiar order of his day. Caroline's behavior was bizarre, but Caroline's behavior had always been bizarre, and this recent turn had many pleasant advantages; he and Emmeline could talk, for instance, which was surely a good thing. For he wanted to speak to Emmeline, not about Caroline, but about his always growing plan for the new building. Emmeline listened carefully, but he could see that she was tired and distracted, her days after all were long, her nights with Caroline a continual strain. He could see the strain, printed in two lines between her thick eyebrows: Caroline's lines.

One night she reported that she had found Caroline asleep in her bed, the night before. Emmeline had slept on the sofa.

'It's got to stop, you know,' Martin said. 'You're just making it worse by giving in.'

'She's trying to replace me,' Emmeline said wearily.

A moment later she said, 'This is wrong. It's very wrong, all of it, and I don't know what to do about it.'

'You can do something about it. Say no to Caroline.'

'I've never been able to say no to Caroline,' Emmeline said.

Two nights later Emmeline reported with a kind of melancholy exasperation that things had really gone too far this time. For Caroline had suggested, had asked outright, really, that Emmeline move into her apartment, to assure that Martin was all right.

'It's all wrong,' she said wearily. 'It's gone too far.'

Martin stood up. 'It's gone far enough. I'll step over and have a few words with Caroline.'

But Emmeline begged him not to. She wouldn't obey the grotesque suggestion, of course. But she knew Caroline, knew when she was up to something, and preferred to let things take their course. Emmeline sat with one elbow on her knee and her chin on her raised hand, frowning in thought so that her eyebrows touched. Caroline, she said, was somehow trying to replace her: to become Emmeline. Not that she really wanted to become Emmeline – but by moving into Emmeline's apartment, by suggesting that Emmeline move into hers, she was attempting to accomplish a reversal. Perhaps it was more accurate to say that in some sense she was trying not to be Caroline. And this was a good thing, up to a point, for wasn't it Caroline's attempt to overcome some obstacle in herself, to leave the old Caroline behind and become new? But if it was good, in this sense, it was good only up to a point, beyond which the wrongness began; for really the whole business was some kind of magic trick. And beyond that she could feel something else at work, some obscure desire working itself out in Caroline, something she didn't like at all, for of course there were three people, not just two, and it was as if – she could just barely seem to see it – it was as if Caroline were attempting to undo her marriage and say that she – that Emmeline – but it was precisely here that she could only grope her way.

The next night she pursued it. It did appear that Caroline, having withdrawn into Emmeline's apartment, was offering Emmeline as a – well, as a wife. This bizarre act, looked at in one way, was an act of generosity. The flaw here was that Caroline was not given to acts of generosity. There was therefore some other motive at work, something that eluded Emmeline; and closing her eyes, she leaned back against the sofa, so that Martin saw very clearly, between her dark eyebrows, the two Caroline-lines, one slightly longer than the other. Martin saw something else: the completed direction of Emmeline's thought. For if Emmeline was correct in her analysis, then it was clear that Caroline was offering Martin a substitute in the marriage bed – that she was presenting Emmeline as a sexual emissary. And an irritation came over Martin, at Emmeline's failure to pursue her own thought to its deepest implication, along with gratitude for being spared that unthinkable discussion. But Emmeline was correct about one thing: Caroline was not generous. Why then would she practically thrust her sister into her own marriage bed? And was it possible that the lines of strain between Emmeline's thick eyebrows were the sign of her secret knowledge, a knowledge she dared not confess to herself?

A night came when there was a second knock on the door. Martin looked at Emmeline, who looked at him anxiously from the sofa across from his chair, but even as he crossed to the door he knew who it had to be. Caroline was wearing a dark dress he had not seen before. She waited to be invited in and then walked in swiftly. Her hair was pulled back tightly from her face but a few tendrils had escaped at the back. Over one arm she carried a shawl. Martin closed the door and walked over to her, where she stood beside his chair.

'Sit down, Caroline. You look tired.'

Caroline ignored him and stood looking at Emmeline, on the sofa, who looked back at her. It seemed to Martin that the two sisters were unable to move, that a spell had been cast, a spell as in an old fairy tale – he tried to remember which one it was. Or did all fairy tales have spells? But within the motionlessness something was growing, something was swelling, Martin could feel it, and turning to Caroline he was struck by a faint glow on her cheek, so that the thought came to him that she looked marvelously healthy, as if lying on the sofa with her arm over her eyes had filled her with health, though an instant later it occurred to him that she was sick, that she really ought to be in bed. But it was Emmeline who looked worn and anxious, there on the couch, while Caroline glowed down at her from beside the chair. It struck him that she looked like a heroine on the stage. And immediately he sensed with his skin what was going to happen, what was bound to happen, what could never happen but was about to happen, it was all nonsense and yet he would have to do something about it, he would have to act fast, very fast, and he tried desperately to struggle out of the spell, as one might struggle up from deep water, while from beneath the shawl Caroline removed a gun, a foolish awkward gun, and with her face aflame, the face of a heroine, she pointed it at Emmeline, who remained motionless but drew her eyebrows together as if in pain. Then a dream-shot rang out, and Martin, still struggling out of the fairy-tale spell, saw high up on the far wall a piece of plaster trickling down, while Emmeline sprang up as if startled from sleep, and Caroline, who had fainted away at the loud sound, fell slowly to the rug, where Emmeline was already kneeling, calling quietly for a damp cloth.

28

THE GRAND
COSMO

Martin sat in a corner of the roof garden of the New Dressler, in a gazebo striped with sun and shade, and raised to his eyes a pair of Jena field glasses. He had ordered the glasses from a German optical company, which advertised a finish of bright black enamel on all metal parts, high-power achromatic lenses ground from special optical glass manufactured in the Jena glass factory, and a covering of fine-grade morocco leather. Through the high-power lenses he directed his gaze eight blocks north toward a group of workmen who were standing near a heavy mat draped over a group of boulders in a deep excavation. They were blasting deeper, day after day, far down, for the new building was to have twelve underground levels and a basement; the consulting engineers had said it could be done. Above-ground the building would rise thirty stories, surpassing the New Dressler not merely in size but in every other way, for Martin had leaped beyond the idea of a hotel to something quite new. The leap had been greeted coldly by Lellyveld, who had refused to support the project unless Martin agreed to grant Lellyveld and White a forty percent interest in the building and the power to appoint the head of accounting – a deal strongly opposed by Rudolf Arling on the ground that Lellyveld wanted to gain control of the Cosmosarium and infect it with his mediocrity. Martin accepted Lellyveld's offer instantly.

He could no longer discuss such matters with Emmeline, who after the inept shooting had resigned her position at the New Dressler to devote herself entirely to the care of Caroline. He had counted on her to return, after a short rest, but it became clear that a change had come over Emmeline: she refused to be alone with Martin, scarcely permitted herself to look at him, and so thoroughly played the part of the guilty woman taken in adultery that he became uneasy and irritable in her presence. As for Caroline, who confessed that the gun had come from Claire Moore in the days of their friendship, for Claire Moore believed in a woman's right to self-protection, the shot had served to jolt her from her sofa-grave; she had returned to her apartment and her marriage bed as if she had come home from a little vacation at the seaside, with a touch of color and a handful of shells. But Martin, who was not unhappy to see an end to the sofa nonsense, felt a slight heaviness in the air of the apartment, now that Caroline had returned. Caroline alone, Caroline without the promise of Emmeline, was a quiet darkening of the air, a delicate and fine-dropped rain, lightly falling. More and more he found himself lingering in his rooms in the New Dressler, one of which he supplied with a bed. At first he had walked down to the Vernons for dinner each evening, with the old pleasurable sense that he was visiting them as a group, was somehow courting them all over again, but Emmeline's fussy and over-anxious attendance on Caroline, Margaret's habit of handling her pearls or fiddling with her dress sleeve as she glanced idly around the room, Caroline's murmured sentences punctuated by long silences, all this grated on his nerves. He began working in his rooms through dinner or taking his meals alone at the New Dressler, so that he found himself eating with the Vernons only once or twice a week.

And Martin was busy: as the excavation deepened, as carpenters began to construct wooden forms for the foundation walls, he moved about the city, visiting art museums, waxwork museums, dime museums that displayed four-legged chickens and bearded ladies, the new nickelodeon parlors with rows of hand-cranked machines, photograph studios, scientific exhibitions, fortunetelling parlors, the mezzanines of public buildings where he looked down at patterns of people moving in parallelograms of light cast by great windows – and one day, up at the building site, a row of cement trucks with revolving drums stopped one after another beside an open space in the hoarding. All over the city, workmen were breaking up streets. Martin liked to stand on boards thrown across torn-up avenues and peer into deep ditches heaped with rubble; sometimes he could see the arch of a subway tunnel. It pleased him that the city was going underground, that even as it strained higher and higher it was smashing its way through avenues and burrowing through blackness; and Martin imagined a new city growing beneath the city, a vast and glimmering under-city, with avenues and department stores and railroad tracks stretching away in every direction.

One day not long after the new building had begun to rise above street level, Martin decided to pay a visit to the old Bellingham Hotel. He hadn't been down that way in more than a year. He had been thinking lately of Marie Haskova; perhaps she would like a job in one of his buildings, he wondered why he hadn't thought of it before. The idea pleased him, even excited him; he wondered how she was getting along, he hadn't really treated her very well, after all she had been a kind of friend, even if their friendship had been ambiguous from the start. As Martin walked down Riverside toward his old street he recalled his wedding night, the sharp-turning stair-flights dropping away, the dark corridor lit by dim gas-jets, her weary startled eyes. She had taken him by the arm, she had led him in. Had he married her that night? Then his other marriage was only a dream-marriage, and Marie Haskova was his bride. He tried to remember the way she looked, the swift sad smile, the slight bitterness about the mouth. It all seemed long ago, more distant than his Sunday walks with his mother to Madison Square Park. In the warm air that smelled of asphalt and riverwater Martin turned onto his old street. He saw at once that he had made a mistake, he had turned onto a different street, and that was strange, it was down-right baffling, because he never made mistakes like that, surely he hadn't forgotten the number of his old street. And even as he stood puzzling it out, looking about and frowning in the bright sunlight, he felt ripples of anxiety passing across his stomach, for already his stomach knew what he himself was only beginning to realize. No, he hadn't made a mistake, it was his old street sure enough, but the Bellingham was no longer there. In its place stood a line of five-story row houses with wrought-iron balconies and street-level front doors. He walked up the cut-stone sidewalk, looking at the doors with their brass knockers and electric bells, and an absurd idea came to him: behind one of those doors was the old Bellingham Hotel, with the little parlor off the main lobby. He became aware of someone looking down at him from an upper window and he walked quickly past. The Bellingham had simply vanished. That was the way of things in New York: they were there one day and gone the next. Even as his new building rose story by story it was already vanishing, the trajectory of the wrecker's ball had been set in motion as the blade of the first bulldozer bit into the earth. And as Martin turned the corner he seemed to hear, in the warm air, a sound of crumbling masonry, he seemed to see, in the summer light, a faint dust of old buildings sifting down.

A fear came over him that the old Vanderlyn was gone, even though he had walked past it not three weeks ago. In its place he saw a heap of rubble, with Mr. Westerhoven's rubbers sticking out. But when he arrived, the Vanderlyn was still there. At lunch Walter

Dundee complained that motorcars were worse than the El trains when it came to scaring horses. Only the other day he had seen a drayhorse start up, toppling a barrel onto the street. Martin saw the horse in Harwinton's ad, the bright red coal burning in its back, the eyes wild with terror. Dundee's blue eyes were sharp, but the skin of his neck was slack, and there was an occasional note of disapproval in his voice; he spoke of retiring soon, fixing up a house he had his eye on, out in Brooklyn. He asked Martin in a reserved way how the new building was coming along. He asked after Martin's wife. And a restlessness came over Martin, through the smoky air he glanced at the clock, somewhere a woman began to laugh, a little rippling phrase that rose in a series of four notes and repeated itself, over and over again, and Martin became enraged: what was so funny, why couldn't she stop laughing like that? But when Dundee set down his empty beer glass streaked with foam and said he ought to be getting back, Martin felt a desire to hold him there, surely it wasn't necessary to rush away, they had barely begun to talk. But Dundee had already risen to his feet. 'Take care of yourself, Martin,' he then said, holding out his hand, and Martin was moved: after all, they had once been partners, even though a lot of water had flowed under the bridge since then. And at the phrase, which he thought distinctly, an image of the great bridge rose up, as he stood by the rail of the ferry with the spray in his face and looked up at the sunny arches, the swoop of the cables, and the dark bridge-pier, sun-striped, where gulls flew in and out of light and shade.

From his lookout station on the roof garden of the New Dressler, Martin watched the skeleton of the new building rise, the Cosmo, the Grand Cosmo: steel beams held by wire cables at the ends of booms swung through the air, cutting torches flared, plumbers and electricians walked on the floors below the ironworkers, and far away Rudolf Arling had only to raise his eyes to see through his window the Brooklyn tower of the suspension bridge, while in another part of town Harwinton was planning a three-part campaign. At lunch Harwinton spoke of image clusters, groups of unrelated images that, presented together, took on special associations. Martin noticed that Harwinton never aged. In thirty years he would have that same look of a schoolboy with blond-lashed blue eyes and small neat teeth. His short straw-colored hair would turn gray so gradually that no one would notice. Omnirama, Cosmacropolis, Unispeculum, Cosmosarium, Stupendeum: he had proposed a long list of names, fretting over each in turn, until Martin woke in the night with the right name ringing in his mind. Consider the fountain pen, Harwinton said. A pretty woman bends over a sheet of paper, smiling as she writes with her fountain pen – all very elementary. Now consider the same woman sitting in a field of daisies. She smiles dreamily as she touches the cap of the pen to her cheek. In the background you see a steamer's funnel, with white smoke puffs blown back against a blue sky. Instantly the pen is associated with the field and the ship, which is to say, with romance and adventure. Buy this pen and you buy love. Buy this pen and you buy life. For the Grand Cosmo he had prepared several sketches with image clusters designed to pique interest. The question at this stage was simply to prepare the public, to create expectation, for after all the Grand Cosmo was so all-embracing, so overwhelming, that one couldn't present it all at once, like a safety razor or a dental cream. Martin looked through a number of sketches and stopped at one. In the foreground stood a skyscraper concealed by an immense white cloth. In the background, small but visible, rose an Egyptian pyramid, the Eiffel Tower, and one tower of the Brooklyn Bridge. draped in cables and suspenders. And Martin was startled: it was as if Harwinton had divined his love for the bridge, as if the image of the bridge suddenly bound him to Harwinton. Was it possible that even Harwinton felt the power of the bridge? But Harwinton, if he felt anything, felt it as a private citizen; as an advertising man he saw the world as a great blankness, a collection of meaningless signs into which he breathed meaning. Then you might say that Harwinton was God. That would explain why he never grew old. The thought interested Martin: he was having a ham sandwich and a cup of coffee with the Lord God, King of the Universe, a youthful American god with light blue eyes and blond lashes. But of course God could not believe in the Grand Cosmo, just as He could not believe in the universe, a blankness without meaning, except as it streamed from Him. For only human creatures believed in things: that much was clear.

As the Grand Cosmo rose to the thirtieth floor, as the steel skeleton began to disappear beneath its sheathing of rusticated stone, ads began to appear in newspapers and weekly magazines, showing the building with the cloth lifted to various heights; and around the half-concealed structure stood phrases such as THE GRAND COSMO: CULTURE, COMMERCE, AND COMMODIOUS LIVING.

The Grand Cosmo opened on September 5, 1905, five days after Martin's thirty-third birthday; the delay was caused by a flaw in the refrigerated-air system, which circulated cool air through wall ducts on every floor and subterranean level. Martin, who had reserved ninety percent of the living quarters for permanent residents and ten percent for transients, noted that fewer than half of the spaces had been rented, but he was certain that the failure was due to the strangeness of the Grand Cosmo: people didn't know exactly what it was. He had forbidden Harwinton to advertise it as a hotel; Harwinton had been forced to make use of teasing hints, such as THE GRAND COSMO: A NEW CONCEPT IN LIVING. The final stage of the campaign had emphasized the completeness of the Grand Cosmo, the sense that it was a world in itself, a city within the city. Harwinton, in his customary way, presented his central idea in a double manner that could only be called contradictory. For if on the one hand he made the claim that the Grand Cosmo, insofar as it contained everything the urban resident could possibly desire, was nothing less than the city itself, so that to dwell within its walls was to be, at every moment, at the very center of the city, yet on the other hand he emphasized that the Grand Cosmo was set apart from the city, he presented it as an exotic place that provided sensations unavailable to the mere city-dweller unfortunate enough not to enter its enchanted walls, he did everything in his power to turn the Grand Cosmo into an attraction, an eighth wonder of the world, a place you simply had to see. These two contradictory images of the Grand Cosmo, which at first threatened to lead the campaign into confusion, were brilliantly reconciled by Harwinton in a third image that began to emerge more strongly: the Grand Cosmo as a place that rendered the city unnecessary. For whether the Grand Cosmo was the city itself, or whether it was the place to which one longed to travel, it was a complete and self-sufficient world, in comparison with which the actual city was not simply inferior, but superfluous.

The newspaper reports were on the whole favorable, though Martin detected a frequent note of puzzlement or bewilderment: the critics, while admiring particular effects, seemed uncertain when the question arose of what exactly the Grand Cosmo was. Some called it a hotel; a few, taking a hint from the ad campaign, called it an experiment in communal living. What struck most of the first wave of observers was the overthrow of the conventional apartment. Instead the Grand Cosmo offered a variety of what it called 'living areas,' in carefully designed settings. Thus on the eighteenth floor you stepped from the elevator into a densely wooded countryside with a scattering of rustic cottages, each with a small garden. The twenty-fourth floor contained walls of rugged rock pierced by caves, each well-furnished and supplied with up-to-date plumbing, steam, and refrigerated air. Those with a hankering after an old-fashioned hotel could find on the fourth and fifth subterranean levels, which formed a single floor, an entire Victorian resort hotel with turrets and flying flags, a grand veranda holding six hundred rattan rockers, and a path leading down through an ash grove to a beach of real sand beside a lake. Still other floors and levels offered a variety of living arrangements: courtyard dwellings (four to six irregular rooms arranged about a central court landscaped with trees and ponds), screen enclosures (large living areas supplied with folding screens that might be variously arranged to form temporary, continually changing divisions), and perspective views (room-like enclosures with windows that provided a three-dimensional view of a detailed scene resembling a museum diorama and supplied with live actors: a jungle with stuffed lions, a New England village with a blacksmith and a spreading oak tree, an urban avenue). In every case an attempt was made to abolish the corridor, to interrupt monotony, to overcome the sense of a series of more or less identical rooms arranged side by side in a rectangle of steel.

The theme of abolishing the expected was taken up by a number of writers, who reported that in order to avoid the tedium of a fixed architectural scheme, the Grand Cosmo employed a staff of designers, carpenters, landscape artists, and architectural assistants who roamed through the building and decided on changes: the removal of an inner wall, the construction of a new summerhouse or tunnel, the transformation of a cafeteria into an Italian garden or a croquet lawn into a street of shops. It was therefore possible to say that the Grand Cosmo was never the same from one day to the next, that its variety was, in a sense, limitless.

While taking note of the unusual living arrangements, and ignoring conventional features such as lobbies, cafeterias, and a very efficient laundry service, many observers preferred to comment on the large amount of space devoted to services and entertainments not generally associated with hotels: the many parks and ponds and gardens, including the Pleasure Park with its artificial moonlight checkering the paths, its mechanical nightingales singing in the branches, its melancholy lagoon and ruined summerhouse; the Haunted Grotto, in which ghosts floated out from behind shadowy stalactites and fluttered toward visitors in a darkness illuminated by lanternlight; the Moorish Bazaar, composed of winding dusty lanes, sales clerks dressed as Arabs and trained in the art of bargaining, and a maze of stalls that sold everything from copper basins to live chickens; the many reconstructions of Hidden New York, including Thieves' Alley in Mulberry Bend, an opium den, a foggy street of river dives (the Tub of Blood, Cat Alley, Dirty Johnny's), and bloody fights between the Bowery Boys and the Dead Rabbits, with a nearby shop called Hell-Cat Maggie's in which one could purchase brass fingernails and have one's teeth filed to points; the Pantheatrikon, a new kind of theater in which actors on a circular stage surrounded a central auditorium that revolved slowly; a Séance Parlor with heavily curtained windows, a spirit cabinet of black muslin, and a round table at which sat, in a high-necked black dress, the medium Florence Kane; the Salon of Phrenological Demonstrations, presided over by Professor Geoffrey St. Hilaire of Geneva; the reconstruction of a gloomy Asylum for the Insane, with barred windows and shafts of pallid moonlight, in which more than two hundred actors and actresses portrayed patients suffering from more than two hundred delusions of melancholia, including the sensation of being on fire, of having one's legs made of glass, of being possessed by the devil, of having horns on the head, of being a fish, of being strangled, of being eaten by worms, of having the head severed from the body; the Temple of Poesy, in which twenty-four young women, led by Miss Fanny Parker, all wearing white Grecian tunics and garlands of green satin vineleaves around their heads, recited one after the other, for an hour at a time, twenty-four hours a day, the best-loved poems of Henry Wadsworth Longfellow, James Russell Lowell, Oliver Wendell Holmes, James Whitcomb Riley, John Greenleaf Whittier, and William Cullen Bryant; the Palace of Wonders, in which were displayed a two-headed calf, a caged griffin, a mermaid in a dark pool, the Human Anvil, a school of trained goldfish fastened by fine wires to toy boats in order to enact naval battles, Little Emily the Armless Wonder, the Heteradelph or Duplex Boy with his second torso and his second set of legs, and the infant Adelaide, a four-year-old musical prodigy who played the complete piano sonatas of Mozart on a specially constructed piano with sixty-four keys; the Museum of Waxworks Vivants, in which waxworks, automated waxworks operated by concealed clockwork, and living actors impersonating waxworks represented tableaux such as The Assassination of Abraham Lincoln by the Actor John Wilkes Booth, Gorilla Seizing a Young Girl, Lazarus Rising from His Grave, and Lizzie Borden Murdering Her Father and Stepmother in Fall River, Massachusetts; the Grand Cosmo Cigar Store, composed of many dusky rooms each opening into the next, as far as the eye could see, including a gaslit workroom where cigars were rolled by authentic German cigarmakers, each room containing one or more wooden Indians automated by clockwork and performing motions such as lifting cigars to their lips and blowing smoke rings, raising and lowering tomahawks, spitting tobacco juice into a brass cuspidor, and in one case walking slowly up and down the length of the room with a menacing expression; elaborate stage sets representing Civilizations of the Solar System, such as the white catacombs of the Selenites, the Venusian gardens, and the glowing palaces of the Empire of the Sun; the Hall of Optical Novelties, including Zemmler's Eidothaumatoscope, a machine for viewing objects just beyond the edges of inserted photographs; a reconstruction of the Heavenly City, based on the reports of more than one hundred mystics; a new kind of department store, designed to disrupt the monotony of displayed merchandise by attractions such as meandering aisles, festive plazas containing striped palmist tents and crystal-gazing booths, and a pygmy village with real pygmies making spears; the Laboratory of Psychical Science, including Professor Blackburn's Ectoplasmosphere (a large hollow glass sphere for attracting and collecting ectoplasmic projections for scientific analysis), a curtained booth for the study of automatic writing in which Miss Eva put visitors in contact with a Persian spirit called Aouda, and a number of recently invented machines for measuring the claims of spiritualism, such as a Phantothermoscope for registering the presence of departed dear ones and a mahogany Telekabinett in which electrodes were attached to the temples of clairvoyants in order to display their mental images on a ground glass screen; the Cine-Theater, which showed short films (four to eleven minutes) featuring tricks and illusions and provided by Black Star Films, including 'The Decapitated Man,' 'Mesmer's Castle,' 'Cleopatra's Resurrection,' and 'Tchin-Chao the Chinese Conjuror'; the Phantorama; the Théâtre des Ombres; the Wonders of the Fairy World, a reassembled plot of genuine Irish forest and glade, including trees and turf shipped in an ocean liner and an authentic woodland stream transported in thirty cedar barrels, the whole illuminated by stage lighting that exactly reproduced the conditions of a moonlit summer night, in order to assist the visitor who wished to search for the fairies who had been observed dancing in a ring on that very plot of ground on May 26, 1904, in County Sligo; and the Theatrum Mundi, a globe-shaped chamber in which black-and-white images from every corner of the known world were projected in everchanging cinematographic montage, showing oncoming trains, the faces of English coal miners, Amazon alligators, cyclists in bloomers, polar bears, the Flatiron Building, a Dutch girl watering a tulip.

Even as journalists attempted to describe the nature of the Grand Cosmo, rumors about the colossal building had begun to circulate in the cheap press, especially rumors about the many subterranean levels, which were said to house darker and more disturbing entertainments as one descended lower and lower. The rumors at first irritated Martin, for hadn't the Grand Cosmo banished the division between upper and lower that had been a feature of the old-fashioned Dresslers? – but Harwinton was pleased: rumor of any kind was a mark of success, to say nothing of its usefulness as a highly effective and entirely free form of advertisement. Martin, looking at Harwinton's cool blue blond-lashed eyes, recalled the plump lady in the fountain pen ad, bending over the desk. It struck him that Harwinton himself had probably had a hand in the spread of certain dubious stories, which in any case had begun to lead a life of their own among guests and visitors and the tabloid dailies, and were even being reported, with a certain disdain, by more responsible journalists as evidence of the building's power to attract attention. It was said that rat-baiting pits flourished in dark corners of the lowest levels, where specially trained rat dogs fought bloody battles against batches of a dozen rats; it was said that a branch of an upstate asylum permitted its inmates to roam the dark in solitary gloom, garbed in the costumes of Napoleon, Marie Antoinette, Jack the Ripper, Edgar Allan Poe. One article reported that the lowest level housed a labyrinthine brothel whose ornate furniture, flowery wallpaper, formidable madam, and thirteen-year-old girls had been smuggled across the Atlantic in the hold of a tramp steamer. Such rumors were to some extent constrained by the very existence of the Grand Cosmo and its verifiable number of subterranean levels, but as if in an effort to evade such constraints, a more fantastic variety of rumor soon began to grow in the rich, shapeless blackness beneath the lowest subterranean level.

It was said that under the thirteenth level a maze of interconnecting passageways had been constructed, each with stairways leading down to still lower levels, unimaginably far down, and there in the world beneath the world, which yet was only the deepest cellar of the cloud-piercing Cosmosarium, black gardens of imagination bloomed. It was said that in the darkness of that sub-subterranean realm, in a forest the color of black tourmaline, wild children, abandoned at birth and speaking no language, were raised by wolves and lived the life of animals. It was said that in moss-stained halls at the ends of crumbling corridors, statues tormented with human longings came to life, roamed the dark with impassioned eyes, and flung themselves upon human lovers, after which they wandered sluggishly until they assumed new and troubling marble poses. There, beneath the world, white and peaceful cities rose in distant river valleys, beckoning the weary of heart and the sick of soul. There, in the Garden of Black Delight, monstrous jet-black blossoms exuded dangerous perfumes, which produced visions of such searing ecstasy that afterward one lost all desire to live. In the House of Metamorphosis, deep in a cave under a hill whose top was an island, Chinese masters trained in secret academies could transform the traveler into a lion, a butterfly, an angel, a waterfall. It was said that to descend into the world beneath the world was to learn the secrets of heaven and hell, to go mad, to speak in tongues, to understand the language of beasts, to rend the veil, to become immortal, to witness the destruction of the universe and the birth of a new order of being; and it was said that if you descended far enough, down past obsidian-black rivers, past caves where dwarves in leather jerkins swung pickaxes against walls veined with gold, down past the lairs of slumbering dragons whose tails were curled around iron treasure-boxes, past regions of ice and fire, past legendary underworlds where the shadowy spirits of the dead set sail for islands of bliss and pain, down and down, past legend and dream, through realms of blackness so dark that it stained the soul black, you would come to a sudden, ravishing brightness.

But whether the writers spoke of the imaginary world beneath the building, or of the many worlds within, they all acknowledged, even in their puzzlement, a sense not simply of abundance or immensity, but of the inexhaustible. It was as if, despite the finite number of stories (thirty) and underground levels (thirteen, including the basement), the Grand Cosmo produced in the visitor a conviction that it could never be fully explored, that around the next corner or down the next stairway existed something unexpected, exciting, and never seen before.

And Martin was pleased: the Grand Cosmo was making an impression. If the impression was still a little unclear, if people remained a little uncertain what to make of it all, that was only to be expected, for after all the Grand Cosmo was a leap beyond the hotel, a leap that was bound to take some getting used to. The building was attracting attention as a vast curiosity, but once people took up residence they would understand that the living arrangements of the good old family hotel were no longer possible.

Martin himself had moved from his rooms in the New Dressler to a living space on the twenty-ninth floor of the Grand Cosmo, where a series of folding screens decorated with Japanese hermits, arched wooden bridges, and waterfalls led past parlor chairs and a concealed bed to a desk with a view of the river. Beyond the farthest screen was a copse of artificial trees, through which a path led to the elevators.

Martin looked forward to the attack in the *Architectural Record*, which did not appear for six weeks and then proved even harsher than he had imagined. For the writer, while briskly acknowledging certain minor technological accomplishments, such as the mechanical singing birds in the parks, refused to see in the Grand Cosmo anything but a culmination of deplorable tendencies. The Grand Cosmo, the article argued, represented in an extreme form the age's love of the grandiose and the eclectic; it brought together so many clashing elements, in so massive a space, as to produce an impression of confusion, of uncertainty. For what, after all, was the Grand Cosmo? Insofar as it pretended to be a place in which people might wish to live, it was uninhabitable. It seemed to combine elements of the hotel, the museum, the department store, the amusement park, and the theater in a colossal enclosure that itself drew on so many styles as to make the worst excesses of late Victorian eclecticism seem a chaste instance of neoclassical restraint. Although the extravagance of the Grand Cosmo, its flamboyance, its sheer hunger for the all-inclusive, might in some sense be deemed praiseworthy as an expression of energy, that extravagance and flamboyance and hunger had been carried to such heights of excess as to turn into the grotesque. What was striking was how the habit of excess, which expressed itself most readily in the form of architectural gigantism, manifested itself in the smallest details, so that the brass doorknobs of the cellar workshops, the numerals in the panels above the elevators, the artificial leaves on the forty-six varieties of artificial tree, were wrought with a Byzantine elaboration. There was thus a paradoxical sense in which the minutiae of the building were expressions of the architect's obsession with the gigantic, and a corresponding sense in which the sheer immensity of the structure was an expression of a miniaturist's tendency toward obsessive elaboration. Both senses betrayed a yearning for the exhaustive, which was the secret malady of the age. In this way the Grand Cosmo might be understood as the ultimate architectural expression of its time, after which a rigorous simplification was inevitable. The article ended with a plea for a return to moderation, reason, and simplicity in the architecture of public buildings.

Martin read the article with close interest, for it

seemed to him that the writer, without a shred of sympathy, had penetrated deeply into the nature of the Grand Cosmo. He wondered whether the addition of sympathy would have permitted a still deeper penetration, or whether sympathy would have prevented understanding by getting in the way. It was just the sort of thing he would have liked to discuss with Emmeline, but he could no longer speak to Emmeline in the old way. She was closed to him, she was blind and deaf and dead. And in one sense that was quite right and proper, for during the course of his marriage she had gradually replaced her sister, and now she must efface herself in order that Caroline might regain her rightful place in the scheme of things. But in another sense it was cruel and wrong, for Caroline could not rise above something cramped in her nature, so that by self-effacement Emmeline was sacrificing a rich form of life to an impoverished one. And therefore the fault must surely be his, for marrying the wrong sister. But at the thought of marrying the right sister an irritation came over him, for he felt repelled by the thick eyebrows, the broad back, the strong hands with their blunt fingernails. For he had been able to desire only the pretty and delicate sister, the sister with the difficult twist in her, the sister lost in dream, who lay motionless beneath him and turned away in silence. And an anger came over Martin, at the mumbo-jumbo of love, the damage of it.

He could discuss the article in the *Architectural Record* only with Rudolf Arling, who strode up and down among his ornate tables heaped with statuettes and ivory animals, denouncing the writer as a fool.

Martin, surprised not by the outburst but by his own severe lack of sympathy for it, defended the writer in silence and understood that Arling sought praise, only praise, and could not tolerate one jot of disapproval. The little ivory animals, the statuettes, the curved legs of the tables, all this had begun to remind him of something, and as Arling paced back and forth, throwing out a hand in angry emphasis, it came to Martin: it was the familiar atmosphere, the secret but unmistakable impression, down to the curving table legs themselves, of Mr. Westerhoven's office. And so the fiery architect with the glittering gray eyes was an emissary of Alexander Westerhoven's – he might have known. It would simply be a matter of time before Arling accepted none but the safest commissions. Martin himself had been stung solely by the charge that the Grand Cosmo was uninhabitable; despite a new burst of publicity, only forty-nine percent of the living spaces had been rented.

He became reluctant to leave the Grand Cosmo, as if the act of passing through its doors were a form of abandonment, of betrayal. The Grand Cosmo needed him, needed him far more than Caroline or Emmeline, who had married each other and shut him out. For really there was no room for him in that dark marriage of sisters, each deep-twisted into each. He imagined Emmeline sitting in his flowered armchair, stepping into a pair of his pajamas, slipping into his side of the bed. He saw his empty chair at the dining room table in the Dressler. Slowly it began to dissolve, to shimmer like a mirage – and suddenly it was gone, like Claire Moore's chair, like the Bellingham Hotel.

One evening Martin was sitting in a small glass-walled alcove of the main lobby, where he could have the double pleasure of being alone and at the same time of participating in the movements of the too-peaceful lobby beyond the glass. He was about to rise when the sense of Emmeline's absence came over him, came so suddenly and so completely that it was as if he hadn't known before that she was gone. It wasn't so much a sensation of missing her as of feeling her absence, sharp and definite as a presence – an absence that continued to fill him until he could feel it as a pressure in his chest and a tingling in his fingertips, as if he were being invaded by something, which streamed steadily into him through a little hole somewhere. It felt like a heaviness, this in-streaming of absence. And indeed he could feel himself bent a little awkwardly in his chair, like a man he had once seen who had suffered a stroke in a lobby armchair and continued sitting awkwardly upright and even smiling, despite the ferocious pain in his arm and chest. In the glass of the alcove he could see the faint reflection of his face, through the face he saw a few lobby chairs and a pillar, and the thought came to him, even as Emmeline's absence began to recede, that he had in fact grown transparent, during the moment he had been entirely filled with her absence.

He took up shifting residence in the Grand Cosmo, living in unrented courtyard dwellings, an unrented cottage in the wooded countryside of the eighteenth floor, an unrented room in the resort hotel on the fourth

272

and fifth subterranean levels. He waited for the public to come. It was bound to come. It had always come. He rode the elevators, strolled through the Pleasure Park and the Palace of Wonders, bought a bag of cherries in the Moorish Bazaar and spat the pits into a stream beside an artful oak tree on the eighteenth floor. He sat in lobbies, tearooms, reading rooms, gardens with weathered marble statues, lecture halls, mossy glades, public parlors – sat listening to residents and visitors, speaking with staff, pondering improvements, observing the change of weather through many windows: gray skies and heavy snow, a sudden blue day, sheets of snow. He had been prepared to operate in the red, two years wasn't uncommon, but the Grand Cosmo was losing too much too fast. On March 5, six months after opening day, he was summoned to a meeting of management in the executive suite on the second floor. The manager, backed by the head of accounting, who kept tapping the ball of a heavy finger against a thick sheaf of pages, urged him to drop his insistence on long-term leases. They were losing nearly thirty thousand a week – a ruinous rate. Irritably Martin agreed. That afternoon he instructed Harwinton to initiate a new campaign of four-color posters and half-page newspaper ads aimed at transient residents. Within a month the ads brought an increase in rentals to seventy-two percent of capacity, but during the spring and summer the numbers gradually diminished, despite new ads in weekly magazines. By September 5, the first anniversary of the Grand Cosmo, rentals had fallen to fifty-five percent of capacity – a rate that could only spell disaster.

The manager told Martin that the Grand Cosmo seemed to confuse people – it didn't appear to be the sort of place they wanted to check into for a few days on a quick trip to the city. And Martin could only agree, for after all the Grand Cosmo was not a hotel, not a hotel at all, but something quite different. One day in a small park on the twenty-third floor he over-heard a woman say to a friend, 'I simply love it here. I wouldn't live anywhere else in the world. And you never have to go out, if you don't want to,' to which her friend replied, 'I love visiting here, Julie, but I could never stay, it's too, it's too –' 'Yes?' the first woman asked, but already they were passing out of earshot along a leafstrewn path. Martin followed them through the deserted park but could hear only murmurs, laughter. For the next two days he brooded savagely over the unfinished sentence as if it contained the secret he had been looking for; one night it struck him that his search for the unspoken words was an acknowledgment that the Grand Cosmo was failing.

Martin strode through the floors of his inexhaustible building, searching for flaws, imagining new entice-ments. Was it the sense of the limitless that prevented people from flocking to the Grand Cosmo as they had to the Dressler? In the largest hotels, vast spaces were divided neatly into small, repeated rectangles – could the secret of such places be monotony itself? Did the public, along with its craving for the up-to-date and the brand-new, also crave not simply the familiar, but the repetitive, the reassuring sense of boredom provided by multiple sameness? Did the Dressler and the New

Dressler flourish not because of their innovations, but precisely because they failed to depart very far from the familiar pattern of the good old family hotel?

It occurred to Martin that perhaps he was being punished for something. The punishment, if that's what it was, struck him as entirely proper, though he wondered a little about the crime. Was he being punished for marrying Caroline and not Emmeline, the pretty sister and not the plain? He had married the sister in dream, the princess asleep in her tower, ignoring the living sister by his side. Was it because he too was a dreamer that he had been drawn to her then, five hundred years ago? She had never woken up. He had stopped trying. Perhaps he was being punished for not loving Caroline enough. Or was it for not desiring Emmeline in the first place? Was that his crime? Or was it the knock on the door of room number 7, on his wedding night? But maybe he was being punished for something much different. When his father grew angry he would harden himself, as if he were holding in an explosion. Was Martin being punished for not stepping carefully among the cigar boxes? Was that it? For surely the Grand Cosmo was an act of disobedience. Or was he being punished for something deeper than crime, for a desire, a forbidden desire, the desire to create the world? For of course only God and Harwinton could do that. Anyone else was bound to fail.

On the first Monday in December the head of accounting met with Martin to urge cuts in staff and the elimination of all inessential services. He further proposed that the six top floors be closed to residents and rented as business offices after a thorough renovation. Removing a bundle of papers from a leather case, he smoothed it over and over with the side of a hand and pushed it toward Martin, who sat down wearily in a chair, began to bend over the papers, and stood up with a curt refusal. He took the elevator down to the laundry, where he walked with his hands behind his back, soothed by the rumble of machines, the heat and steam of winding passageways. The next afternoon he found himself sitting in a public parlor on the twenty-sixth floor, looking at the first snow falling lightly. The lightly falling flakes of snow seemed the dust of vanished buildings; he understood that the Grand Cosmo was a commercial failure and would vanish like the Bellingham.

And again he strode through the floors of his building, but the doors, the walls, the lobby chairs, the artful gardens with their pools and statues, all turned as he watched the flakes of lightly falling snow. He remembered his ride with Emmeline to the building site of the Dressler, the man knocking his stick against the side of his snowy shoe, white ice on the black river: one by one the mansions of snow and ice would melt away, leaving no trace of what had once been there.

He came to the main lobby and sat down heavily in a corner chair. Behind the high windows snow was slanting down. One by one the Dressler, the New Dressler, and the Grand Cosmo would melt away, like the Bellingham before them. Marie Haskova had melted away, his marriage had melted away, Walter Dundee, Louise Hamilton, Bill Baer, gone, all gone. He would have liked to talk to Emmeline, but she too had melted away. And at the thought that Emmeline had melted away, a pity came over him, for poor Martin, lost in the falling snow. Poor Martin! He saw Emmeline standing beside his coffin, Caroline in a black veil looking coldly down. His face was calm in the coffin. He recognized that calm face. Tecumseh.

By the end of January it was clear that he would no longer be able to meet his payments. On the morning of February first he went over the figures with the head of accounting, consulted briefly with the manager, took a stroll along a forest path, and stepped into the brown dusk of the Grand Cosmo Cigar Store, where under the fierce gaze of an Indian who kept raising and lowering a tomahawk he purchased a first-rate Havana. He ran the cigar slowly under his nose and placed it in his jacket pocket as if he were saving it for a celebration. In the afternoon he canceled his account with Harwinton and informed the front office that the Grand Cosmo would no longer accept short-term guests. Only permanent residents who signed long-term leases would be admitted to the community of the Grand Cosmo. The general public would no longer be permitted to make use of the main lobby, of the ground-floor cafeterias and concessions, of the Moorish Bazaar and the winding aisles of the department store, but were to be excluded entirely from the domain of the Grand Cosmo. For the Grand Cosmo was not a tourist attraction or a hotel for transients, but a world within the world, rivaling the world; and whoever entered its walls had no further need of that other world.

The sense of failure filled him with an odd energy – he wasn't going to sit in a melancholy stupor and watch the snow come sifting down. For after all he had done what he wanted to do, it could not have been different, his only error was to have dreamed the wrong dream. And Martin embraced his failure, threw himself into the idea of failure as into a new and soaring creation.

In order to prevent foreclosure, he offered Lellyveld and White a forty-nine percent interest in the New Dressler. He was determined to keep the Grand Cosmo open, to hasten its rush toward disaster; and he was prepared if necessary to transfer to Lellyveld and White the ownership of both Dresslers. For there could be no half-measures, in failure as in success.

As Martin watched his losses mount, as he waited for the Grand Cosmo to swallow up the two Dresslers and for all three to pass into the hands of Lellyveld and White, he spent his days roaming the floors and levels of his domain, eating lunch in cafeterias where three or four diners sat at widely separated tables, giving instructions to gardeners and electricians, playing checkers with the groundskeeper in a small park on the fourteenth floor, taking a light dinner in the main dining room, which seemed to grow larger and whiter as guests dropped away. After the elimination of short-term rentals, the Grand Cosmo was able to fill barely forty percent of its living areas, though a third of these had been rented for one-year terms that might not be renewed; and in the large parks and shady gardens, in the lanes of the Moorish Bazaar, in the public parlors, in the dusky rooms of the Grand Cosmo Cigar Store,

Martin would wander for hours without seeing anyone at all.

In the remote reaches of upper floors he would sometimes pass a couple walking side by side, or a woman walking alone; and in their faces he would see a look of shyness or faint puzzlement, as if they had not expected to meet anyone in such a place, at such an hour.

He liked to roam the meandering aisles of the nearly deserted department store, ablaze with electric lights late into the night. Slowly he walked among the empty glittering aisles, stopping to examine a pocket watch or a pair of gloves, while a clerk, rising hastily from a chair behind the counter, quickly slipped a jacket over a vest and, rubbing his eyes, proceeded to answer questions about 17-jewel Elgin movements, damascened gold-and-nickel top plates, and oil-tanned calfskin with snap buttons.

Throughout the day, but especially after dinner, a number of residents sat in the main lobby, which rose two stories and stretched away behind pillars and arches, disappearing around corners, forming nooks and glass-walled alcoves, little half-concealed places with dark-gleaming lamp tables. If you chose your chair carefully, you could have the sense of a festive and crowded place, full of dark wood-glints and laughter, or of a hushed and polished vastness stretching emptily away.

One evening when the lobby seemed emptier than usual, as if the remaining residents had wakened from a dream to rejoin their actual lives, while the abandoned dream, still vivid from the life that had glowed in it only moments before, was left behind to fade slowly into the blue-gray mist of dawn, Martin had an idea. In return for free room and board he would invite a troupe of out-of-work actors to sit in the lobby chairs, stroll about, play billiards in the billiard rooms and write letters in the writing rooms, to talk, to laugh – to create, in short, the atmosphere of a peacefully flourishing community. It was arranged easily by telephone the next morning, and that evening new faces appeared in the lobby. People strolled about or sat lazily on armchairs and couches, here and there little bursts of laughter could be heard, from a suddenly opened door came a click of billiard balls. And Martin liked the effect, the rather complicated little effect of false life that, in the acting, became less false, that spilled into the real, since the actors knew each other and were pleased to talk, to walk about, to go on with their lives in a pleasant new setting. There was a new liveliness in the main dining room, in the cafeterias and tearooms, in the parks and woods; the Cine-Theater flourished, the actor-residents strolled through the Palace of Wonders and the Hall of Optical Novelties and bought postcards in the giftshop of the Museum of Waxworks Vivants, and always the elevator doors opened and closed.

One evening in the dining room Martin saw at a nearby table three women absorbed in conversation. One of the women, who appeared to be older than the other two, wore an old-fashioned wide-brimmed hat with fresh flowers; the two younger were bareheaded. Martin did not know whether the three were actresses or residents. They were quiet and soft-spoken, so that he could hear only a murmur broken by soft laughter, and as he ate his roast beef and read his folded newspaper he could not prevent himself from glancing over at them from time to time. Once the older woman caught his eye before looking away; as he lowered his eyes he had the sense that she was leaning over to whisper something to her daughters, for one of them, the dark-haired one, made a movement that he caught out of the corner of his eye, she had turned her head to glance toward him, in a not unfriendly way. After a while the three women rose, and he studied his paper, only raising his eyes to give a nod as they passed his table. And later, when he entered the lobby, he saw them sitting by themselves, as he knew they would be. He caught a glance of invitation, dreamily he sank down in a chair in their little circle, and as he did so he had the sense that across the room something had changed, as if a slightly unnatural quiet had invaded the Grand Cosmo, the sort of quiet that accompanies an effort to listen. For surely the women were actresses, playing a daring part, though they presented themselves as a mother and two daughters. The daughters were young, they couldn't have been more than twenty, the dark-haired and the light, the mother seemed scarcely ten years older, it was a daring and outrageous game they were playing, and yet perhaps they were mother and daughters after all, it wasn't unusual to find such combinations in hotels all over the city. It occurred to Martin that he could check at the front desk, it was the simplest thing in the world, but when they rose he sat for a long time in the armchair, starting up once to see that the lobby was nearly empty – he must have dozed off.

And indeed he was tired, so tired that he could barely lift his head, though at the same time he felt intensely alert. The Grand Cosmo would soon pass away, even now it was fading, becoming dreamlike as he watched. Already he could hear it falling, falling like white snow. The three women were a sign, demon-women summoned up from deepest dream. For a building was a dream, a dream made stone, the dream lurking in the stone so that the stone wasn't stone only but dream, more dream than stone, dream-stone and dream-steel, forever unlasting. Friendly powers had led him along dark paths of dream, they had been good to him – to him, Martin Dressler, son of Otto Dressler, seller of cigars and tobacco. For really he had traveled a long way, since the days when he rolled out old Tecumseh into the warm shade. For he had done as he liked, he had gone his own way, built his castle in the air. And if in the end he had dreamed the wrong dream, the dream that others didn't wish to enter, then that was the way of dreams, it was only to be expected, he had no desire to have dreamt otherwise. And as Martin in his chair sat deeply asleep and yet entirely awake, for so it seemed to him, as Martin in his dream-chair slipped in and out of dream-thoughts that were the clear thoughts of day, he became aware of something just out of reach of his mind, something that needed attending to. And it came to him: a man, one of the actors whom he had noticed from the beginning, a man whom he had picked out without giving him much thought, simply nodding to him now and then, one actor among others. Maybe it was the full brown mustache, maybe it was the erect posture, or some gesture of the hands, but what had struck him was the resemblance, slight to be sure, between himself and that stranger. But now in his dream-waking, in his sleep-alertness, he seemed to grasp the slippery meaning of the man, who until this night had been scarcely in his thoughts at all.

The next day he had a private interview with the actor, a thoughtful and humorous fellow a little older than the others, a little down on his luck; it might well have been another, but Martin wanted only him. And in Martin's vest and jacket, with his hair combed back off his forehead, with Martin's habit of thrusting a hand in his pants pocket and jiggling loose change, he really did, in a way, at a short distance, look like Martin, though anyone could see it was only an actor. In the course of the day Martin explained to the man, whose name was John Painter, everything he needed to know: the habits of Martin's day, the morning meetings with the manager, his favorite soup. Of course the idea wasn't to fool anyone, but only to complete the cast of characters. During the afternoon he took Painter with him on his rounds, pointing out an attractive courtyard dwelling on the twenty-sixth floor that he might wish to occupy, lingering over a wooden Indian who raised a cigar to his mouth and blew a thick, slowly turning smoke ring, presenting the actor with a key to the boiler room. In the evening Martin took the elevator down to the department store and wandered among the deserted, brightly lit aisles before stopping at the clothing department to buy a shirt collar.

The next morning he went down early to buy his paper in the lobby and wait for the barbershop to open. In the barber's chair he closed his eyes for a moment and at once he was back in the Vanderlyn: his bellboy jacket felt tight around the chest, luggage creaked, buzzers rang, from the street came a clatter of wheels and hooves. He would transfer the title of the Vanderlyn to Emmeline Vernon, she could do with it as she liked. At breakfast he read his paper over steak and eggs, then folded it twice and left it beside his plate. He pushed back his chair and nodded at the three dream-women, who were just then entering with their demon-smiles, and as he stood up there rose to his nostrils a faint, pleasant odor of violet water and scented soap from his close-shaved cheeks.

He walked through the lobby to the heavy glass entrance doors, and when he pushed one open he stopped: the light was so bright that he had to shut his eyes, even though at this early hour he stood in the building's shade. Suns danced in the red of his closed eyes. He hadn't left the Grand Cosmo for a long time.

Carefully shading his eyes he made his way down the steps and across the light-filled warm shade of the avenue to the low wall of the park. On a dark green bench a white-haired woman in a black dress sat feeding pigeons from a paper bag. The fat sleek birds strutted about with their chests stuck out, their shot-silk throats shimmering pink and green. Martin entered the park and walked along a sunny-and-shady path matted with blackish-brown leaves. Through the trees he could see flashes of the river. After a while he stepped off the path onto a downward slope, into green-black shade spattered with spots of sun. Only then did he look up: through branches crowded with little green leaves he saw a patch of blue – a blue so blue, so richly and strangely blue, that it seemed the kind of blue you might find in pictures of castles in books of fairy tales, after you peeled away the crackly thin paper. It occurred to Martin that it was early spring.

He came to a place where the trees were more widely spaced, and sitting down in the grass he leaned back against a trunk and took off his hat. A light smell of hair oil rose from the leather sweatband. Carefully he placed the hat on one knee. The dark hatband had a silky shimmer that brought to mind the throats of the pigeons. Through the trees he could see the river and the red-brown Palisades. A sunny barge was moving slowly along. Sometimes it failed to come out from behind a trunk at the precise moment he imagined it should, and then he wished it wouldn't emerge at all, that it would vanish entirely behind a single tree and never be found again, as though it had slipped through a rent in the world and come out in another place, but immediately it would appear, barely moving, a great cat lazing in the sun. Before him he could see a more open place among the trees, where some boys were playing ball. They had laid down their caps and jackets to serve as bases. At his foot grew a single dandelion, a dark stem bursting into a blaze of yellow.

He had slipped out of his life, he had passed through a

crack in the world, into this place. By turning his head slightly he could see the Grand Cosmo through clutches of upper branches. It was still there, it hadn't vanished quite yet. But neither was it entirely there, half hidden as it was behind the leaves, the faintly moving little leaves, which perhaps were moving only to prevent him from attending closely to the crumbling masonry and falling steel behind them. His neck began to hurt. He turned back to the boys, the trees, and the river.

Martin closed his eyes for a moment, and when he opened them he was aware of a change in the light. The sky was brighter, the sun higher – the day was getting hot. He felt light, transparent. Here in the other world, here in the world beyond the world, anything was possible. For when the friendly powers let go of your hand, so gently that you were barely aware of it, then you needed to hold on to something, or you would surely be lost. You might float up into the too blue sky and never come back. You might dissolve into flickering spots of sun and shade. For when you woke from a long dream of stone, then you wanted to lie there with closed eyes, trying not to hear the sounds of morning, pressing back into your pillow as if by the sheer pressure of your head you could sink back beyond sleep, into your own childhood. But the light was too bright, his left buttock hurt, his calves itched. Martin shifted against the tree. The ridges of bark, long diamonds, pressed into his back. He felt like walking.

Martin got up and brushed off the seat of his pants with his hat. He put his hat on his head and started back toward the path. For when you woke from a long dream, into the new morning, then try as you might you couldn't not hear, beyond your door, the sounds of the new day, the drawer opening in your father's bureau, the bang of a pot, you couldn't not see, through your trembling lashes, the stripe of light on the bedroom wall. Boys shouted in the park, on a sunny tree-root he saw a cigar band, red and gold. One of these days he might find something to do in a cigar store, after all he still knew his tobacco, you never forgot a thing like that. But not just yet. Boats moved on the river, somewhere a car horn sounded, on the path a piece of broken glass glowed in a patch of sun as if at any second it would burst into flame. Everything stood out sharply: the red stem of a green leaf, horse clops and the distant clatter of a pneumatic drill, a smell of riverwater and asphalt. Martin felt hungry: chops and beer in a little place he remembered on Columbus Avenue. But not yet. For the time being he would just walk along, keeping a little out of the way of things, admiring the view. It was a warm day. He was in no hurry.

All Orion/Phoenix titles are available at your local bookshop or from the following address:

Mail Order Department
Littlehampton Book Services
FREEPOST BR535
Worthing, West Sussex, BNI3 3BR
telephone 01903 828503, *facsimile* 01903 828802
e-mail MailOrders@lbsltd.co.uk
(Please ensure that you include full postal address details)

Payment can be made either by credit/debit card (Visa, Mastercard, Access and Switch accepted) or by sending a £ Sterling cheque or postal order made payable to *Littlehampton Book Services*.
DO NOT SEND CASH OR CURRENCY.

Please add the following to cover postage and packing

UK and BFPO:
£1.50 for the first book, and 50p for each additional book to a maximum of £3.50

Overseas and Eire:
£2.50 for the first book plus £1.00 for the second book and 50p for each additional book ordered

---

BLOCK CAPITALS PLEASE

name of cardholder ....

address of cardholder ....

....

....

postcode ....

delivery address
(if different from cardholder)

....

....

....

postcode ....

☐ I enclose my remittance for £ ....

☐ please debit my Mastercard/Visa/Access/Switch (delete as appropriate)

card number ☐☐☐☐☐☐☐☐☐☐☐☐☐☐☐☐

expiry date ☐☐☐☐   Switch issue no. ☐☐

signature ....

prices and availability are subject to change without notice